Paradise on the Pike

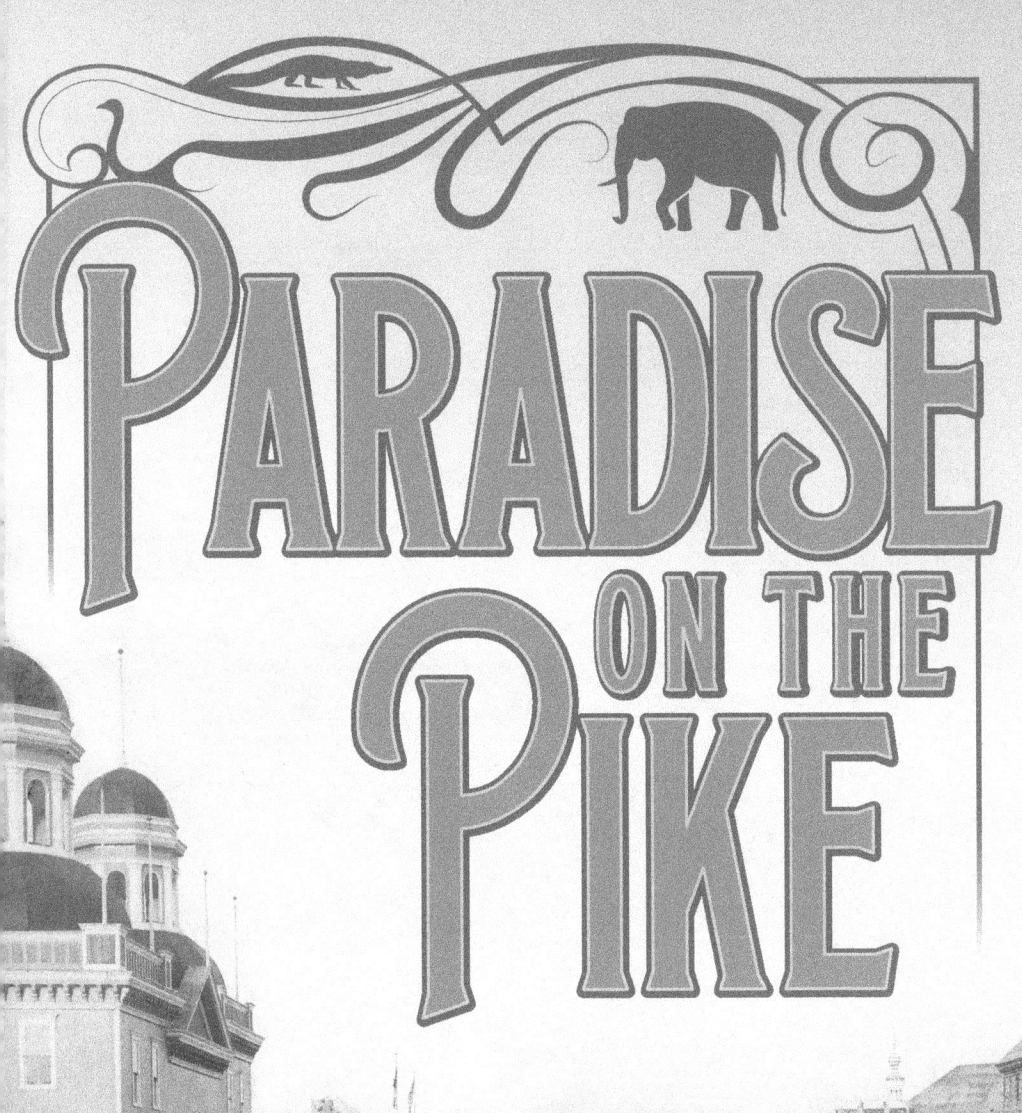

Sarah Angleton

PARADISE ON THE PIKE

Sarah Angleton

bright
button
press

ST. LOUIS, MISSOURI

Copyright © 2024 by Sarah Angleton

Cover Design by Steve Varble

All rights reserved. No part of this publication may be reproduced, distributed, or transmitted in any form or by any means, without prior written permission, except in the case of brief excerpts for the purpose of review. No artificial intelligence technology was used in the any way in the writing of this work, and no use may be made of this publication for the training of generative artificial intelligence (AI) technologies without express written consent from the author.

Published by Bright Button Press: PO Box 203 Foristell, Missouri 63348 (United States of America)

This is a work of fiction. All names, places, and incidents are either products of the author's imagination or used factiously. Any resemblance to actual incidents or persons, living or dead, is coincidental.

Publisher's Cataloging-in-Publication Data
provided by Five Rainbows Cataloging Services

Names: Angleton, Sarah, author.
Title: Paradise on the Pike / Sarah Angleton.
Description: Wentzville, MO : Bright Button Press, 2024.
Identifiers: LCCN 2024901442 (print) | ISBN 978-0-9987853-0-1 (paperback) | ISBN 978-0-9987853-9-4 (ebook)
Subjects: LCSH: Immigrants--Fiction. | Zoo animals--Fiction. | Circus animals--Fiction. | Louisiana Purchase Exposition (1904 : Saint Louis, Mo.)--Fiction. | Human trafficking--Fiction. | Historical fiction. | BISAC: FICTION / Historical / 20th Century / General. | GSAFD: Historical fiction.
Classification: LCC PS3601.N64 P37 2024 (print) | LCC PS3601.N64 (ebook) | DDC 813/.6--dc23.

Dedication

To all those who work so diligently
to maintain the memories of the
1904 World's Fair.
Thank you.

Dedication

Chapter 1

Eight days after his father had thrown back his final glass of vodka and keeled over dead in the barn, Max Eyer finished building a chicken coop that closely approximated a perfect miniature of the small stone farmhouse he now shared with only his mother.

The coop had been Mutti's idea, a project to occupy Max's mind in the days following his father's untimely, if not entirely unexpected, end. That a drunkard had drunk himself to death in some unknown corner of Prussia was not particularly shocking. If anyone were to miss Felix, it would only have been his string of customers whose dependence on his foul, oily brand of homemade vodka indicated they were likely to one day share his fate.

But one could also never discount the grief of the son of even an undeserving father, and Max's grief was intense. It captured him in odd moments, in the thwack of the hammer that recalled the sound of Felix's melon head landing with a thud on the earthen floor.

The young man stepped back to admire his completed work, hammer in shaking hand, a burning sensation clawing up the inside of his throat as a confusing mix of emotions threatened to overwhelm him.

"That's a nice coop."

Max flinched and, tightening his grip on the hammer, turned to find a stranger riding slowly toward him on the back of the most beautiful chestnut horse he'd ever seen. As steady as a statue, the man wore a crisp, gray suit, a close-trimmed silver beard, and a smile so genuinely lit by joy,

Max wished he could return it.

"Fine looking birds, too." The man slid from the saddle with the agility of one twenty years his junior and gestured toward the dull black chickens picking through the grass inside the fence. "Krüper if I'm not mistaken. Good layers?"

"Yes, sir."

The stranger offered his hand. Max forced himself to grasp it in a firm shake, his own skin dingy by comparison, though the stranger's hand was more calloused than expected. "My name is Carl Hagenbeck," he said. "I'm looking for Felix Eyer. Is that you?"

The bile began to rise once again. Max swallowed it back, his gaze drifting involuntarily to the barn that held his father's beloved still and where Felix's body had so recently crumpled to the ground. Max coughed to clear the stinging inside of him. "No, sir. My name is Max Eyer. Felix was my father."

A shadow darkened Herr Hagenbeck's features. "Oh, I see." The horse shook out its mane and stamped but settled again at a whispered word from its master. "I do see. I am tremendously sorry for your loss. If I might ask, when did he pass?"

"Just over a week ago."

Hagenbeck frowned. Thin creases etched his cheeks. The expression did not suit him at all, and Max regretted so bluntly delivering the news of Felix's death.

"Why did you need to see him?" This man did not strike him as a vodka drinker, at least not the kind who would be interested in the swill Felix produced with the recent potato harvest. The tubers should have made their way from the Eyer farm to more traditional markets. Perhaps this well-dressed stranger was in the potato business.

"I had hoped to see him about an opportunity to sell his land, but it appears that will no longer be possible." Hagenbeck reached into the breast pocket of his coat and pulled out a card. "Thank you for your time. I'll take my leave for now, but perhaps when your family is better prepared for a business conversation, you might contact me?"

He patted the horse's neck. As he did so, Max looked down at the card in his grimy hand where he read words that didn't make sense to him. His head snapped up, catching the visitor's attention.

"Wait," he said to the man who had placed one foot in the stirrup but now removed it. "You're not a farmer."

Amusement danced upon Hagenbeck's brow. "No, young man. I'm not a farmer."

"But what does this mean? You are a dealer in animals?"

"As it says. I am a collector and supplier of animals from all over the world, every kind of creature you can imagine, and some you've probably not dreamt of."

Max tried to picture the animals Hagenbeck might be talking about. As a young boy, he'd seen pictures in schoolbooks of elephants and giraffes and lions, the giant whales of the oceans and the great apes of other lands. He'd pored over drawings of them, and copied them, too, spending long hours hiding from his father, and from the anxiety of his mother, by sketching such wonderful, mythical creatures. For as far back as he could remember, he'd also longed to see them in the flesh.

He licked his lips, momentarily drawn from his harsh life as the son of a harsh man, into his past as an innocent child with dreams and ambitions beyond the unhappy home that consisted of twelve acres of flat fields, streaked with meticulous rows of potato plants, a sagging stone house that remained cold in the winter, and a barn where his father made the vodka that in turn made him mean.

"Elephants?" he asked, quietly at first, not quite daring to put voice to his hope.

A bubble of laughter burst from Hagenbeck's chest. "Yes, elephants. In fact, I have twenty of them currently housed in my tierpark in Hamburg. As you can surely imagine, we are somewhat cramped for space."

Max could not imagine it.

"I take it you've never been to the zoological garden?" Herr Hagenbeck asked.

The young man shook his head. "I've never even been to Hamburg. I haven't been anywhere."

It was true, though Max could hardly believe he'd volunteered the information to a stranger. Though the city of Hamburg loomed to the southwest of his home, from where Max stood in the close confines of the Village of Stellingen, it might as well have been across an ocean.

Hagenbeck studied Max with narrowed, thoughtful eyes. "May I ask how old you are?"

"I'm twenty in a month."

"Your father's only son?"

"His only child."

"And his heir, may I presume?" Hagenbeck's prodding sent an uncomfortable tingle through Max's limbs. He pictured his mother, trying to imagine what she might want him to say. He could have sworn he'd seen the kitchen curtain move under the pull of her slender fingers. Max fidgeted. He and Mutti had not yet had this conversation, but it must be true. Felix Eyer was not the type of man who would fight to jointly own property with his wife. Legally the farm would belong to his son, who would now bear the responsibility of caring for his mother.

Max nodded.

"Well, then," Hagenbeck said as he motioned to the card firmly gripped in Max's dirty fingers. "If I may, I suggest when you are ready, you consider whether you wish to dream of a different future than the one tied to this farm, and if you decide you might, let me know."

Max tucked the card into the pocket of his pants and shook his head. "But you still haven't explained what an animal dealer and keeper of elephants wants with a small potato farm."

Hagenbeck brought his pointer finger to the side of his nose and then aimed it toward Max and grinned. "Where you see potatoes, my friend, I see a world landscape." He spread his fingers and stretched his arm out toward the sky. "I see an expansive African savannah filled with roaring lions, Arctic glaciers climbed upon by fierce polar bears, a jungle filled with swinging monkeys."

"In a potato field?" Max could not picture such things anywhere, least of all in the countryside of northern Germany.

Hagenbeck brought his hands together with a clap. "Yes! In a potato field. In many potato fields if I'm lucky. My Hamburg zoological garden is landlocked. We cannot expand and I have such fantastical plans. It is my hope that Stellingen may become the site of a new kind of tierpark, one where animals from all over the world can be displayed not behind bars, but in their natural environments, separated by non-obstructive means." The man now paced in his excitement, and his motion caused the horse to stomp in agitation.

Max held his hands out toward the animal in a show of reassuring calm he couldn't manifest for himself. He maintained eye contact and the horse began to settle. Out of the side of his mouth, he said, "I don't know what any of that means."

The animal trader stopped pacing. He'd stopped behind Max, facing the aging farmhouse. Now that Max had built the chicken coop, he would have to start thinking about repairs to the home, especially since it occurred to him it was his responsibility. The weighty realization threatened to steal his breath.

"I apologize. I get so excited," Hagenbeck said. "I really don't wish to impose upon your grief, but I'd welcome the opportunity to tell you more about it. And your mother, too, of course."

The man's attention drifted beyond Max and the horse to the kitchen door where Mutti stood in a day dress printed with faded yellow flowers that washed out her pale features. She'd always been slim, but somehow, she'd grown more insubstantial each day since Felix's death. Max hadn't heard the whine of the door hinges as she'd stepped out. It was as if she'd simply moved through the solid door like a ghost—a ghost that now considered the odd scene before her.

Hagenbeck hustled toward her, his hand outstretched. "You must be Frau Eyer. I'm Carl Hagenbeck of the Hagenbeck Tierpark in Hamburg. I am so very sorry for the recent loss of your husband."

She did not move, even as the animal dealer reached her, and he was forced to lower his hand again. Max secured the horse to one of the chicken yard's fence posts and hurried toward them.

"If you are sorry my husband is dead, Herr Hagenbeck, then you must not have known him."

At her words, a now familiar sour tang coated the back of Max's tongue. His parents' marriage had been an unhappy one. In his memory, Mutti was light and love and everything a mother should be, but as he'd grown, she'd become this husk of a woman, hollowed out by the miscarriage of several would-be brothers and sisters and the never-ending struggle to wrest Felix from his demons.

Hagenbeck's head tilted to the side, as if considering her words. "If that is the case, then I am terribly sorry to hear that as well."

Mutti shocked Max by offering a small head bob in reply, revealing a cautious openness. To his surprise, she invited their visitor inside.

"Call me Emmi, please, Herr Hagenbeck." She indicated that he should sit in the wooden chair at the head of their small kitchen table, the one where Felix used to sit.

"Only if you will call me Carl."

Max grew dizzy. His mother, who had spoken little over the past week, who had barely slept or eaten, by comparison appeared animated in front of this man, his enthusiasm contagious. She placed a cup in front of Herr Hagenbeck, now Carl, and another in front of Max, who slid into the seat across from him. With a clink, she dropped a piece of caked sugar into each and then lifted the kettle from the cooktop to pour tea for both of them.

"*Did* you know Felix?" she asked him.

"Ah," he said, taking a sip, not waiting for cream. He replaced the cup on the table and sucked his upper lip with a soft hiss. Curls of earthy steam rose from his cup. "No. I'm afraid I am nothing but an intruder on your home."

"Nonsense," Mutti said. She poured herself a cup and returned the kettle to the cooktop, grabbing cream for herself and for Max before settling at the table. "Judging by the way my son's demeanor lit up as you were speaking outside, I would say you are a welcome relief to our sorrows."

"That's very kind of you to say."

"So," Mutti looked from Hagenbeck to Max and back. "Why are you here, Carl?"

It was Max who answered, surprised by his own interjection and at the thrilling rush he received from the words he spoke. "Herr Hagenbeck wants to make our land part of his new zoological garden."

Mutti ran a thumb around the rim of her teacup and became as unreadable to Max as if a veil had been lowered over her face. Regret flooded him. Their visitor had wanted to wait, to make his offer another day, when their grief was not so fresh, when they could better think of their future. Max should have listened to the older man, should not have pushed him to talk for so long, his extended presence coaxing Mutti from the house.

But then, the corners of Mutti's mouth twitched upwards, her eyes sharp and purposeful. She whispered something so softly, Max wasn't sure he was meant to listen.

Hagenbeck, perhaps sensing an opening, volunteered, "It would be a good offer, of course, above market value. I will be purchasing land from some of your neighbors as well."

Mutti barely seemed to hear him, lost as she became in the consideration of such a shocking suggestion. Then to his surprise, she said, "That's not a bad idea at all."

She wrapped her hands around her teacup and squeezed, her shoulders lifting, and she shifted in her chair toward Max. "We should accept."

She said it without hesitation, without caveat, as if the value of the offer meant nothing, and not a thing in the world would make her happier than forever letting go of the land she had worked with her recently deceased husband. Max drew a hand across his forehead, unsure what to think.

"Well," Hagenbeck lightly punched the table in celebration of sudden victory. "I only need the land. You can keep the house, of course, and if Max is interested in a job, I could certainly use another strong back, especially a worker who is good with animals and has a good sense for design—"

"No." Mutti's back stiffened and the muscles of her jaw tightened. "The house, too. We don't wish to stay."

"We don't?" Max's question slipped out in the high-pitched crack that betrayed his youthfulness.

In what could only be the energy of excitement, Mutti appeared unmoved by his obvious discomfort. "This is a wonderful opportunity, Maxie. We can start fresh. We'll go to America."

"America," he repeated. All Max knew about America was that it was much farther away than Hamburg. "What will we do in America?"

"Oh," said Hagenbeck, mirroring Mutti's jittery excitement. "You'll love America. They call it the land of opportunity. Anything you can dream you can do there."

"You've been?" Max asked, both awed and frightened by the worldliness of their visitor.

"Yes, I have!" Herr Hagenbeck's voice rose in volume and enthusiasm. "I was in Chicago for the World's Fair back in '93. Absolutely exhilarating."

Max couldn't begin to formulate a response to this mystifying claim before Mutti spoke again.

"My brother Reinhardt is in America with his family." Mutti patted Max's arm, an unsuccessful attempt to reassure him.

He flipped through his memories for an Uncle Reinhardt. Max vaguely recalled from his childhood his mother talking of her brother in America, perhaps reading aloud from letters and sharing tales of mischievous siblings romping around the countryside. As the years progressed and Felix's angry grip tightened, Mutti spoke less and less of her family of origin. until Max's knowledge of them contained no more than a few disconnected scraps of this American uncle.

"If you have family there, then everything is much easier," Hagenbeck said.

"So, your offer will include the house?" Mutti asked.

Max's airway constricted, his breaths becoming shallow at his mother's casual suggestion they would leave their home. The prospect, once a thrilling dream, had become a terrifying reality.

"Of course! The house, the land, I'll even take those fine chickens and any other animals you have."

Mutti stood and held out her hand, which Hagenbeck shook vigorously as he also stood. "This has all worked out very nicely," he said. "I'll have my man write up an offer, a generous one I hope you'll find, for a mother and son stepping toward adventure. I wish you both great fortune."

Hagenbeck drained the rest of his barely cool tea and set the cup on the table. "Max, it was a pleasure to meet you and Emmi. Thank you for your hospitality and your openness. You'll be hearing from me soon."

The animal trader, with his impeccable suit, clean calloused hands, and kind demeanor, walked out of their kitchen to mount his horse and head back down the lane away from the farm.

Behind him, Mutti clapped her hands together with unnerving energy. "I guess I'd better start packing, now that's all settled."

"Nothing is settled." Max shoved back his chair and stood. Broad like his father had been, Max could not be called particularly tall even though he loomed over his diminutive mother. "This is our home. It's my home."

Mutti raised her pointed chin in defiance, then cupped his cheek in her palm. "Maxie," she addressed him with a tenderness that melted his indignation. "We cannot stay here. Not here, with the ghost of your father, haunting us for all our days. We have been given an opportunity, and we will take it. It is settled."

Max stepped back from her, leaving her hand briefly hanging in the air before she lowered it to return to her fluttering. He looked on as she mumbled her way through a list of looming tasks, happier than he'd seen her in more than a week, or years, or perhaps his entire life. She'd transformed from fearful shadow, the tragic widow, into light itself, fluid and hopeful.

He tried to capture this zeal for himself, but a breeze caught up the curtain and drew his eye to the window and to the sight of their strange visitor skillfully trotting out of view at the end of the road. Max chewed the inside of his cheek until it hurt, fearful nothing had been settled at all.

Chapter 2

It took approximately one month for every circumstance in Max's life to change so dramatically he no longer recognized it as his own. Not one week passed before the ink dried on a deal with Carl Hagenbeck to purchase the farm, and it was all the time Mutti had needed to decide very few of their possessions would travel with them to the new world.

They sold off what few things they could, gave away others, and left the rest, their pockets lined with enough of Hagenbeck's money to settle up Felix's debts, buy new traveling clothes for each of them, and purchase passage on a steamship from Hamburg to New York City. From there, they made their way to the great city of St. Louis on the banks of the Mississippi.

"I never understood how large the earth was, nor how small it could feel," he remarked to Mutti as they pulled into Union Station, a structure Max had difficulty accepting could exist in the same world as the fields and forests surrounding Stellingen. She squeezed his hand and studied him with an intensity so bright it threatened to shatter him. He steeled his nerves and retrieved their travel trunk.

He'd thought Hamburg confusing and New York maddingly loud, but St. Louis's Union Station was the most overwhelming of all. The fact that mere weeks ago he'd been building a chicken coop, attempting to assemble the pieces of his father's death through the fog of a complicated grief, and that now he lived on the other side of the world in the middle of what he could only describe as fantasy threatened to engulf what remained of himself.

The train station, if one could call it such, buzzed with human industry and glowed with luxury. Well-appointed brick archways adorned by unnecessary artistic touches unnerved him. In the middle of the immense ceiling hung a crystal chandelier better suited to an emperor's palace or grand ballroom than a train station filled with smoke and soot.

Max gaped at it all, blindly trusting his mother to guide him through the bustle, his hand firmly gripped in hers as though he were a small child instead of a grown man, for that is how this place, this climactic slip of time between their old lives to their new, overwhelmed him, and as when he was small, Max stood in awe of his mother's calm capability.

Somehow this slight, overburdened woman with cracked hands and a watery gaze had once again become a person of power. Her visage held the hard lines of determination and purpose shared by the people around them, each returning from or about to embark upon important journeys. Even the unhurried wore anxious expressions as they hugged and waved goodbye to companions or waited, scanning the surge, for anticipated arrivals.

Uncle Reinhardt wore such a look when they finally spotted him just inside the entrance to the building. Max had never met his mother's eldest brother but couldn't have mistaken him. The two possessed identical pale gray eyes and the same wispy blond hair lacking much trace of color at all, the only difference being that Mutti could tease and fluff her hair to give the illusion of volume while Reinhardt's had given way substantially to the pink of his scalp.

Reinhardt was taller than his sister, broader certainly across the shoulders, and his middle ballooned into a comfortable beer belly, but he was not a large man. Beside Felix, whom Max strongly resembled, his uncle would have been difficult to notice.

He'd always thought the same thing about Mutti, though he'd not dared whisper it aloud, choosing instead to indulge his irrational fear that if he gave voice to the way his father overshadowed her, she might vanish altogether. Now, however, no fleeting thought about his mother could ever make this reinvigorated version of her smaller.

"Emmi!" Uncle Reinhardt opened his arms to embrace his long-lost but clearly beloved sister. They fit together, these two halves of a symbiotic pair, even after having not seen one another in the span of a lifetime, if Max's own life were used as the unit of measure. He'd once measured the passage of time by the seasons of the farm, in the birthing of animals, the harvesting of the crop. From this instant on, time would exist as before America and after. Max feared he'd become untethered with no notion of time at all. He could not fathom what seasons lie ahead in the vast unknown of this immense city named for a saint, with a train station as ornate as a palace.

The hum of the crowd and Max's own growing apprehension muffled much of the reunited siblings' long-anticipated greeting, but soon Mutti squeezed Max's elbow. A joyous tear spilled down her cheek as she said, "This is my son Max."

Reinhardt clasped Max's other elbow and pulled his nephew into an unwelcome hug. Max's pulse pounded in his ears.

"I see what you mean," Reinhardt said to Mutti, releasing Max and proceeding to speak of him as if he weren't there at all. "He resembles his father very much. Strong and healthy. It's good to meet you, my boy."

Stunned at the physical contact with this oddly familiar stranger, Max didn't know how to respond. Reinhardt bounced subtly as he spoke, overflowing with unabated delight at welcoming them. He took the traveling case Mutti had carried from the train platform and continued to chat, leading them out of the grand hall into the bright sunshine to a street lined with waiting coaches for hire.

Max trailed them, half listening as he struggled with the heavy trunk containing the rest of their meager belongings.

"How was your journey? You made good time on your passage?"

"Yes," Mutti responded. "Thirteen days from Hamburg to New York."

"Ach, in my day it was much longer. Matilda and I were on a sailing ship for more than a month."

"The world is changing, big brother. It's a good thing, too. I don't think Max would have managed much longer."

"Not much of a traveler, young man?"

Max's cheeks grew hot under his uncle's scrutiny. He adjusted his grip on the trunk and somehow summoned a response. "My first time on a ship."

"First time on a train as well, I assume?"

"Yes," Max grunted.

Reinhardt's brow furrowed in what Max assumed was meant to be an implication of empathy but served instead to increase Max's wariness. What about his uncle's mannerisms bothered him so, Max couldn't have said, until Reinhardt spoke to the driver of one of the nearby carriages and placed Mutti's bag inside the passenger compartment.

It was his uncle's German that troubled Max. The man's English nearly matched in lilt and cadence that of the coach driver; his German comparatively slow and careful and punctuated by timing not entirely natural to Max's ear. Reinhardt was a man who seldom spoke German, or at least spoke a garbled version of it peppered with pieces of the language of his adopted country. This realization hit Max almost as a physical blow. He staggered and would have dropped the trunk had Reinhardt not reacted quickly to relieve Max of one end of it.

"Danke," said Max, heat rising up the back of his neck.

Reinhardt adjusted his grip on the trunk and helped Max heave it into the coach. "You're welcome."

Max understood the meaning of the phrase, had heard and practiced using it on the journey from Hamburg, but he cringed inwardly to hear it trip so casually from his uncle's lips. Reinhardt, clearly unaware of his nephew's scrutiny, reached for Mutti's hand to help her into the coach. When Max made to follow them, another sight beyond the row of coaches captured his attention—some sort of train cars, connected to overhead wires and without an engine to pull them. He'd seen similar vehicles in both Hamburg and New York but hadn't been able to satisfy his curiosity about them.

Reinhardt traced his nephew's open-mouthed stare. "Streetcars." Max accepted the unfamiliar word without comment and adjusted his grip on the trunk. His uncle continued in his unusual German, "They cross all over the city and are a convenient way to travel, though you have to know the routes and be aware of the stations. I chose a carriage for this ride from the station because I thought it might be easier with your luggage to end directly at home."

"Very thoughtful," Mutti said.

Max agreed, though he'd have liked to climb aboard one of the small trains and experience them for himself. Still, he could appreciate that his uncle, who like himself would have been expected to help lug their baggage an unknown number of city blocks from streetcar stop to home, had indeed made a thoughtful decision, however self-serving it might have been.

They soon left the nicely paved streets around the station and turned onto those that were narrower and dustier, more similar to the country roads with which Max was familiar, though busier and lined with homes that, if not as grand as he might have expected based on his initial impression of the city, appeared tidy and well maintained.

"Many of the city streets have been recently paved," Reinhardt explained to them as they rode along. "Not all, of course, but Mayor Wells has made it a personal project as the city prepares to host the World's Fair."

"What is a World's Fair?" asked Max, glad for the opportunity to explore the phrase the animal trader Hagenbeck had used. "Is it similar to a county fair with farm goods on display?"

"Something like it, on a larger scale." His uncle, distracted, did not elaborate as the coach stopped on a paved road at a two-story brick home with numerous genial windows and spacious front steps leading up to a set of double doors, out of which spilled two women, each carrying a baby and leading a waddling line of small children all tumbling forward to greet the new arrivals.

One of the women, older and lumpier than the other, handed her babe to Reinhardt who lifted the squealing tot above his head, eliciting a fountain of giggles. Her hands free of their burden, the woman stepped forward and threw her arms around Mutti, swallowing her with ample flesh.

Next, the woman turned to Max and crushed in an exuberant expression of love from a squealing stranger.

"Willkommen!" She backed up from the hug, her grip still firm on Max's forearms as her eyes swept from his head to his toes. She turned to Mutti. "What a handsome young man he is, Emmi."

Mutti came to life at the words, pulled the woman's hands from Max and squeezed them. "These must be your grandchildren," she said, indicating the squiggling brood.

"These are most of them, yes. There's an older boy in school."

Max snatched the name Matilda from his memory of Mutti's ramblings during their journey. This would be Reinhardt's wife, a woman of whom Mutti was fond. Max could see why. He liked her immediately. Aunt Matilda spoke a less sluggish German than her husband did, as if she took greater pride in her heritage, and for her, speech was a full body experience.

She waved her arms around in large, animated gestures as she talked, eventually pointing to the younger woman who stood beside her with a second, even younger babe cradled to her. "Frieda helps me care for the little ones while their parents work."

Frieda had to be barely older than Max and she was very pretty, with chestnut brown hair, rosy cheeks, and womanly curves he regretted noticing. His shame dissipated only somewhat when Mutti asked if Frieda was one of their daughters and Reinhardt clarified she was a daughter-in-law, married to their youngest son Ernst, and mother now to their newest granddaughter.

Mutti cooed at the tiny babe and reached to pull the little girl from her mother's grasp. Frieda flinched with surprise, but she yielded to the older woman's insistence. The baby barely stirred during the transfer to those wiry arms that remembered how to perfectly cradle such a precious bundle.

Max eyed his mother as she drank in the essence of the sleeping infant, blissfully unaware of a stranger's embrace. He leaned toward Frieda. "Das tut mir Lied," he said quietly.

"No need to apologize," she responded, waving away his concern with a flick of a slender wrist. "She is family. You both are family." She stressed the "you" with a familiarity that made his stomach clench.

He willed himself to shrug off his discomfort. "She has not had such a young one in her life for many years."

Frieda chuckled and surveyed him. "I suppose it has been a while. She'll find no shortage of young ones around here."

Her statement was true enough. Max counted three children in addition to the two babies. He could not venture a guess at their ages, but they consisted of a boy and a girl of similar height and a smaller boy. He thought of asking Frieda their names but feared he would not remember them. Instead, he asked, "Do you all live here, then, with Reinhardt and Matilda and all the children?" Max couldn't imagine living in such a crowded space.

She shook her head. "Nein," she assured him. "My husband and I live here for now, along with little Marguerite, but there are three brothers. The other two live nearby in their own homes."

"But not you?" Her language was clumsy, but it contained no trace of regret as she explained her living situation.

"Not yet." An enchanting dimple appeared on her right cheek.

The elder generation had begun to move inside the house, shooing the children in front of them. Max would have gladly remained in the front yard speaking to his cousin's charming wife but was happy to follow her as she continued to talk. "We are the newest married, and we're saving for a house of our own, but my pregnancy was difficult. Matilda has been wonderful, and she can use the help with the busier children. The twins especially can be a lot to handle for an Oma."

As if to illustrate the point, the little girl ran back outside and down the stairs with a shriek. Her brother followed, head down and hands stretched wide, ready to tackle her into the grassy lawn.

Frieda snatched him by his shirt collar and soon had the girl with her other hand. "Martha and Otto," Frieda hissed. "You will stop this behavior at once."

She knelt on the grass to be at eye level with the children and pulled them around to face her. They each focused on her, but their reactions were different. Otto's innocent blue eyes brimmed with nearly shed tears, while Martha's otherwise identical eyes narrowed and her lower lip protruded into an obstinate pout. Freida swatted each of them gently on their bottoms. "What an impression you both have made. You must apologize to our guests. Say you are sorry to Cousin Max."

Max might have been standing in a spotlight as the children both glared up at him. They spoke at the same time, a quick, "We're sorry, Cousin Max," recited in English and without sincerity.

"Now go say it as if you mean it to your Tante Emmi."

The children wiggled their way back into the house, leaving Frieda shaking her head and unsuccessfully fighting a grin.

"Where is their mother?" Max asked.

"Annmarie works as a server at the family's biergarten. Her husband Hugh manages it now as Reinhardt has gotten older, but most of us help out from time to time." A question formed in Max's mind, but Frieda anticipated it and explained, "Hugh is Reinhardt and Matilda's second son. Richard is the oldest. He's an attorney." This was said with a sigh.

"And the other boy is his?"

"We call him Johnny. He's got a school-age brother as well." Frieda crumpled into a fleeting frown at the mention of Richard's older boy. Max decided not to pry.

"And there's a family biergarten. Is that what your husband does, too?"

"Actually, no," she said, climbing the steps toward the double front doors. "Ernst has never cared for it. He works in construction. He's much better with his hands, and doesn't care for the hospitality part of the business."

"Too grumpy?" Max asked, a twinge of hope in the question. The more he talked with Frieda, the more determined he became to dislike her husband.

"Oh, no." She pushed open the door and stepped aside, holding it open for Max to lug the trunk up the stairs and into an entryway. "It's not that. I wouldn't say that at all. He's more introspective; he's an artist. He likes to build things, and though he is funny and charming and certainly very good with people when he needs to be, I think he prefers when he can get away from them, too."

Max's shoulders slumped along with his hopes. Ernst sounded a bit similar to himself—like a man Max might admire. "When will I get to meet the wonderful Ernst?"

"You'll see him this evening along with the rest of the family. They'll all be coming here to meet you. Your arrival has created a stir."

In front of him and to the right as he walked through the door, Max saw a wide staircase. To the left, a hallway led to a back room of some sort, from which he could hear the noisy chatter of the children. To his immediate left, a short wall stretched to an archway leading to a sitting room. On the entryway wall hung a large photograph of a family, Uncle Reinhardt and Aunt Matilda in the center, surrounded by three men, each paired with a woman. Spaced among them, the children didn't correspond to their parents, but when he discovered Frieda who stood beside the man who Max assumed was Ernst, he realized he saw no infant. The photograph must have been taken before she was born.

"It seems to be a close family," Max observed.

"It is," Frieda said. "Sometimes a little too close, if it's not too disloyal for me to say so."

"I don't think it's disloyal at all. You love them, yes? I am overwhelmed by them, too, and I haven't even met them all yet. I come from a small home where my family consisted of me and my parents. The chattiest members of our household were the chickens."

She beamed at him. "I'm from a small family, too."

"German?" he asked.

"Yes," she answered with a slight hesitation. "My father immigrated from Germany. My mother, from France. I was born here."

"That explains it."

"Explains what?"

"Your German," he said. "It's—"

"It's what, exactly?" A crinkle formed above her nose and her body stiffened. He barely managed to stop himself from laughing at the offended manner she adopted. He threw a hand up in defeat.

"I only meant it sounds distinctly American."

"Well," she huffed. "What's wrong with that? I am American."

"Nothing." He lowered his hand and his voice, a warm glow rising in her cheeks and making her all the more fetching. He almost wanted to make her angry. Almost. "I hadn't meant to imply there was anything wrong with the way you speak. It was merely an observation."

"I would bet my German is better than your English."

"I have no doubt." Max's English continued to be limited to a few phrases he'd picked up to aid him and his mother in their travel. He could ask for water or for food as long as he didn't need to be specific. He understood when someone asked him for his travel papers or required to know his name. He knew how to ask which train to take to St. Louis and could exchange a limited nicety or two.

"You'll need to learn," Freida said, this time with a hand on one hip so she resembled a cranky school matron.

"Yes," he grudgingly admitted. "I will have to learn."

"And rapidly," she added, "if you are to get a job. There are a lot of Germans in the city. Even the mayor is German, but you will not easily secure a position if you cannot speak the language of the majority."

Max chewed the inside of his cheek. She was truly lovely, this sort of cousin of his, and she was concerned for him. In a busy home filled with children and joy, and her own child held by nearly a stranger, she focused intently on him. "I'm sure you're right. And I will need a teacher."

"Yes. You will need a teacher."

"Someone who speaks fluent German but is distinctly American. Someone with patience for my sluggish tongue and thickheadedness, but also stern enough to keep me on task."

"All those things," she agreed.

"I think you'd be perfect for the job."

"Yes, I would be perfect for the job."

He raised an eyebrow. "We start tomorrow?"

"Yes," she said. "When I put Marguerite down for her nap in the afternoon, then we will begin."

Chapter 3

Max's anxiety at finding himself both the son of a dead man and thousands of miles away from home began to recede the instant he developed an inappropriate crush on his cousin's wife. What had been a constant crash of waves in his mind, muting all other stimuli, had softened to little more than a dull thrum, and the fluttery sensation of it buoyed him through the afternoon.

Aunt Matilda had settled Mutti into a comfortable upstairs bedroom across a hallway from the room Frieda shared with her husband, while Uncle Reinhardt escorted Max to the attic which held a narrow bed, wash basin, and small wardrobe with little floor space between.

"It's not much, I'm afraid." Reinhardt tucked his hands inside the pockets of his pants and hunched to avoid bumping his head on the slanted ceiling. Max, taller by at least two inches, did the same. "We're short on space, but it should do for a young bachelor."

"Danke."

Reinhardt cleared his throat and waited an expectant beat before continuing to speak. "We'd have had a larger room for you, but Richard, our eldest, lost his wife a few months ago. His boys are with us quite often."

Max opened his mouth to offer condolences, but the thought of vulnerable children losing a parent stymied his voice. The edges of his vision blurred, and the rush of his own blood pounded through his veins.

"Are you okay, son?" Reinhardt reached a hand out toward him, but

Max sidestepped his touch, skirting the edge of the bed. He focused on a small round window that sparkled in the late afternoon sun, suggesting a recent cleaning.

Reinhardt returned his hand to his pocket. "You have a nice view of the city," he said.

Max leaned close to look out the window. What he saw was not exactly the good view of the city his uncle suggested, but he could see the front lawn and the street beyond. Max bobbed his head.

"You're a man of few words, which I respect." Reinhardt waited a full minute before he turned and walked out of the room, but before he closed the door behind him, he looked back and said, "You know, Max, we all get a little lost sometimes, but it is possible to locate ourselves again. I think you'll be happy here. I really do."

Reinhardt did not wait for a response. When the door thumped closed behind him, Max released a long exhale, grateful to be alone. The sound of footsteps faded on the stairs, and he turned back to the window to watch the twins run shrieking across the yard below and wish he might see Frieda run after them. She didn't appear, but he closed his eyes and conjured the bright-eyed, rosy-cheeked image of her and could nearly believe his uncle's words were true.

Max hadn't managed to string together more than a few hours of restless sleep since Felix's death, but here in the attic bedroom of his uncle's house half a world away from his troubles, easy, dreamless sleep finally overtook him.

It didn't last very long.

Despite the darkening of the sky outside the little round window, Mutti's knock on the door might have come only a few minutes later. Max shook off the dizziness of sleep, told his mother he would be downstairs soon, and did his best to smooth his rumpled shirt.

When he did descend to the first floor of the house, it was as if he'd been lowered into a boiling cauldron of chaos. The house had filled in his absence, its cacophony growing with a multigenerational chorus that assaulted his ears and would have forced him back up the stairs had he not spotted Frieda in the corner of the sitting room. She beamed at him, which urged him forward with rhythmic steps echoing the pounding in his head that began the moment he realized her delight wasn't reserved only for him but extended to another who'd now stepped through the door.

Max recognized Ernst Winkler from the family portrait. The man possessed an open, honest face more reminiscent of his mother than his father, and he sported a red beard in need of a trim. His hair, too, stuck haphazardly from a cap that, once removed, unveiled an unkempt mass of greasy curls. He crossed the room toward his wife with long, eager strides, kissed her cheek, and thrust his hand toward Max, who begrudgingly shook it. He was the first of the three brothers Max would meet that night, and the one, much to Max's dismay, he liked the best.

The eldest, Richard, had studied law both in order to advise the business and evidently to prove his superiority to the rest of his less educated family. He stood tall, with his nose in the air as though he smelled something foul, and did not lower his gaze to meet Max's when the two were introduced. Richard laid claim to the little boy Johnny and a school aged boy whose name passed like water through Max's brain. Later he would remember him as the sullen boy, whose own attitude he might have mistaken for an arrogance similar to his father's if he'd not known of the recent loss of his mother. For Richard, too, he could muster some small amount of sympathy. Max knew perhaps better than anyone that a heavy heart can alter a man.

He found the second brother more difficult to take in and could have best described him as boisterous. His name was Hugo, though he introduced himself as the Americanized Hugh, and he was the kind of man to be openly amused at his own jokes so everyone in the room would understand he was having a good time and that they should, too. Probably he made a wonderful restaurateur, always the life of the party, ready to ensure a good time for all. Max didn't care for such men.

Ernst, on the other hand, Max could understand. This cousin had kicked off his work boots before entering the house and wiped his dusty hands on his dirt-smudged pants. Frieda tolerated the one kiss, introduced him to Max, and shooed her husband off to wash up. By the time the others had introduced themselves to Max in one roiling, confusing mass, Ernst had made his way back into the sitting room scrubbed clean and in fresh clothes. He'd also rescued his baby daughter from her eager new great aunt and handed her now to Frieda, who excused herself to go and feed the little girl, leaving the two cousins to get to know one another.

"Frieda says you're a builder?" Max asked, not knowing what else to say. He hadn't truthfully wanted to know the details of his cousin's life when Frieda offered them, as he'd been predisposed to dislike him.

"I am. The beer business is for men like my brothers."

"Softer men?" Max asked, not sure why he relished the opportunity to sow discord among the men of the Winkler family.

Ernst rubbed a rough hand over his beard and sank back onto the sofa. "Friendlier men, perhaps. They are more naturally interested in knowing others. They work hard. Their families work hard, but it's not for me."

"Because you're not naturally friendly?"

Ernst crossed his arms and tipped his head. "That's right."

"Yet, you are the one in the corner of the room getting to know your newly arrived foreign cousin, whom everyone else gawked at and abandoned."

A smirk formed beneath Ernst's scraggly beard. "You're family. And Frieda likes you. That's enough for me. It's not that I don't enjoy people. I prefer to keep myself to myself is all."

"Me too," Max said, touched that the man had so eagerly claimed this new cousin as family. Max could grudgingly see why Frieda might love this man.

Ernst studied him with intensity. "This family can be too much for men like us, I think, but your mother has fallen right into step." He gestured toward Mutti at the other end of the room, chatting away with Hugh's wife, Ann-something. As they watched, Mutti threw her head back and chuckled, exuding the kind of joy that comes from the soul and cannot be contained. Max tried to recall the last time he'd seen her so genuinely delighted about anything and couldn't conjure it.

"She's happy to be here."

"You're not?" Ernst asked.

For a man who preferred to keep himself to himself, Max's cousin certainly didn't hesitate to pry into someone else's business. An ember of resentment dropped into Max's stomach where it threatened to flare.

He swallowed and summoned a lie, meant not only for Ernst but for himself as well. "It's different here is all. For one thing, it's big. I'm sure I'll adjust eventually."

"You need to find something to do with yourself," Ernst said. "You're a farmer, yes?"

"I grew up farming with my father." Max shrugged. "I guess that makes me a farmer."

"I'd say so. You don't strike me as a beer man. Have you any building experience?"

"A little. Fences, chicken coops, barns." The last was a stretch. Felix hadn't so much as patched the roof of the barn since Max had been old enough to help. He did assist his father in maintaining the still from time to time but thought better of mentioning an experience that might demonstrate his suitability for working in the family brewing business.

Ernst leaned forward and bent his head toward Max as if to share a secret, too close for Max's comfort. His nose twitched at the stench of a working man who'd washed with haste and not well. "Any interest in working on a building site?"

Max pulled back a little and swiped at his nose. "I don't know. What kind of building site? I really don't have much experience."

"That doesn't matter. I can see you're a hard worker, or at least you must be to have grown up farming. No stranger to hard work, I assume."

"No," Max agreed.

"You can learn the rest. We could use another good man on the crew."

"Do you have your own building firm?"

"Someday I will. But I can talk to my foreman and I'm sure he'll have a place for you."

Max did enjoy working with his hands, creating beautiful things. Perhaps building would soothe the beast inside him and make this whole American experience less strange and more comfortable. "Will I have to speak English?"

"The foreman and some of the men speak German, but it will be a lot of English on the job. You'll have to learn."

Max straightened his back to sit up tall. "Frieda said she would teach me."

Ernst's serious countenance gave way to a happy pride. "There's no one better for the job. So, are you interested? Should I talk to the foreman?"

"I think I could be," Max said. "What kind of building is it?"

"We're working on the fairgrounds."

The tilt of Max's head must have revealed his ignorance about such things, because Ernst explained, "St. Louis is preparing to host a great world exposition starting next spring. It'll be more than 1,200 acres of exhibit halls and attractions, all of them designed to impress and inspire, and all in need of strong backs and careful hands to complete them."

"Oh, are you speaking of the fair?" Frieda walked up behind Max and reached over the back of his chair to hand the baby to Ernst before sliding onto the sofa beside him and injecting herself further into their conversation with admirable ease.

"We were." Ernst brought his tiny daughter up to his shoulder and began gently patting her back. Frieda tried to drape a dish towel next to the little head, but Ernst brushed it away and it fell back onto Frieda's aproned lap. "I'm going to see if we can hire Max to work on the grounds with me."

"What a wonderful idea." Frieda beamed. You'll absolutely love it. It's the most amazing spectacle."

Ernst began to protest. "Well, you might be overselling—" he said but was interrupted when the baby released a substantial belch and with it a white, mucous substance splatted onto her father's shirt collar.

"Guess we know what Marguerite thinks of your negativity."

"I'm not negative," he said, staring into the eyes of his captivated daughter. "You just ought to manage your expectations. The project has a long way to go."

Frieda gave no acknowledgement to his caution and focused entirely on Max, sending a thrill all through him. "It's going to be the biggest, most extravagant exposition the world has ever seen, and it's going to be right here in our city."

How big or extravagant other world expositions might have been, Max had no way of knowing, but Frieda's passion was contagious, her pride in her city washing over him even if he could not yet fully understand it. That he wanted to would have to be enough for now.

A few minutes later, Matilda called the family to gather around a long dining room table. When he tucked into a feast of sauerbraten and potato dumplings as delicious as any Mutti ever made along with warm apple tart for dessert and accompanied by plenty of the family's own dark brew, a sensation resembling contentment washed over Max, mingling with the aromas of home. The family was keen to take up the fair as the topic of conversation, which nicely deflected the attention they might otherwise have lavished on Max and Mutti.

Once the whole crowd of them got going, Max could recede into the private spaces of his own thoughts and eat in a semblance of peace while quietly attempting to replace dark thoughts with light. He and Mutti were alive and safe and together, welcomed by a family who loved them without even knowing them. He would learn the language of his new home with the help of a beautiful new friend, and he would help to build the greatest exposition the world had ever seen.

Chapter 4

In less than a week, equipped with little more than a handful of English phrases, Max stepped off a streetcar in St. Louis, Missouri, and onto the grounds of what would become the Louisiana Purchase Exposition.

His boots sank into the earth.

"Rubber mud," Ernst said by way of inadequate explanation as he pulled his own boot from its deep impression with a loud squelch.

Unhelpful as it was, the description was an apt one. Before them rose a forest of construction. Piles of lumber, stones, and other building materials stretched up like trees from the doughy ground, kneaded and abused by the treads of the giant cranes and steam-belching excavators now silently awaiting operators to call them to life for the busy workday ahead.

Amid the skeleton promises of grand structures to come stood other more completed façades, marble palaces overseeing the work with dignity. Regal pillars, grandiloquent towers, expansive archways, detailed scrollwork, and a dizzying array of statuettes emerged from the chaos as Max took it all in.

"It's a fairytale kingdom," he said. "These are exhibition halls?" As far as he understood, fairs were places to display farm animals and crops, goods of the countryside. These structures were not barns to be filled with prize pigs. They were mansions fit for dignitaries.

"The largest ones. I'm not sure what's what. It's the head architect's job to worry about that. Some will be concessions, many of them restaurants or shops. Others will be theaters or exhibition halls where people from all over America and the rest of the world will display their latest inventions and innovations." Ernst shrugged. "That's what they say anyway."

"And what are we to be working on?"

"Ah, follow me. We have the best part—Festival Hall, the focal point of the fair. Two hundred feet tall with an auditorium big enough to seat more than three-thousand people. By opening day, it will sit atop cascading waterfalls, and at night its gilded dome will be lit by electric lights that will shine bright enough to be seen miles away."

Ernst stretched his hand across the sky and through the man's vibrancy, as though he could actually see this shining building outlined in stars like a constellation in the night sky.

For now, scaffolding veiled much of the building itself which resembled a cake with a large frosted dome sitting atop a ring of columns. Sweeping stairs, lined by carved white railings, opened up into a large muddy pit where at most a few feet of water had collected and partially frozen over in the December chill.

His cousin led the way through the mud toward the stairs, pointing as he went. "This will be the Grand Basin. A system of pumps will pull water up from a diverted river to cascade in waterfalls along the sides of the stairs here. It's going to be spectacular."

Max could envision the stately dome standing guard over the massive buildings that would soon emerge from their bony outlines, each worthy to be called a palace. Most of the exterior walls of Festival Hall were already in place.

Workers streamed in from all directions, tools and lunch pails in hand, but every one of them walked with purpose on this crisp, clear morning. Max watched one man don a hard hat and begin to climb the side of the scaffolding. Another man emerged from the building carrying a bucket and proceeded to smear one of the pillars with a thick white paste.

"What is he applying to the walls? Some kind of paint?"

"It's called staff," Ernst explained as he pushed open one side of the massive double doors and the two of them stepped together into the array of construction inside the building. "A mixture of lime and cement, some glycerin, too. Gives the buildings a uniform look. Resembles an ivory-colored marble when it's hard."

Max stopped beside a pile of hand tools, his ears ringing from the scope of it all. "None of it is real?"

Ernst took a few steps back to meet Max's eye. "It's real enough, cousin. The buildings on the fairgrounds are meant to be temporary but create the illusion of permanence. When the fair is over, the grounds will return to what they were before, a large city park. Very little of the structure will remain. But for the duration of the fair, it will be a land of fantasy."

"That doesn't seem right." The entire city worked to create this magical dream and in the end they'd all wake up and it would be gone, nothing more than a faint whiff in the air, an echo of something once beautiful.

"Fairs don't last forever, and the city can't afford to build all permanent structures. Come on. I'll introduce you to the foreman and get you working."

Max met many men that day, including the one Ernst identified as the foreman. His cousin's insistence that the man spoke German had been an exaggeration, but then Ernst's own German was often a haphazard blend of unfamiliar expressions, peppered with English. The men's banter often only vaguely recalled the language of Max's homeland, as if they were speaking underwater, and he spent his day trying to decipher their muffled words.

The work was simple at least. His assigned crew worked on plastering some of the interior walls. He caught on well without a great need for complicated instructions, though the immense space swallowed him. Several times he had to steady himself, experiencing vertigo when he scanned the expanse of the auditorium with its high ceiling and massive platform that awaited the installation of the largest pipe organ in the world, with more than ten-thousand pipes.

Festival Hall was the largest building Max had ever spent time in and the prospect of its destruction after the duration of the fair was more than he could comprehend. His boss and fellow workers kept the building's fate well in mind, however, as they worked hurriedly when patience should have been required. Max struggled initially to embrace the furious pace and said as much to Ernst when the two met on their lunch break.

Over cold sausages, thick slices of dark bread, and flasks of strong coffee, Ernst explained, "The fair was supposed to open last spring. It got delayed because it became too much of an undertaking to complete. The city won't delay again. We work as fast as we can, as competently as speed will allow, and no more. In four months, this fair will open, whether we're ready or not."

"I see," said Max. And he did. More craftsman than builder, he considered the rushed nature of the work less than perfectly satisfying, but if he understood the project as a work of art under a hard deadline, it was more tolerable, even enjoyable at times. The days were long, the work draining, but Max appreciated solace in the one advantage this lent him. Between the grueling work on the fair site during the day and the mental exercise of English lessons each evening, he had little time to long for the farm in Stellingen, or to brood about the dark circumstances that had brought him to this place so far from his home.

Frieda drove him as hard as the foreman ever did. Each day after the evening meal, he sat down at the dining room table with her to practice his English while Matilda and Mutti cleaned up from supper and Ernst put the baby to bed.

"Ich kann diese Sprache nicht lernen," Max said, as he did every night. After the fourth time he could have given her response in English, but he enjoyed hearing her do it.

"You can learn this language, Max. You will learn this language."

This night he decided to impress her. "I can learn this language," he said in English. "I will learn this language."

The pleased reaction he'd anticipated paled in comparison to the delight she demonstrated by pulling her hands together with a squeal. "Excellent! Sehr gut!"

In fact, Max found English less difficult than he'd first imagined. The structure of it was strange, but words translated easily from one to the other, and it made a sort of logical sense now when he heard his German family and coworkers flowing easily between the two, sometimes in the middle of a sentence.

Wisely, Frieda had begun teaching him first the phrases he was most likely to use on the job site, including the English names of tools and construction materials, simple instructions like direction commands, time references, and warnings of danger. He dutifully watched her mouth form each sound, her soft pink lips molding the perfect letter O, the way her tongue kissed the back of her teeth to make an L. He copied each, forcing his own mouth into awkward shapes until his letters parroted her own.

Each day, at her command, he practiced a new phrase or two with the other workers on the job, enduring their merciless teasing when he misplaced his verbs or volunteered a phrase in the wrong context. The men were eager enough to correct him, and in this way, he learned to comprehend their conversations. After several weeks, he ventured to join them with more confidence.

"I can learn this language," he said one night in late January as Aunt Matilda cleared the dishes and he sat beside Frieda. She was fresh and beautiful in a blue dress that accentuated her waistline, slim and lovely eight months after her daughter's birth, and made her eyes sparkle all the more in the fluttery light of the room's gas sconces. "I will learn this language. I have learned this language."

"Oh, Max." She placed a delicate hand on his arm. "You have worked so hard and have learned so much. I'm very proud of you."

She blushed, and he felt his cheeks match hers. He slid his arm from her hand and clasped her fingers instead. "Thank you for teaching me."

His words neither slow nor sluggish, he knew what he wished to say and saw the phrases forming in his mind before he said them. They materialized as English words, rather than translations from German. He could at times now think in a new language, and it was all thanks to this wonderful, encouraging woman in front of him.

If his thoughts had been more generous, he might have realized he perhaps owed much of his success to the men he worked with who conversed with him day after day, correcting his missteps and poor pronunciations with friendly ridicule and grace. It might have occurred to him that Ernst had been a part of this process, that during their daily lunches on the fairgrounds, their conversations had transitioned to include more and more English. But Max wasn't thinking of his crew of workmen, and he definitely wasn't thinking of Ernst.

At that moment he focused only on Frieda. He squeezed her fingers, leaned forward, imagined her lips demonstrating for him the shapes of foreign sounds, and in the shimmering light, with no one else in the dining room of his uncle's St. Louis home, he met those lips with his.

Chapter 5

The sting of the well-deserved slap Max received from his cousin's wife didn't hurt nearly as much as the sharp look of betrayal she flashed at him.

"What were you thinking?"

The words carried not even a hint of the slight German accent that usually haunted her English, and it gave him pause to wonder whether she put it on for the benefit of the family into which she had married.

"I am sorry."

He spoke in English, because his response required careful reining, and he feared his native tongue would run as wild as the thump of his heart. His first instinct was to confess his adoration of her, but his impropriety had already done much to communicate his affections and had not been well received. He hadn't meant to kiss her. He'd never have dared had he not been blinded by an overwhelming sense of intimacy. She'd tasted of the sugared fruit Aunt Matilda had served for dessert. He licked his own lips in remembrance and fought the urge to lean toward her for another.

"Are you?" she snapped and he straightened, forcing himself to back away from her.

"It was a mistake. I was so happy, pleased with how well I had learned from your teaching. I—" He couldn't conjure the English words to express that she was the greatest source of light in his dark world, that her belief in his abilities buoyed his heavy spirit. He wanted to express that, while the image of her patiently demanding lips danced through the quiet spaces of his mind, he respected her marriage and did not wish to cause her embarrassment. Instead, he said, "It will never happen again."

"It most certainly will not." Red blotches formed across her porcelain complexion. Frieda brought delicate fingers to her mouth to wipe away the shocking kiss and reached to scoop up the primer they had been working with from the table. "Our lessons are over. I have to tend to the baby."

She turned on her heel and stormed out of the room, the swish of her skirt echoing in the empty dining room. For that, at least, he could be grateful. There had been no witnesses to his folly. She might not tell her husband of the unfortunate encounter. No one but the two of them would ever need to know.

Or perhaps, he realized with a start, she would tell Ernst of his mistake. Even after working with him for months on the fairgrounds, Max couldn't be sure how the man would react to such a revelation. Ernst was sensible, reasonable. He kept his private life private. While the men around him complained of their wives and families, Ernst remained ever loyal. He worked hard because he desired to save up for the future he and his wife dreamed of for themselves and their daughter, a responsibility he carried on broad shoulders and a strong back. His presence instilled confidence, and his bearing commanded respect. Ernst had been nothing but kind to his strange foreign cousin, and as repayment for that kindness, Max betrayed him.

Max tried to swallow the lump now lodged in his gullet. It didn't matter whether Frieda chose to share his indiscretion with her husband. Max could not bring himself to face Ernst either way.

The next morning, Max did not descend from his small attic room in time for the predawn breakfast he and Ernst usually ate together before heading to the fairgrounds. When the inevitable knock came on his door and his cousin's voice called his name, Max did not detect the malice that would surely be present if the man knew his shameful secret.

Somehow that didn't make him feel better.

"I'm sick," he grumbled. "Go on without me."

Ernst offered muffled well wishes and his heavy footsteps echoed on the stairs.

Max turned over on his mattress and buried his head beneath a pillow. He wanted no part of a confrontation with Ernst, but just as difficult would be an encounter with Frieda after her husband had already left for work. He lay still and listened to the noises of the house—the distant clank of pots and pans being scrubbed in the kitchen, the happy squeal of a content baby. As he focused in, separating strings of sound, he heard the thud of the heavy front door and the rapid footsteps of children streaming into the sitting room and straight through to the dining room and the kitchen. The rest of the brood had arrived.

Light, feminine steps approached his door, and his ears grew hot. He wasn't prepared to see Frieda again and when the knock came, he nearly cried out that he wished to be left alone, but the creak of the hinges he'd meant to oil told him his time had run out.

He lifted the pillow enough to peek at the intruder. Mutti stood beside his bed—lips pursed, hands on hips—her brow creased with worry.

"Maxie?" she said with caution. She did not reach for him, but he suspected she knew, in that uncanny way she always did, that he was awake.

Sunlight streamed through the slats in the round window that provided the only peephole from the attic to the greater world.

When he didn't respond, she stepped into the room and sat beside him on the bed, lifting the pillow to place her hand upon his forehead.

"Ernst said you were ill." She spoke in the soft, familiar German of his childhood, but even she had been influenced by their surroundings in this new land. Hints of a lazy American flatness had begun to tear at the edges of her words. The sound of it brought tears down his cheeks, which Mutti wiped away with her soft hand.

"You do not have a fever. What's going on, Maxie?"

How could he tell her he had kissed Frieda, attacked her even, for that is what it had become in his mind. She was the defenseless damsel and he the ravenous villain.

"I'll be okay," he finally said. "I'm a little sluggish this morning."

Mutti swept the hair from his forehead and sighed. "You have been working yourself too hard."

"No." He shook his head. He pushed himself up on his elbows. "I enjoy the work."

Mutti's hand dropped to her lap and her gaze met his. "Yes," she said. "I can see that. Ernst has been good to you, setting you up with a job using your hands and creativity."

"I don't know about creativity," he answered, not wanting to comment upon how good Ernst had been to him. She was right. He had been a champion for Max, getting him work satisfying enough to distract him from the weariness of life so far from home and from the dread he'd tried to leave there. "I only paste plaster on buildings. Temporary buildings."

"Palaces. Temporary or not, they are works of art that will hold precious treasures from around the world."

"I suppose so," Max said and pulled himself the rest of the way to sitting.

The thin blanket slid down to his waist, revealing a stained undershirt. Mutti tucked the edge of the blanket around him as if he were a child, and the impulse to cry nearly overwhelmed him.

"Mutti," he said, and she stared into his soul, her expression soft and loving, prepared to forgive him anything as she had always done. Never had he looked at her and found anything but devotion, complete and all-consuming. "I miss home."

He made this confession in such a low whisper he couldn't be sure he'd voiced it aloud at all until she brought her hand to his cheek and cupped it lightly. The callouses had eased from her fingers, though he knew she was not a lady of leisure. Most days she worked in the beer garden with her brother and his sons. She had taken over the responsibility of cooking and had expanded their menu to include a wide variety of classic German foods that appealed to their clientele who yearned, as Max did, for a taste of home. But he couldn't deny she'd been happy. As long as her days might have become, they were nothing compared to the difficult life of the farm—the hard life of being the wife of a hard man whose ambition never reached further than his temper.

Mutti's thumb stroked his stubbled jaw line, transferring to him the weight of a guilt so heavy he had difficulty breathing. "We live here now, Maxie."

"You do," he said and could barely believe the next words that fell from his mouth without his permission. "But must I?"

She dropped her hand from his cheek and pulled away from him, her complexion a pale mask of fatigue. She pinched the bridge of her nose and exhaled before looking back to him, a flash of anger etched across her brow. The source of her fury hid beyond his reach. "Yes, Max," she said, jaw clenched. "You live here now as well. Neither of us will ever look back to Germany. We move forward." And the next bit she said in English, as sternly as Aunt Matilda reprimanding one of her grandchildren. "Get up and wash yourself. You are going to work."

Within the hour, Max shaved and dressed and boarded a streetcar bound for the fairgrounds. He'd not paused for breakfast, desperate as he'd been to avoid Frieda as he rushed down the stairs and from the house.

The crisp air of that late morning in January helped to clear his mind. He needed to be out of the house, away from the structure that sheltered his sin.

The fairgrounds bustled with activity as always. The mud had hardened in the cold, making the walk across deep construction ruts easier. In some places, too, the landscaping team had already begun to level paths marked out with brick edging and sparse examples of evergreen foliage hardy enough to bear the conditions of a Missouri winter.

It did Max good, he decided, to be walking the grounds. The fair, or the outline of it, had become a sort of home after all, with its familiar balanced whir of industriousness and dream, the friendly banter, even that which he did not quite understand, of his colleagues, a comfort into which he could fit and experience peace.

If he were honest, Mutti's change in mood when he mentioned the possibility of returning home had frightened him, the implication of it pounding through his head with every step. It did not surprise him she'd be determined to stay far from Stellingen, the scene of her sad life with Felix. He understood as much. What he could not make sense of was the flare of dangerous anger behind her eyes. She must have been haunted more than he realized by her past if the mere hint of possibly returning could instantly shatter her contentment.

PARADISE ON THE PIKE

Max tried to swallow the lump of suspicion now stuck in his throat as an awful idea he refused to allow to fully form in his brain. As free as Mutti lived now in this new life of contentment, he could see the oppressive weight of an intense guilt bending her. Unbidden, the image rose in his mind of his father's slumped figure on the barn floor, the crumpled heap that had so recently been a hard and stubborn man. Max shook his head. He would not connect Felix's misfortune and Mutti's guilt.

This fully formed determination made him shudder, and he realized while he had been lost in his swirling thoughts, he'd also become lost on the fairgrounds. Instead of heading south past the Electricity and Machinery Palaces toward Festival Hall where Ernst and an entirely new source of guilt lay, he had veered to the west and now entered what was known as the Pike, a long street of sorts lined with the peculiar and more strictly entertaining elements of the fair. Behind him the stone giants of the larger exhibit buildings waited for him; in front of him, a choice.

To his right, a replica of a great mountain range loomed over an expansive swath of construction. He could see the peak of a cone roof with a distinctly German flair, and his breath caught as he took in the sight.

He turned his back to it and walked down the longer length of the Pike, passing plots which each contained great incomplete structures, surrounded by fences and signs that probably identified what their completed building would be, what wonders they might hold. Max did not try to read them. The letters jumbled into foreign combinations he feared he wouldn't comprehend. Not an especially strong reader in his native tongue, Max's grasp of reading English remained at best tenuous even as his conversational skills improved.

On the south side of the street stood a row of unique structures, not the great marble-like palaces that surrounded the basin yet buildings that looked as if they might belong somewhere very different than the places they now sat. Then, from somewhere to his right, on the north side of the Pike, came the familiar sound of his native tongue. It wasn't the broken and sewn haphazardly back together speech patterns of his American relatives, but the genuine German of his former life.

He spun toward the sound to discover a flat area, surrounded on two sides by scaffolding set against framed, two-story structures, each with a peaked roof. Workers rushed about in the space, tools in hand, some of them climbing the scaffolding to nail boards into place. Max felt the pull to return to his own place of work, but not before he traced the source of the German. He approached the fencing surrounding the construction site, and on it he discovered a sign similar to those he'd passed on other lots. This one, too, held unfamiliar words, but one stood out to him as something he recognized: Hagenbeck.

Max's cheeks tightened and his lips stretched into a wide smile. The man in his neat gray suit on the back of a fine horse popped into his mind. Max had traveled thousands of miles away from home, and somehow, home had followed him here.

Chapter 6

Half a year and half a world away from the death of his father, Max's world began to right itself again. Delirious with the unexpected delight of it, he approached the sound of his native tongue, which emanated from the mouth of a man who might have been Herr Hagenbeck himself.

Like his counterpart, the man wore a crisp suit and carried himself with quiet dignity. He was clean shaven, a bit broader than the man Max remembered from Stellingen, but younger. Max waited for him to finish issuing instructions to a small band of coverall-clad, pink-cheeked construction workers, who hung on their boss's words, drinking them in completely even though they consisted of nothing more than measurements of a trench they were evidently supposed to dig.

"Herr Hagenbeck?" Max asked tentatively when the man had finished speaking.

The boss turned his back on his work crew and returned the greeting in the fluent German of home. "Guten tag. Do I know you?"

Max hesitated. The more he studied the man the less he resembled the Hagenbeck Max remembered, but then there was something in the line of his jaw, the shape of his nose, the way he moved his hands as he spoke.

"I don't think so." Max pointed to the sign. "I know this Herr Hagenbeck."

"Ah, I see. I recognize a Hamburg accent. May I assume we share a homeland?"

"No, sir." Max fumbled for an explanation. "I am from the village of Stellingen, outside Hamburg. My farm, we—"

"Stellingen? That must be where you met my father, then."

That made sense. The man was indeed an imperfect reflection of the self-identified animal dealer who had purchased Max's home to make a place for his creatures, and he'd sent his son to St. Louis to do the same.

Max grew lighter with the discovery of the connection, as if a weight lifted from his chest. "He purchased our farm for his tierpark."

"And now you are in St. Louis. How wonderful! Have you arrived recently?"

"Yes," Max said. He explained that he was now living with his mother's brother, that they were using Herr Hagenbeck's generosity to begin a new life in America. The younger Hagenbeck listened attentively, not once interrupting as Max spilled more of his story than he'd intended. It felt good to describe the journey to America in his native language to someone who knew so much about his home—so good he even let slip that his father's sudden death pushed them to sell the farm and leave Stellingen.

Hagenbeck did not focus on that part of the story beyond offering a brief word of condolence.

"It does my heart good," he said, "to meet you and hear of your enthusiasm for the tierpark project. It's coming along well, you'll be glad to know."

Max welcomed the news, but disappointment he would not see the completed park stabbed at him.

"Thank you, Herr Hagenbeck," he said. "It was nice to meet you." Max glanced back toward the end of the street, toward the peaks of the palaces beyond. He couldn't be sure how much time had passed, but guilt over his absence from work tainted the joy of encountering a piece of home. He'd have to be getting back to Ernst and Festival Hall, to make his excuses for begging off the morning's work, and somehow face his cousin.

Hagenbeck must have noticed his discomfort because his demeanor changed from friendly to concerned. His brow furrowed. "What did you say your name was, son?"

"Max Eyer."

"Well, now Max, my name is Lorenz, or as my American friends often say, Lawrence. Are you working on the fairgrounds?"

"I'm on one of the construction crews, currently assigned to Festival Hall. I'm doing the final plastering."

"Good, good. Do you have a lot of construction skills?"

"I have some," Max said, not quite daring to get excited by the line of questioning. "Working on the farm requires a lot of different skills. And I am a fast learner."

"I'm sure both of those statements are quite true." Lorenz rubbed his chin in thought. "Did you care for a lot of animals on your farm as well?"

Max rubbed a hand across the back of his neck. "Äh, yes, we had some farm animals."

"Because I could use a good German lad like you, both during our construction process and as the Hagenbeck Animal Show gets underway. Might that interest you?"

"Perhaps." Max chose caution, unable to quite grasp the opportunity he was being handed. "What kind of help would you be looking for?"

"Well, we can always use hands in construction, and some familiarity with animal care and training would be handy even in the designing stage. My father and I have drawn up the plans for the best possible enclosures, without bars, to provide our visitors with up close animal experiences. We're calling it the Animal Paradise on the Pike. Of course, now that we are finally here on the fairgrounds, I need men who can make adjustments as necessary and who might know a thing or two about making sure the animals are well cared for and also managed by a firm hand."

"I could do that. Thank you, Herr Hagenbeck."

"Think nothing of it, my boy. It would be a pleasure to have a fellow countryman and a farm animal expert on hand, but I'm Lorenz around here. Herr Hagenbeck is my father. I admire him, but I can't fill his big shoes. I've not often been Herr Hagenbeck when we work so closely alongside one another. It would be confusing. I don't wish to make a thing of that here, either."

Max doubted taking care of chickens, a milk cow, and a horse made him a farm animal expert, and he certainly had no special knowledge about the more exotic creatures that would populate the concession, but he was also quite certain Lorenz Hagenbeck wasn't truly expecting him to be experienced. Max was, for him, surely a sense of home, just as Lorenz would be for Max.

"Is your crew German?" They must have been, for Max had heard his language well spoken, as if the speakers never bothered with any other tongues.

"Some of us, yes, but not all. It's a varied group." Lorenz leaned closer and with the hint of a sneer he said, "We have an American business partner who hired most of the construction crew. They all speak primarily English. Do you speak English, Max?"

"Somewhat." He thought of his lessons with Frieda, of her perfect lips, and of the devastating way his lessons had ended. The skin on the back of his neck burned. "I was taking lessons."

"The way to get better is to throw yourself into it. Our head animal trainer is an Englishman." Lorenz raised his gaze as if he expected the man to appear. "He'll help you out, I'm sure. You'll find it a valuable skill as you settle into your new home."

"Will your father be at the fair?" Max asked, hopeful. The creator of tierpark had become a larger-than-life figure in Max's mind. He belonged in the fantastical setting of the fair.

Lorenz beamed. "He's here now, in fact. I had to unload some elephants in New York and then he met me and we traveled here together to oversee the finishing touches of the concession. He'll be here for a few weeks and then will have to head back to his project in Stellingen. I'd take you to him now, but he's in a business meeting for a little while yet. You can wait if you like. I can have one of the men show you around."

Max would have liked nothing more than to stay with Lorenz Hagenbeck in the shadow of the Tyrolean Alps, but he could not avoid Ernst forever, and receiving an offer for an exciting new job inspired bravery. "I should be getting back for now."

"Of course. Don't let me keep you. I'll have our man reach out to the building manager and make arrangements for your transfer to our site. Continue to report to your current assignment and we'll let you know when you can start with us." He reached out a hand for a shake, which Max met with his own firm grip. "Welcome aboard, Max."

"Danke. Vielen Dank."

Max left the grounds of the Hagenbeck Animal Paradise with his heart lifted, but the farther he got from it, and from his new friend and the old familiarity of home, the more his spirits began to sink again. His steps became heavy, the toe of his boot catching on the tortured ground. He made it nearly half the distance toward Festival Hall before he turned instead toward the entrance he'd arrived at on the streetcar at Lindell Boulevard.

When he emerged from the fairgrounds, he didn't bother to wait for a ride but instead followed the road toward the main part of the city in the direction of the Mississippi River. He'd not taken much time before to observe the city beyond the grounds of the fair.

Nothing could be more different than the Village of Stellingen, with its rolling potato fields and homes pieced together by bricks saturated with the stories of generations. The City of St. Louis ranked fourth in size in the United States, Max had been told by an overly proud Ernst. Yet the noxious odor of rendering plants and the foul grunge of industry choked the air in the city, rife with the competing concerns and cultural clashes of a wild and messy tableau of humanity.

Despite this, the city possessed a certain beauty, and an optimism for the future, perhaps aided by the anticipation of the Exposition during which St Louis would be on display for the whole world. Lindell Boulevard, which led from downtown to the northern border of the fairgrounds and to the campus of Washington University beyond, had, in anticipation of the Fair, become a street lined with fine, new houses, attracting many of the city's wealthier citizens who had relocated to be closer to the action.

Max walked along the edge of the shaded road for more than an hour, his observations made hollow by his own roiling thoughts, as jumbled and conflicting as the atmosphere of the city he supposed he now had to call home.

Mutti's dramatic shift in mood when he'd expressed a desire to return to Stellingen niggled at the edges of his mind, attempting to wrest his attention away from the excitement of his new position with Hagenbeck's Animal Paradise on the Pike and the dread of telling Ernst about it. His cousin would surely ask why Max was making the change, and he spent the afternoon concocting a plausible story that might lead away from his indiscretion with the man's wife.

When his feet began to ache in his work boots, Max at last chose a place to hop onto a street car. He switched lines twice, winding through several parts of the city he'd not yet seen, admiring the various architectural designs and cultural vibes of the city's varied citizenry before he finally wound his way back to his uncle's Central West End neighborhood. Once there, he continued to walk until the shadows grew long, the gas street lamps glowed, and he could no longer justify to himself the need to stay away.

"Max! Feeling better?" Ernst greeted him as he pushed through the door, slipping into the kitchen from the alley in back of the house. His cousin stood there with Mutti who laughed following something Ernst must have said as she stirred a pot steaming with a spicy aroma. Max's empty stomach grumbled, and his hunger overwhelmed his anxiety with the more pressing drive to eat.

Mutti ladled stew into a bowl and handed it to him with a spoon. He sat at the table, spoon half lifted when Frieda entered the room.

"You're back," she said, her voice edging toward forced cheerfulness.

"I needed some air," Max explained, a weak excuse, but all he could muster standing beside his barrel-chested cousin and rosy-cheeked Frieda.

"Understandable," Ernst said, evidently oblivious to the increased tension in the room. "Nothing like a brisk walk in the cool air to set you right after a bout of sickness."

Frieda released a huff and, without saying anything, crossed the room to retrieve a kitchen towel she carried back out with her. If Ernst noticed anything unusual in her behavior, he did not comment on it. Instead, he squeezed Max on the shoulder and said, "I made your excuses to the supervisor. He's a longtime friend and was understanding, but you will be on the job again tomorrow?"

Max nodded before he thought about it. In fact, he had hoped he wouldn't be on the job tomorrow. He hoped he would be at the Animal Paradise concession working with Lorenz and his crew, but despite the hours he'd spent mulling over and practicing exactly how he could explain that he'd been on the fair site today and had not come to work, but instead had gotten another job, he hesitated to form the words.

"Thank you, Ernst. I am much better. I will be at the fairgrounds tomorrow." Max spoke in English, slowly and carefully. If he somehow failed to communicate in a way his family could understand, he could always blame the difficulties of the language.

Ernst met his effort with approval. "Ah, your English is getting good. You almost sound comfortable speaking it. Frieda has beaten you into shape, ya?"

A flush crawled up Max's neck, but his cousin's cheerfulness did not waver. He could not know that Frieda had justifiably slapped Max the previous night and that shame for his inappropriate behavior had kept him away today.

"Yes," he managed, his teeth clenched. "She is a good teacher. In fact," an idea occurred to him. If he could couch his new experience, his new job, in terms of Frieda's ability, perhaps hide it among a series of compliments, the pill would be more easily swallowed. "I think her tutoring has helped me get another job."

"What are you talking about?" Mutti stopped her stirring and squinted at him. "You won't be working with Ernst anymore?"

Ernst folded his thick muscled arms. His brow furrowed.

"Äh, no," Max began to explain. "Well, yes, actually. For a little while longer, but today when I recovered, I decided to go to the worksite and put in a few hours, but I never made it."

Neither Mutti nor Ernst said anything, waiting for him to continue.

He swallowed hard. "I made it to the grounds in the late afternoon, but then had second thoughts about going to the job site, as I didn't know if I might continue to feel sick and if it might be better if I didn't go at all. While I thought it over, I walked along the Pike area, past the construction there, and spotted a familiar name."

Max explained to them how he'd seen a sign with Hagenbeck's name and then heard German in a familiar accent and introduced himself to Lorenz who'd been both excited to encounter a fellow countryman and impressed with his English. When he identified his new friend as the son of Carl Hagenbeck, Mutti brought the back of her hand to her mouth in surprise, and when Max said he'd accepted a job from the man, she cried out.

"Nein!" she scolded, stern and insistent. "You did not tell him you would work for him, did you? You already have a job, a commitment, to Ernst."

"It's okay," Ernst said quickly.

"It is not. He gave you his word."

"No, no, it's not so serious. Crews trade men across the grounds sometimes. This Hagenbeck will need to work it out with the foreman. There shouldn't be too much trouble." He gestured toward Max. "I'm happy for you, cousin. I'll miss having you on the job site, but this could be a good opportunity for a farmer like you."

Max didn't care for the tone his cousin adopted when the word farmer slid off his tongue resembling an insult, but at least this news would distract from any other things that might attract the man's notice, like the fact that his famer cousin dreamt of kissing Ernst's wife.

Chapter 7

Max loved everything about Hagenbeck's Animal Paradise on the Pike except for the snakes.

Two days after meeting Lorenz for the first time, Max began working for the Hagenbeck family on the grounds of the Louisiana Purchase Exposition and received a proper tour of the concession.

Without plaster to mix or fake marble to sculpt into the mirage of permanence, construction took on a different look on the Pike where imagination ran more wild. What the fair's primary entertainment district lacked in cascading fountains and grand palaces, it made up for in bold variety and creative fun.

Across from the Animal Paradise stood a Japanese pagoda beside a gigantic statue of Atlas holding up a miniature world. Down the way from them, a path wound through a model neighborhood complete with hospital and shops, and in the distance to the west loomed the Tyrolean Alps rising above a Bavarian castle slated to feature high-end German cuisine.

But nothing else captured the fantasy of it all quite like the Animal Paradise itself, which consisted of a wide-open arena in the center with high wooden risers, and numerous animal enclosures without bars to impede the visitor's view of exotic animals in approximations of their natural environments.

To one side of the arena, seals frolicked beside a pond on slick rocks covered with a thin layer of ice in the chill of early March while white birds with long beaks perched on overlooking boulders. Another area, separated by a trench and low partition, held two bears lazing about in the sun. At the rear of the concession, a manufactured forest and swampland featured a walkway around which alligators would soon swim, and behind them a wall of glass-fronted vivaria awaited the arrival of numerous lizards and snakes.

"Snakes?" Max asked Lorenz on the tour, stopping in the middle of the walkway to shake off the sensation one had slithered across his foot. "Poisonous?"

"Some will be venomous." Lorenz wrinkled his brow in thought. "We'll have at least one Indian King Cobra for certain, but I'm not sure what else we'll receive. It depends on what the animal catchers manage and how many survive the trip. Snakes can be tricky. It also depends on whether any might be promised to other collectors."

"There are places that want them?" Max's voice cracked.

"Many people want venomous snakes, my friend—an element of danger to their zoological attractions."

"Will I have to care for such creatures?"

"Have no fear. You'll receive training from the best." He pointed at himself first. "Me, and of course our head trainer Reuben, who I know you'll get along with very well. We have experience handling these kinds of animals, and more impressive ones as well. We'll have you comfortable even with lions in no time. Hagenbeck's Animal Paradise on the Pike is a place to mingle with animals, not to fear them."

"And that's why there are no bars." Max had been told this would be the case at the tierpark that by now enveloped his home, but he hadn't been able to picture it until standing in this space.

Though not yet fully populated, the presence of several species already released into their new homes allowed Max to understand and appreciate the huge undertaking of such a concession design. Designed specifically for the comfort of each animal inhabitant as well as for the education of human visitors, the enclosures were separated from one another and from guest walkways by trenches, the width of which had been calculated based on careful observations of each animal's natural behaviors and abilities. Around these trenches, the landscape molded into cliffs and rock faces, pools and false icebergs, forming a backdrop precise in design for each animal inhabitant. The ingenuity of it delighted Max's artistic sensibilities. His fingers itched to create and complete such landscapes, though he hesitated at the idea of there being no bars between himself and a hungry lion. He said as much to Lorenz now.

"Oh, we have one here already," Lorenz said, then added, "Trieste. Brought him over myself."

"Trieste is the lion?" Max swallowed.

"Yes. He's quite tame, in fact. Come on. I'll show you."

Max followed Lorenz around the outside of the arena and across the swamp walkway through another gate they'd not yet explored, beyond which waited a series of large cages, tall enough for a man to stand in and deep enough to hold many wondrous creatures. Lorenz explained, "Some of the animals are waiting to move into their more permanent enclosures. There's still building work to do. It can be helpful, too, for them to acclimatize to the environment before they have too much freedom."

Max kept pace with Lorenz, wishing he could slow down instead and study the cages. Each held one or more exotic animal, some of which Max could confidently identify and some he could not be sure about. Two held enormous turtles, and in another, a creature with red-brown fur and resembling something between a bear and a racoon. He wanted to ask Lorenz what it was, but the man kept up a rapid pace to the very last cage in the row where a soft growl greeted him. Max backed away.

"Oh, no, that's nothing to worry about. He'll really roar at you if he's angry. That was more of a whispered greeting." He motioned for Max to come closer and he took a few careful, shuffling steps to peer into the cage.

Inside he saw a glorious creature, so clearly feline but larger than any cat Max had ever seen. "It's something like an overgrown barn cat." The comparison grew more remarkable as Lorenz reached his hand into the cage to scratch behind the beast's ear, tangling his fingers in its wild mane of brown fur. "It's a lion," Max said, stunned.

"Your first?" Lorenz asked.

He couldn't imagine adequate words. The creature was larger and more majestic than he'd imagined but also somehow less fearsome. He nodded. "He's nothing but an overgrown kitty."

"Well," Lorenz said, sliding his hand from the cage, "it's not quite that simple. He's a wild animal at heart. He would rip your throat out if he had a mind to. But he's mostly a sweetheart, aren't you, Trieste?"

Max took a larger step back and bumped into a crate behind him. Something hissed from inside.

"Nothing to fear," Lorenz reassured him. "Most animals behave in predictable ways. They get hungry. They get frightened. They get tired. And they crave affection. As long as you respect them, they will respect you. Animals never frighten me as much as people do."

A fine sheen of sweat slicked Max's forehead. He stared into the lion's enormous amber eyes. Trieste stared back, his large pupil narrowing, and licked his lips.

"Ah, this must be Max!" A man's warm, enthusiastic voice caused the lion to raise his head and push up on his front paws to see around his new acquaintance. Max, uneasy about displaying his back to even a caged and seemingly friendly lion, turned only his head to find a slender man with a long nose, wide grin, and dark, piercing eyes.

"Rube," Lorenz greeted him. "Perfect timing. Yes, this is Max, the young man from Stellingen. Max, this is Reuben Castang, practically my brother and, second to my father, the best animal trainer in the world. He can train any animal to amaze and delight. You should see what he can do with the humble goat."

The newcomer, at most ten years older than Max and similar in age to Lorenz, beamed at Max and shot a friendly scowl at Lorenz. "On about my goats again." He explained in English with a strong British accent, "Lorrie is a brother in spirit certainly, and I did spend many years in Hamburg under the tutelage of the elder Hagenbeck, who was gracious enough to treat me as one of his sons."

"Most often better than." Lorenz gently elbowed his friend in the ribs. The men held obvious affection for one another, making Max, for an instant, the uncomfortable outsider.

The sensation didn't last. Reuben turned to him and said, "Can't tell you how pleased I am to meet you and hear of your enthusiasm for the tierpark project. It's coming along well, you'll be glad to know. Carl had a letter yesterday and said he was pleased with the progress."

"Where is the old man?" Lorenz asked. "I was hoping he'd be here to greet Max." Then he added to Max, "He was particularly delighted to hear you were in St. Louis and you'd be working with us."

Reuben rubbed a hand across his forehead. "Williamson is keeping him busy."

"Pete Williamson," Lorenz clarified to Max. "The American business partner. He can be a little difficult to work with."

"A pain in our ass is what he is. Fancy man thinks it should be his name on the entrance. Trouble is he doesn't know a damned thing about animals or about the cost of keeping them healthy and happy."

"I'm sure Father is taking him in hand," Lorenz said.

"If anyone could, it'd be Carl. I've seen him train many a cantankerous beast, but this man is more stubborn than the most obstinate jackass I've ever known."

"Come on now." Lorenz adjusted his hat. "You'll scare poor Max."

"Good," Reuben answered. He pointed to Trieste, alert in his cage, his predator eyes tracking among the three of them. "This one probably wouldn't hurt you if you jumped up on his back and dug spurs into his side, but you need to watch your back with that beast Willamson. He'll stab it the minute he gets a chance. I hope Carl understands that."

"He does," Lorenz said. "But let's not challenge the new guy to ride the lion like a horse. You know not to do that. Right?"

"Course he does," Reuben insisted with a clap on Max's back. "But just in case, I'll start you off with the goats. We need to get them into their enclosure, which is in need of some final touches. Sound good?"

Max blinked. "Ja. Goats." He lacked first-hand experience with goats as well but doubted they wished to eat him. Trieste, still glowering at the men, might do so if given the chance, and Max promised himself he would show the animal nothing but the utmost respect.

He also silently vowed to give this American business partner, Williamson, a wide berth. Max might not know much about exotic animals, but with beastly men, he had no shortage of experience.

─── ∞ ───

"How was your first day on the new job? Did you meet the animals?" Kindly Aunt Matilda, at least, did not hesitate to speak to him. Frieda busied herself in the kitchen and had largely avoided his presence since he'd arrived home. Mutti was at the biergarten, leaving Max relieved he didn't have to navigate her bizarre anger and grudging acceptance of his new job.

The children, as anxious as their grandmother to hear from their cousin, the wild beast tamer, turned their energy toward him. Four of the young ones—Hugh's twins Martha and Otto and Richard's two sons, Clyde and little Johnny—gathered around him in the sitting room, awaiting his reply. Matilda sat on the sofa behind them, poised to offer encouragement they didn't require to ask a hundred questions of their new cousin. They spoke in rapid-fire English and Max could not keep up, but it did not seem to matter. He answered Matilda's question, which was exciting enough.

"I met a lion," he said. Four bright faces glowed at his carefully pronounced words, setting off a new flood of unintelligible excitement. "His name is Trieste and he has great big, yellow eyes." Max circled his own eyes with his thumbs and fingers curled into large Cs to illustrate. The children gaped at him, suitably impressed.

"But a lot of the animals have yet to arrive at the grounds. My job right now is to finish making the places for them to stay."

"You're building a house for a lion?" asked Clyde with tight-jawed incredulity. His blond hair was mussed and the tail of his school uniform shirt had come untucked. Normally an unnerving miniature of his stoic father, the boy appeared surprisingly unkempt, which Max thought a nice change.

"Well, not a house, exactly." Max sifted through the English at his disposal for an apt description. "It's more of a yard. Though he will have a cave so he can hide from the crowds when he is frightened."

"Why would he be scared?"

This was a sensible question, but Max attempted to reproduce Lorenz Hagenbeck's explanation when he'd asked a similar one. "Lions are not used to many people. In Africa, where they are from, people avoid them, so when all the crowds at the fair gape at them, it will feel. . ." Max searched for a different, better word, but could find none.

"Frightened," Clyde finished for him, equipped now with a new knowledge about lions and a burst of puffed up confidence.

"Exactly," Max agreed, glad to see the boy's childish grin which contained several gaps where baby teeth had recently been. "The lion's enclosure is nearly finished and soon he will be able to stretch his legs and roar over the whole fairgrounds."

"Where is he now?" another child asked. This one was Martha, one of Hugh's twins, a pretty little thing with dark, curly hair, long lashes, and an endearing mischievous streak.

"He's in a large cage for now."

"But that's mean," she cried, her little chin quivering. The other children added their agreement.

"It's for a short while," Max assured them. "And he is comfortable for now, well taken care of by people he trusts." Max believed this much was true. However it had been forged, Lorenz clearly enjoyed a relationship with the lion. Max also understood he hadn't yet earned such trust from the beast. When Trieste looked at Lorenz, the animal's demeanor softened, its muscles relaxed and, had it the capacity to purr, Max did not doubt it would have.

When the animal made eye contact with Max, however, its jaws began to clench with a tension that filled the air. He'd spent his first day on the job putting the finishing touches on the large sculpted cave beside the open trench that would separate Trieste from himself and from the thousands of fairgoers the lion also had no reason to trust and every reason to attack. Despite Lorenz and Reuben's assurances the big cat probably wouldn't hurt anyone, Max questioned while he worked whether the trench would be enough.

These concerns he did not share with the children. Instead, he pivoted to descriptions of animals he felt much more comfortable around. "The head trainer at the animal show is a man named Reuben," he explained. "And he is very good with goats."

Martha quirked one eyebrow and wrinkled her nose. "Goats?"

"Äh." Max extended his pointer finger and touched the little girl's nose. "Yes, stubborn goats that he convinced to stack one on top of the other like this." He got up on his hands and knees and gestured for the children to do the same. Then, one at a time, he helped them to carefully pile the smallest ones on the backs of the larger until they formed a clumsy pyramid. Soon they became a herd of tumbling, giggling goats romping across the floor of the sitting room.

Max sat back on his haunches and watched, joining Matilda in the first deep belly laugh he could remember experiencing in a long time. Content, his gaze drifted to the archway leading to the entry hallway to discover, hovering above the wild goats, a smiling Frieda. The moment he caught her attention, she turned away and disappeared down the hallway toward the kitchen.

Chapter 8

Lions, seals, goats, and children tramped through Max's thoughts while the streetcar rolled toward Forest Park and Ernst prattled on about the humongous steel wheel taking shape on the fairgrounds.

"Have you seen it yet?" he asked Max as they approached the Lindell entrance to the fairgrounds, where they both hopped off.

Max attempted to recall his cousin's monologue, unsuccessfully searching the piled up words for meaning. "I haven't," Max volunteered. "What is that?"

"The Ferris Wheel? It's precisely what the name suggests—an enormous wheel, originally designed for the Chicago fair, but we'll make better use of it. There are boxes along the outside for people to ride in as it revolves. They say you'll be able to see the entire fairgrounds from the top of it."

"Sounds terrifying." Max hoped this was the correct response.

"Perhaps," Ernst agreed. "But it sure is impressive. It's northwest of Festival Hall. The round frame is about half complete. It's a sight to see."

"I'll try to take a look. Will it be finished by the opening?"

Ernst shrugged. "Will any of it?"

Max doubted it. There was still so much to do, but then the many weeks he'd been on the grounds were marked with rapid change at what should have been an impossible pace. The construction-torn grounds he'd first stepped onto had become a garden of pathways and thoughtful landscaping, of sculptures and buildings with complete albeit temporary façades.

He could envision a day on the horizon when he might pluck up the courage to stand in a box atop a tall wheel to see it all in one spectacular view.

He wished Ernst a good day and skittered around the backside of the Pike along the northern edge of the fairgrounds to enter through a smaller entrance that cut in right beside Hagenbeck's Animal Paradise.

Morning had become Max's favorite time on the fairgrounds, before the activity of the day really got going and the air filled with the sounds of construction and the hum of hundreds of workers bustling about. The calls of foremen, the hammering and saws, the mechanical belches of heavy equipment were enough to drown out a man's thoughts, but before any of that began, the sun rose on a burgeoning masterpiece of ingenuity and craftsmanship, of dreams and imagination.

Max could have believed the nearly completed pagoda on the Pike had come straight out of Japan. The fake mountains rising at the end of the brick roadway might have been wild and dangerous and capped with real snow. In front of them, the great castle where hungry fairgoers would soon grab a bite to eat might have housed a great prince who oversaw a sea of columned structures made of real marble that caught the light of the sun.

He'd arrived at the Animal Paradise earlier than he was expected, and he used his extra few minutes to climb the stairs to the right of the entrance and stand on the elevated walkway. It wasn't tall enough to see over the entire fairgrounds, but he could take in the view of the animal concession which was in itself spectacular.

In a relatively small space, here in the middle of America, the Hagenbecks had created a miniature of the world, complete with cliff sides and pools for all manner of creatures, and it stood across from a Japanese pagoda and in the shadow of a castle and the Tyrolean Alps.

"What do you think of it?" Carl Hagenbeck stepped up onto the platform and threw a fatherly arm over Max's shoulders.

Max warmed at the casual display of affection from this man who loomed so large in the memory of one of the most pivotal moments in his life, the surprise of seeing him now gluing Max's tongue inside his mouth.

Carl Hagenbeck continued as if Max's silence had answered his question. "It's nothing, you know, compared to the wonder that will be my tierpark at Stellingen."

"How's that project coming along?" Max asked with a pang of longing for the farm that had been his home and was now undergoing a transformation of its own, unfathomable to him until he'd seen the magic occurring in Forest Park.

Hagenbeck dropped his arm from Max's shoulders and placed his hands on the railing. "Not as beautifully as things are progressing here, but then there will always be delays when one is attempting to perfect a vision. We should be open in a couple of years, give or take."

"What kind of delays?" Max asked, sincere in his desire to know.

The man studied Max and sucked in his lower lip without answering. Voices rose from below them and Hagenbeck's attention shifted toward the concession entrance below. "Nothing to worry about, my young friend. All will work out."

He moved toward the stairs, and added, "Our Sinhalese have arrived! If you'll excuse me, I need to save them from Williamson. That cocky American is already trying to sink his claws in them."

Carl Hagenbeck hurried down the stairs without another word, leaving Max to wonder what kind of animal a Sinhalese might be. In his weeks at the Animal Paradise concession, he'd discovered at least a dozen species he'd never known to exist, but visions of bears and tigers melted the instant Max leaned over the railing to see a collection not of captured beasts, but of people like none he'd ever seen before—dark-skinned people in strange dress standing inside the entrance gate. Two white men stood with them, one tall and slender, the other short and round. The shorter man beamed and shook Carl's hand. The tall man did neither.

The brown-skinned arrivals included five young men clad in long skirts that wrapped around their middles, paired with slim, long-sleeved jackets that hung well below the waist. Atop the head of each sat a round, flat hat with an ornate band. An older man among them differed in appearance by his weathered, wrinkled skin and speckled hair visible below his cap. The seventh of the party was a young woman, slender and alluring in a rose-colored skirt that flowed around her waist and hips more than did those of her male companions. Her blouse, as far as Max could tell, was little more than an extension of the skirt fabric looped up around her neck and tucked back into the waist, though it was difficult to see precisely as she also shivered inside a woolen wrap.

The air did carry a slight spring nip, but Max, bound for mucking elephant stalls to start his workday, appreciated it in a way this woman clearly did not. The newcomers evidently preferred warmer weather.

So captivated was he by the brown-skinned woman that Max barely registered the movement when Herr Hagenbeck brought his palms together beneath his chin and bowed his head to the elder who did the same in return. Then the two embraced.

"Pamu, my friend!" Hagenbeck exclaimed in English, his words floating up to Max, suddenly embarrassed to be listening in. "How was your journey?"

"Very good, Mr. Hagenbeck. Thank you." The dark-skinned man answered in a strangely lilting English. "Your man escorted us to St. Louis and saw that we were very comfortable."

"Excellent, excellent."

"I thought there would be more of them," said the tall white man. He wore a tailored suit with pinstripes and a neat bowler hat in the precise shade to match and stood apart from the rest of them, suggesting that he was not the man who had ever seen to anyone's comfort but his own. He examined his fingernails as if the conversation bored him. The sun glinted off a jeweled ring on his pinkie.

Hagenbeck grumbled, "They are a perfectly sufficient number."

The older man said, his voice grown meeker, "I had hoped we would be a larger party, but I have brought you the finest mahouts I know." Four of the foreigners bowed as the elder man had done. Pamu then indicated the other man and the woman. "Your brother John said you also wished for a snake charmer, and so I have brought you one. Inesh is the finest charmer I know, and he travels with his sister Shehani. She is the most graceful dancer, and she fears nothing."

"We are thankful for all of you, and I know the fair visitors will be as well." Carl cut through his guest's discomfort with an easy grace. "Mr. Williamson meant no disrespect, I'm sure."

Williamson's pinched expression, from Max's vantage point, implied a lack of concern about his level of disrespect. Max didn't wait to hear whether he uttered an apology. The morning had grown long, and it was time to get to work.

He crossed the elevated walkway in the opposite direction toward the stairs and met Reuben at the bottom just exiting a tool shed that doubled as his office and butted up against the backside of the arena.

"Ah, good morning, Max! How are we looking from above?"

"The rocks look real," Max said, motioning to the backdrop of the enclosures along the edge of the space. The finishing touches on these fake boulders had been Max's first task on the job, but his comment was honest. They really did give one the illusion of a wild landscape.

"Yes, excellent workmanship." Reuben smirked. "Could you get started with the grazers this morning? We'll put off the elephants for now. They're picky about people and I need to get you properly introduced, but we're expecting our mahouts from Ceylon to arrive today, and the elephants will be put to work in the arena once they get here. Your job will be easier without their help." Reuben pulled a set of jingling keys from his coat pocket and handed them to Max, who took them with slight hesitation and no small amount of relief that he wouldn't meet the elephants immediately. He'd watched them the day before and while they struck him as gentle creatures, they were also large ones with a great deal of strength. He was not anxious to rake the ground around their stout legs and beneath their sagging bellies.

He studied the keys before commenting, "The mahouts have arrived already. Herr Hagenbeck is with them now at the entrance, along with Herr Williamson."

"Pete's there, too? That man has to have his hands in everything." Reuben shook his head and stomped off in the direction of the entrance. Before leaving Max's view, the trainer called back a reminder, "Grazers first, then elephants when we get them out. Ostriches after that. When you've finished with those, come help finish the arena benches. The crew there will be glad for another set of hands."

"Yes, sir," Max said to the space where Reuben had been.

He switched the keys to his other hand and wiped a sweaty palm on his trousers. Though he'd been shown how to properly clean the enclosures and care for the animals on his assigned list, Max had yet to perform these actions on his own. He tingled with nervous energy as he walked toward the door leading behind the grassland enclosure.

The unique Hagenbeck design called for no bars or fences to block the animals from the view of the public, but a hollow rock wall formed the background of the series of enclosures along the far end of the concession.

PARADISE ON THE PIKE

Aesthetically, the wall appeared as a natural barrier between the Animal Paradise and the neighboring Streets of Seville concession on the Pike. The wall served a practical purpose as well, however, as it contained the inner workings of the Hagenbeck open containment system.

Behind the rocks hid a backstage area arranged like a wide hallway with a series of indoor caged spaces connected to each outdoor enclosure through sliding doors that could be opened or closed with a pulley system on the outside of the cage. Max's limbs trembled slightly as he unlocked the entrance to this backstage space and flipped a switch to turn on an electric light.

The dank air smelled strongly of animal, the pungent aromas of each enclosure emptying into this one space. Max took a few shallow breaths to adjust to the stink of musk and a salty hint of fish. These mingled with the foul odor of feces and the sweet notes of hay that transported him to the farm in Stellingen, to the barn where his father had crumpled cold and lifeless on the dirt floor. Max's vision blurred and he swayed, his heart pounding, until he caught himself against a nearby shelf.

By the time he'd calmed and stood steady enough to let himself through the double set of doors into the herbivore exhibit with a shovel, rake, broom, and wheelbarrow, he was covered in sweat and had never been so happy to see a cow.

In fact, the animal that greeted him was a zebu, which he'd recently learned was an Indian type of cattle with a camel-like hump on its back. The creature nuzzled into Max's side and, when he gave it a scratch behind its pointed ear, it offered a greeting that more closely resembled a growl than the typical lowing familiar to Max. The animal was not aggressive, but it was determined and, Max decided, hungry.

He worked as hastily as he could with a variety of curious four-legged supervisors. One surly camel stayed well away, but all the others approached, determined to be wherever he was. Llamas, muntjacs, and Reuben's favorite two ornery goats took turns blocking his progress and forcing their ways between the broom and the pile of old hay and dry droppings.

"If you get them fresh food first, they'll let you get on with it."

Max turned to discover the source of this advice was the tall American from earlier in the morning. He stood directly across the trench, the jacket of his pinstriped suit slung casually over his shoulder. His bowler hat had been knocked askew, but still he looked out of place in the concession designed to house wild animals.

"I have to clean first. Then they get fed. Those were my instructions."

"Oh, Lord," the man said. "Another German. They get you right off the boat?"

"What?"

"What's your name, kid?"

"Max, sir."

"Well, Max, I'm Pete Williamson, one of the partners around here. We're getting ready to lead the elephants to the arena. You wanna help?"

"Herr Castang told me to clean the enclosure while they're at the arena, and I have to get the ostriches, too."

Pete leaned back and let out a low whistle. "If Mr. Castang said so, I guess you better get on with it then. See you around, Max."

Max thought to wave, but the man had already turned his back and headed down the path toward the elephants.

∞

It took Max another half hour to sweep and rake the grounds of the grassland enclosure. Then he unwound the hose from the storage room and sprayed down all the surfaces before spreading fresh hay. Later in the day he would return with a selection of vegetables most of the animals would enjoy, but for now he did a rushed cleanup in the empty elephant enclosure and headed to the ostriches.

The Pike contained a separate ostrich farm he was told would eventually house twenty or thirty of the large birds. Max couldn't imagine that many. Hagenbeck's Animal Paradise already had three of the cantankerous creatures that, along with camels, giant tortoises, and elephants, fairgoers would have the opportunity to ride around a track if they wished. Hopping on the back of any of the creatures didn't appeal to Max, but he especially didn't understand why anyone would want to ride an ostrich. They were moodier than grazers and substantially less patient for food, snapping at him as he worked. It was a relief when at last he finished with them and headed to the arena.

All eight of the elephants had been gathered in the arena, including Mataga, a baby born on the crossing from Hamburg. The elephants stood accompanied by the mahouts, each bearing a jewel-encrusted pole with a gleaming metal hook at the end. As Max watched, the largest elephant bent its front legs and brought its head down into a bow and the Sinhalese woman, no longer wearing her woolen wrap, walked out from behind the animal and leaned in to its ear as though she were whispering a secret.

"Pretty girl, isn't she?" The deep abrasive voice crawled over him, making Max want to flee. He turned to discover Pete Williamson had slid up beside him. "I mean, if you like them exotic."

He over-enunciated the last word, one Max did not know, though he caught the gist from Pete's demeanor.

"*Do* you like them exotic, Max?"

He couldn't possibly answer the question, even if he'd wanted to engage the man in conversation, but it soon became apparent Pete had no interest in his answer anyway. He gave Max a nudge and said, "Better get to work,

Max. Wouldn't want the boss thinking you were only here to sling your juice over his ethnographic exhibits."

Max shivered at this comment, though its precise meaning eluded him, and he was relieved to follow the man's advice about getting to work. He gave Pete a stiff nod, hopped up on the bleachers, and made his way to the far end where one of the workmen smoothed the topside of the bench with rough glass paper.

At his approach, the worker sat back on his haunches. "You're the new man?" Shaggy red hair escaped the edges of his flat cap. A too-trimmed beard failed to hide round, pockmarked cheeks.

Max squatted down beside him and held out his hand. "Max."

The worker shook his hand. "Finn." He turned and pointed to the top corner of the stands where bare scaffolding awaited bleacher seats. "The boys are cutting the last boards now and will get them nailed into place. We could use a hand with the smoothing, though. Can't have some dolled-up lady getting a splinter in her arse."

Max agreed and picked up another sheet of glass paper.

"I'm working my way up. You can start at the top of this section and we'll meet in the middle, yeah? Just the really rough spots."

Max, already on his way up, stopped and looked back at the sound of Finn's voice again, saying, "And hey, Max?" The redhead stepped toward him and leaned in close. "Don't let that Pete bother you too much. He's nothin' but a worthless rat. Even Lorenz says he'd get rid of him if he could."

Finn glanced toward the center of the arena where Pete had stepped too close to the dancing girl and rested a hand against her back. The elephant beside her fidgeted and stomped the ground. Pete pulled back, snickering. The girl's stony look suggested she had not enjoyed his touch.

"And I'll tell you what," Finn said. "If Old Man Hagenbeck thinks Pete's interfering with the ethnographic display, the old man will be none too pleased."

There was that word again. Max ventured the question he'd not have dared ask Pete. "What is this word—ethnographic?"

"That's what Old Man Hagenbeck calls his people exhibits. Likes to put the people and the animals together from the same parts of the world so the audience sees them more natural-like. That's why he brought all these Indians to handle the elephant, same way they do in their country."

"They're Sinhalese," Max corrected, carefully repeating the word Carl Hagenbeck had used for the foreign visitors.

"That not the same thing?"

"I don't think so."

Finn shrugged. "Anyway, they're handling the elephants. I'm glad to let them. I'll smooth the benches and not get trampled to death, thank you."

Max took one last look at the elephants, calm and compliant with the exception of the one Pete had approached which shuffled its large feet in the dirt and resisted falling into line with the others now marching around the arena edge. Reuben Castang approached the beast and said something to Pete, who moved away from the dancer and the elephant then walked out of Max's sight. Next, Reuben spoke to the elephant, stroking its long trunk as he did so. Max couldn't hear what the trainer said, but the last things he saw before he turned to the mundane work of smoothing bench seats were the animal falling into line behind the rest of its herd, and the Sinhalese woman, head bowed and arms wrapped around her middle.

Chapter 9

"Max! Got a second? I want you to come meet Lizzie."

Max finished smoothing the last board in the current section and waved to Reuben to signal that he'd heard. Finn and the other workers had packed up and left nearly twenty minutes earlier, but Max hadn't been at it for long, as he'd had to stop to feed and water some of the animals in the late afternoon. He wanted to get to a logical stopping place, but it had been a long day. It occurred to him that at this hour he could probably excuse himself from whatever else Reuben had in store for him. Only the thought of an awkward supper with Frieda stopped him.

Lizzie, it turned out, was one of the elephants, the last one to remain in the arena with Reuben. The mahouts had already led the rest back to their shelter for the evening. It had been a long day for them, too, and Max approached Reuben and Lizzie with caution.

"Not to worry, old chap." Reuben stroked the elephant's trunk, which she curled around his arm. "Lizzie's a good gal. You can come give her a pat."

He didn't move. Not the largest of the elephants in the concession, Lizzie stood an impressive three feet taller than Max and had to outweigh him by several tons.

"Come on now, I've known this elephant since she was a baby. She's as gentle as they come. That's why I'm introducing you to her first. If she loves you, and she will, then the rest will love you, too."

Max trembled and reached a slow, tentative hand toward Lizzy's trunk, still gently wrapped around Reuben. The lightest touch of Max's fingers on the elephant's rough, dry skin caused her to loosen her grip on the other man and turn instead to the newcomer. Max ran his hand along the length of her trunk twice. Lizzie closed her large eyes and swished her tail. Then she swung her trunk up and over Max's shoulder as if claiming him as her own.

"She likes you."

A chuckle bubbled up out of Max, both nervous and delighted by the encounter.

"The great secret to elephants is that you always treat them with respect and consistency. If they learn to trust you, then you can usually trust them."

"Usually?" Max attempted to back out of Lizzie's embrace. She tugged him back with a gentle flex of her trunk, giving him no choice but to comply. He froze in place and tried to ignore the nearness of her gigantic mouth.

"They're big animals, Max. Sometimes they forget how small we are by comparison and are not as careful as they should be, but I doubt our elephants would hurt you intentionally. Especially if this one has taken a shine to you."

"Am I to care for them, then?" A hard lump formed in the back of his throat.

"Not exclusively, but it's always good for them to be familiar with anyone who may take part in their care. They got on well with the mahouts today, which is good."

"Who exactly are the mahouts?" Max had understood that this was a word for a kind of elephant handler, a foreign one, but he'd not heard the word before this day, and he was curious to know more about the odd collection of foreign arrivals.

"Elephant handlers from Ceylon. Here to form the ethnographic portion of the animal show. Carl Hagenbeck has made a name for himself by displaying both animals and people from around the world as they would be seen interacting in their homelands." Reuben pulled an apple from his coat pocket and at once Lizzie slipped her trunk from around Max, her attention captured by the shiny red fruit. He exhaled in relief. Gentle or not, she'd caused his muscles to tense.

"You speak of the people as if they are animals." Max winced as the elephant snatched the apple from Reuben's grip with her trunk and placed it into her gigantic mouth. The trainer's brow wrinkled, but he retained his composure.

"Man is a type of beast, it could be said. And like the animals from different environments, there are many varied adaptations and habits of men as well. It's good to see them together."

Max allowed the uncomfortable notion to roll around in his brain, seeking a place to settle. He feared that to question the man's assertions would be to appear ignorant, but there was one simple question that loomed large.

"Where is Ceylon? I suppose I should know."

Reuben shook his head. "Nonsense. Most people don't know. That's the point." He added in a more commanding tone to Lizzie, "Nach vorne."

The elephant stepped forward and continued to follow Reuben toward the open back gate of the arena and onto the concession grounds.

Max caught up with the animal trainer, tickled by this unexpected turn in events. "She understands German!"

"Of course. She was raised from a baby in Hamburg."

"And the mahouts?" Max wondered what he might say to the pretty dancer if he knew she could understand him.

"Do they speak German?" Reuben pulled an apple from his other coat pocket and gave it to Lizzie. "A few phrases, perhaps, but not really. They speak their own dialect, and they speak English. Ceylon is a British-controlled island off the tip of India."

"So, it is India," Max said mostly to himself, remembering his conversation with Finn.

"I wouldn't recommend you say that to them." As if to emphasize the point, the elephant stamped one of her enormous feet and shook her head. "Steady, girl, I don't have any more apples with me. You can have more in the enclosure."

Lizzie demonstrated acceptance of this with renewed vigor in her steps as she progressed toward the open gate at the back of the arena, leaving Reuben to trail behind. As soon as they drew close enough to see the enclosure, another of the elephants bellowed out a greeting.

Max picked up his own pace to match that of Reuben and his charge. "They're not so different from horses," he said once he'd caught up.

"More opinionated than most horses, and rather larger so they can more easily force the point if they've a mind to." Reuben reached up to touch Lizzie's flank. "But not entirely dissimilar."

Lizzie stopped at her trainer's gentle touch and waited at the gate that led back into the elephant enclosure, behind a large chute down which the elephants could slide into a deep pool. At a gesture from Reuben, Max withdrew the keys he'd been given earlier and fit one into the lock. The gate swung open before Max had time to wonder whether the other elephants might take advantage of the circumstance to come back out, but all seven of them—six adults and one baby—stood well back and waited for Lizzie to enter. She did so without complaint.

Max swung the gate shut and secured the lock while Reuben opened the door of a nearby storage shed to retrieve a bucket filled to the brim with apples. These he flung into the enclosure where they scattered among the excited herd. "They love most fruits," he explained. "Apples are the simplest to get hold of right now, but I've never seen an elephant turn up its long nose at any variety."

Reuben handed the empty bucket to Max. "Mind running that to the food trailer before you head home? I've got to check in on the goats before I head out. Going to the Cowboy Bar to meet up with Carl and Lorenz. You'd be welcome to come along. It's north of the Pike, part of the Rough Riders concession."

Max took the bucket. "I should get home. My mother will worry."

"Some other night, then. I'm thinking about bringing Lizzie one of these times."

Max laughed as he pictured the large elephant stepping through the door of a local watering hole. Reuben didn't even crack a smile.

"Well." The Englishman brought his hands together. "I appreciate you staying to meet Lizzie. I'll introduce you to the rest of the herd tomorrow."

"I look forward to it." Max nearly convinced himself he meant it. The successful interaction with his first elephant, though stressful, had buoyed his spirits and he walked with light steps as he parted ways with Reuben and made his way back to the arena. He entered the performance space intending to cross to the seating area and let himself out there near the concession entrance. The sun had sunk from the sky, but several gas lamps lit both performance space and stands.

He thought to put them out before he left, but movement caught the corner of his eye. In front of the far-right end of the stands he spied the Sinhalese woman. Her back to him, she hadn't seen him enter and he drew back toward the gate, sliding into the shadow that clung to the outer edge of the performance space. From there he watched, his heart pounding, as she swayed to a rhythm she alone could hear. The dancer's movements resembled nothing Max had ever seen. Her legs stretched long and she glided rather than stepped, her arms flowing around her in patterns that made him dizzy. From side to side her hips swayed beneath the fluid fabric of her rose-colored skirt. She no longer wore the woolen wrap from earlier, and the smooth brown of her bare skin shimmered in the soft light of the lamps.

From some place beyond her rose piercing notes, pinched and wavering and not entirely melodious but supported by a softer and deeper continuous tone. Max moved closer to investigate, stretched up on his toes to see around the dancer Shehani, and spotted the source of the strange sound. The Sinhalese man, identified earlier as Inesh the snake charmer, sat on the ground, his back against the front edge of the bleachers, his legs crossed so that his knees jutted in front of him, and he perched on his own feet. To his lips he held an unfamiliar instrument consisting of a small, bulbous body with two long, thin pipes, up and down which the fingers of one hand flitted. The music, once begun, contained no pauses for breath, and Max's own respiration paused as he took in the full sight. The musician's other hand waved the lid of a shallow basket back and forth in front of a snake with a wide head like a spoon that swayed with the movement.

Shehani continued to dance, matching the rhythm of the strange flute, her skirts swirling within inches of the back of the snake's head. The creature swiveled, its stare ripped from the snake charmer. Without pausing his music, Inesh dropped the lid, grabbed the snake halfway up its long body, and pulled it away from her until the creature's head landed in the basket. Only after he replaced the lid loosely on top of the basket and the serpent slithered the rest of its body inside did the music stop. Shehani's dance continued uninterrupted as if the music she required emanated not from any instrument but from the depths of her soul.

PARADISE ON THE PIKE

Max tore himself from this enchanting vision, at once so beautiful he could cry and so intimate his stomach knotted with shame that she remained unaware of his presence. Careful not to attract either sibling's notice, he tightened his grip on the empty apple bucket and snuck back out the gate he had previously entered.

He followed the path around the edge of the arena, stopped outside a pool of lamplight, hugged the empty apple bucket to himself, and attempted to slow his wild, racing heart as he considered the beautiful but disturbing image he'd witnessed—that of the Sinhalese dancer and the snake charmer as if they themselves were animals in the zoo and he, a visitor, ogling nature's perfect creatures transplanted to a false world to perform for his pleasure.

Chapter 10

By the time Max made it home to his uncle's house, a light blazed on the front porch, illuminating a small, lone figure slumped on the stoop.

"You missed supper," said Clyde at the very instance Max's stomach growled the same lament.

"Did I miss something good?" Max stood at the bottom of the steps eye-to-eye with the young man, whose back straightened under the scrutiny of an adult.

Clyde's nose wrinkled. "Bratwurst and potato cakes."

"That sounds good to me."

Clyde propped his elbows on bent knees and dropped his chin onto his hands. "Yeah, I guess so."

Max's imagination conjured the dishes and his stomach rumbled. He wished he could say goodbye to the child and make his way to the kitchen where he hoped a plate waited for him, but something about Clyde's demeanor stopped him. He lowered himself onto the step beside the boy. "Is it the bratwurst, or the potato cakes you dislike?"

"I—I don't dislike them. I just miss my mother's cooking."

"Hm." Max removed his cap and placed it on his knee, taking a beat to determine how best to respond to the grieving child. "I didn't know her. What was she like?"

Clyde chewed on his lower lip. "Not like Oma."

"Not German?"

The boy shrugged. "She didn't speak it, and neither did Father when she was around. She didn't want us to pick it up. She'd hate it that me and Johnny spend so much time at Oma's now." He scrutinized Max with a contemplative frown. "She wouldn't have liked you very much, either."

That made Max laugh. "You cannot know that."

"I can," Clyde said without a hint of humor. "She was very stuck-up."

Max didn't know this phrase, but he understood what the boy had meant. "You know, I lost a parent, too, probably around the same time as you." He picked up his cap and crumpled it in his hands. A dark pit opened in his stomach and swallowed any desire for food. "My father died, and I ended up here, too. At your Oma's house."

The little boy looked him straight in the eye and asked, "What was your father like?"

Max's tongue turned to sand. "Tja. He wouldn't have liked you very much." He leaned back against his elbows, propped on the next step up.

Cold perspiration had broken out on Max's neck and he shivered. Clyde grabbed his hand and squeezed. The two sat brooding in silence under the glow of the porchlight until the door opened behind them and Aunt Matilda leaned out, red faced and stern with one hand on her hip and the other pointing a stiff finger at Clyde. "We've been looking everywhere for you, young man. Inside and straight to bed. Your father will come for you in the morning."

Clyde didn't argue. He snatched his fingers from Max's grip and whispered a goodnight before disappearing into the house.

Matilda's jaw relaxed as she watched her grandchild climb the stairs. Then she turned to Max. "I'm glad to know he was with you this whole time." She stepped back inside and held the door for Max. "Frieda's left you a plate in the kitchen if you're hungry."

PARADISE ON THE PIKE

Requiring no second invitation, Max stepped into the house. As he passed, her hand caught his elbow with a light touch. "Thank you for talking to him. He's had a difficult time. I think you two probably have a lot in common."

Max's stomach gurgled in response, more from discomfort now than hunger, but he mumbled a dismissal of her misplaced gratitude before making his way to the kitchen and hoped what she said wasn't true.

The kitchen was empty, cleaned after the meal he'd missed, but as promised, a plate sat on the counter. He lifted the tea towel that covered it to find two cold potato cakes, a portion of sausage, and a thick slice of dark, crusty bread. He took a fork from the flatware drawer and slumped into a chair at the small kitchen table.

He'd managed three bites when the muffled sound of voices pulled his attention to the back door. A glance told him the lock stood bolted against the night. He scooted back his chair so he might unlock it and identified one of the voices as Mutti's. When he couldn't place the second male voice, he hesitated.

Mutti spoke barely above a whisper, but he couldn't mistake her. Her German drifted along to the rhythm of Stellingen and remained relatively untouched by America, though her English had progressed nicely under Frieda's tutelage.

But Mutti spoke now. No, she whispered German, sweetly, in the way a lover might do, and her utterings received answers in a silky tenor, harsh and grating to Max's ear—the German thick and slow as if it struggled to glide over the man's tongue. Even so, Max could understand it, and his jaw clenched with the realization of the story unfolding on the other side of the door.

"You are a beautiful woman, Emmi. I want nothing more than to be with you."

Max seethed, but his chest expanded with warmth when his mother rebuffed the advance.

"You are too much, Henry. I am barely widowed."

"A year? More now, isn't it?"

"And I have a son."

"A grown son who will one day soon have to see that his mother is a vibrant woman with much love to give."

"You speak as if you know me." Mutti's teasing tone tempered the harshness of her words. The three bites of cold sausage soured in Max's gut.

"I want to know you." They were words sticky with lust.

Max crept to the kitchen window. If he stood in exactly the right place, he could see a corner of the back step, the lace trim of Mutti's skirt, practically entangled with a trousered leg connected to a foot in a polished shoe.

"Enough," she said. Another shoe appeared, backstepping onto the next step down. Max exhaled in relief. Mutti had clearly pushed the man away. Not aggressively enough for Max's full satisfaction, but she was resisting this obnoxious, forward man. Max would help her if he must and pictured himself throwing open the door to land a solid punch across the polished shoe man's jaw. "I must say goodnight."

"I wish you wouldn't."

"Good night."

Max recognized the weight of finality in Mutti's statement, apparently the same whether she played the part of a strict mother or secret lover. He knew it from the times he had pushed his luck too far, gotten into a fight with one of the other village boys or, worse, picked a fight with his father.

The mystery man seemed to accept it, too, this universally recognized resoluteness. He slowly stepped down from the porch and as he more fully came into view, Max could see his hands raised in defeat. The dim back porchlight revealed a decently dressed man, tall, too—probably taller than Max—and slim. Like a snake.

The snake man in polished shoes observed from the yard while Mutti fumbled with a key in the door. Max rushed away from the window and placed his hand on the knob just as Mutti pushed to let herself in. She uttered a strangled, "Max."

"Mutti," he replied and pointed to the man who glanced back briefly before disappearing around the corner of the house. "Who is that?"

Mutti looked behind her as if surprised to hear that anyone was there. "No one."

"You were talking to no one?"

"You heard us talking?"

"I heard mumbling outside the door."

She sighed, dropped her key into her handbag and the bag on the table beside his supper. "Eating late, are you? I didn't expect anyone to be in the kitchen."

"It was a long day. I had to introduce myself to an elephant. Someone was kind enough to leave me food."

"Matilda is always so thoughtful."

Max didn't correct her. He'd been touched that Frieda had made him a plate, but he deserved no such consideration and had found her kindness unnerving. But he would not be distracted from his mother's back porch visitor.

"Who were you talking to out there?" he persisted.

She rolled her eyes at him and sat at the table across from his food, indicating that he should also sit and continue eating. He did claim his chair but did not touch the food again until she began to speak.

"His name is Henry Duncan. He frequents the biergarten in the evenings. He struck up a conversation with me a few weeks ago and was kind enough to walk me home tonight because it had gotten late, as you know."

"Shouldn't Reinhardt or Hugh walk you home?"

"They are working still. I could have waited, but Henry offered, as he was coming this direction anyway. He's a nice man. A police detective."

Max nearly spit a piece of sausage back on his plate. "It's Henry, is it? This man you met so recently? And a detective?"

Mutti's cheeks glowed red in the dim light and her expression hardened. "Lower your voice this instant. You'll disturb the whole house."

Max did as he was told, dropping to a forceful whisper. "Do you think it wise, spending time with a man—"

Max paused and a jolt of fear shot through him, a sensation he couldn't justify to himself. He didn't begrudge his mother happiness, could perhaps have even considered it a good development that she'd met a man, but something about the notion of this man, a police detective, rankled.

"A man like him," he hissed.

"You are overreacting, son." Mutti put her hand on his arm, a gesture that would have reassured him when he was younger but that now struck him as patronizing. He could see that she liked this detective. Max would have thought she'd had enough of men in her life after her disastrous marriage.

"Duncan doesn't sound German," he said in an attempt to ease the tension mounting between them.

"No, it doesn't. I asked him about that. Most of our customers are German. Apparently his mother immigrated from Berlin and married an American. When he feels nostalgic for her cooking and the for the culture of his German family, he comes to the biergarten."

That at least made sense to Max. Homesickness for his own culture is what had driven him to Hagenbeck's Animal Paradise, after all, a move Mutti had not exactly approved of. "And he walks you home."

"Once. He walked me home once. That's all. It's not some grand romance."

The very word sent a shiver of revulsion slivering down his spine. "Are you hoping it will become one?"

Mutti's lips contorted, and she glared at him with an intensity he didn't dare try to interpret. Then she reached across the table to squeeze his hand. "I'm not some silly young girl looking for romance. I've played that hand. It ended badly."

Max bowed his head in relief.

"However," she continued, "if a kind and handsome police detective offers to see me home safely on a dark night, I'm not going to turn him down."

"I suppose I should be grateful for him, then," Max admitted. "Is he going to walk you home again, do you think?"

Mutti pulled her hand away from his and smiled as she leaned against the back of her chair. "I wouldn't be surprised if he did. And I also wouldn't mind. You shouldn't either. It might be nice to be close to a police detective. I'm not of a mind to discourage him."

Chapter 11

Ten days after a late season snowfall that threatened the coming festivities, the opening day of the Louisiana Purchase Exposition finally arrived on April 30, 1904. Max made his way to the grounds early that day, slipping through the partially obstructed Pike entrance that remained unopened to the public before the sun had fully risen. Despite the early hour and a light drizzle, the grounds crawled with flustered workers frantically clearing debris and scrambling with finishing touches. Ernst had not come home the previous night, working late to help with the last-minute paving of roads through the grounds.

Carl and Lorenz Hagenbeck were pleased enough with the concession, with only a few more animals yet to arrive in the coming weeks. Still, Max sensed a palpable unease as he let himself through the front gate to the high-pitched trill of the ostriches and the deep-throated groan of a lion greeting the morning.

He drew in the chilly damp air and let it coat his lungs until they hurt, then moved along the path around the outside of the arena, heading first for the elephants. He'd met all of them by now, and while he didn't trust a single one, only Lizzie paid him much notice anyway.

His ability to easily distinguish between them surprised him. The elephant known as Moms was the simplest to identify, and the wariest of him, given that she had a baby in her care. Max would not dare approach Josky and Monte, the giants among the herd, without the presence of either Reuben or one of the mahouts with their jeweled hooks. The other three—Pinto, Topsy, and Trilby—must have found him unworthy of their notice. They treated him with a disdain that implied they thought of him as nothing more than the servant who brought them fresh water and food. They never deigned to come close to him as Lizzie did, her trunk reaching out to him for a scratch.

This morning several of the giants lay sleeping, unconcerned with the nervous energy of the grounds. Lizzie stood, however, her feet shuffling across the damp earth of the enclosure, and beside her Max saw the Sinhalese woman who whispered something in the elephant's large ear when Max approached. Lizzie shook her head in response and lifted her trunk, stretching it in the direction of Max. The woman's head turned in response and she startled when she saw him leaning against the short barrier on the other side of the trench.

"Good morning," he said.

She dropped her gaze and then raised it again, but said nothing.

"You speak elephant," he said, trying to affect a light tone. Her forehead wrinkled as if she didn't understand. He followed up by pointing to Lizzie and asking, "What did you say to her?" It occurred to him that the woman might speak only her native dialect and not English, though he supposed German was even more unlikely.

He studied her, as she did him. Her dark hair, the sides tied back in an intricate knot, cascaded down her back in waves of silken perfection.

"I told her to be aware of strange men who might strike up a conversation with her." Then she grinned. "You are Max, yes?"

Max blushed and sputtered, defensive, though he couldn't have said why. "You know my name?"

She wobbled her head. "Mr. Reuben pointed you out to me. You are the German animal keeper who came from the farm where Mr. Carl is building his new zoo."

Her English flowed more readily than his, contained a wider range of vocabulary, and followed an unusual rhythm, her words more evenly spaced than he'd become accustomed to hearing, which lent a bounciness to her speech he could have listened to for hours, even if he couldn't understand every syllable.

"You speak beautiful English," he said.

"Thank you. I have been speaking it my whole life. And Sinhala. And elephant, though that is more about tone and a few command words, which are either English or German because Mr. Castang is English and has trained them in Hamburg from a young age." She gave Lizzie a pat on the trunk. "Mr. Pambu does speak a fair amount of German. He's the older gentleman with us. He's worked with Mr. Carl Hagenbeck before in his ethnographic exhibits. It was kind of him to bring me and my brother with him to America."

Max watched her speak as much as he listened, noting the way small movements curled around the sounds coming from her lips as if she expressed ideas with her entire body, her words nothing more than an enchanting enhancement. And she was beautiful, not with the same kind of beauty Frieda possessed, but in a mysterious sort of way that made Max want to unwrap all of her secrets.

"What is your name?" he asked, too ashamed to admit he already knew and only wanted to hear her say it.

"Shehani."

And that in itself was a mystery. Max repeated her name, rolling the strange sounds around his tongue, testing them. She giggled at his effort.

She brought her hands together again and bowed her head. "It's a pleasure to meet you,

Max."

He didn't know whether she expected him to mimic her actions or not, but Lizzie saved him from any awkwardness by tapping him on the shoulder with her trunk. He stroked her, thankful for the distraction and turned to look at her. "What is it, girl?"

Lizzie answered with a flick of her ears.

"She wants attention. I suspect she is hungry. I assume that's why you're here?"

"It is, but first to clean," Max responded and turned toward the door that led to the back room and the supplies for his morning cleaning duties. Before he got there, however, he thought to ask, "Why are you here so early, Shehani?" Her name came together more fluidly in his mouth this time, and he treasured the shape of it.

"I wanted to spend some extra time letting Lizzie get to know me. It's a big day. We will be together in the parade later for opening day. I want her to be comfortable."

"She looks comfortable to me." He thought of Reuben's words to him about this elephant the day he'd met her. "I think she likes you."

"And I like her very much, but every elephant is different. It's best not to take their friendship for granted. I admit, I am nervous to be riding her in the parade for the opening. We are starting to get to know one another, but one of the mahouts would be better suited. They have much more experience than I do." Shehani patted the elephant on her side and stepped away from the giant. "But I think she is a gentle soul."

Her words echoed in his ears as he let himself through the locked door leading behind the enclosures and he heard her call out, "It was a pleasure to meet you, Max."

In the enclosed space where little light had yet penetrated through the windows above equipment shelves, a tingling warmth spread happily through his chest.

PARADISE ON THE PIKE

Under an overcast sky and in the midst of a spring chill that made one grateful for the denseness of the finely dressed crowd, David R. Francis, president of the fair, stood in coat and tails above an enthusiastic throng, and upon receiving a telegraph signal from US President Theodore Roosevelt in Washington, DC, Francis stretched out his hands and declared the opening of the fair with the words, "Open Ye Gates! Swing Wide Ye Portals!"

Water cascaded from Festival Hall into the Grand Basin where fountains sprung up to mirror the swell of people pushing their way onto the grounds. Max hadn't listened to all two hours of speeches delivered by various dignitaries whose titles meant little to him, but for this opening moment, he'd claimed a place on the steps of the Palace of Varied Industries. There he stood with hundreds of workers, gathered to take in the scene. From his vantage point he could see the parade progressing toward him from the administrative building beyond the far end of the cobblestone Pike toward the Plaza of St. Louis at the foot of the Grand Basin. Into view marched a long line of many of the delights the fair promised its visitors—strangely clad foreigners, uniformed soldiers, a high-stepping brass band, and three Hagenbeck elephants under the direction of their Sinhalese mahouts. One of those elephants was Lizzie and on her back rode Shehani decked out in her colorful dress.

Max strained to see her better but could not wait for them to reach his position. He now had to rush to keep ahead of the crowd and make it back to the Animal Paradise concession before the crowd poured onto the Pike. He whispered a silent wish for them both, that Lizzie would behave gently, though after observing Shehani dance, her delicately floating limbs within easy reach of the snake, he suspected her bravery could extend to handle anything.

He had little time that first day to appreciate the excitement of the crowds entering the gates onto the grounds of the largest fair the world had ever seen. The Hagenbecks insisted on animal shows starting at noon and every hour after on most days, but immediately following opening on this opening day of the exposition, a feat that proved incredibly difficult to coordinate.

Reuben ran himself ragged managing the logistics of shows, directing the mahouts and attempting to keep the animals calm and cooperative. More than usual of the mundane tasks of animal care fell to Max. After hosing out enclosures, feeding, and watering, Reuben recruited him several times to help move animals to and from the arena. The concession employed more than enough workers for smooth operation, but the excitement of the long-anticipated opening day proved too much for some of them, who were overwhelmed and less helpful than they needed to be.

Max didn't exactly mind the furious pace of the day and even enjoyed the tumble of tasks that distracted him from more difficult thoughts. He welcomed the growing fatigue settling into his muscles, and it might have been a perfect day if Pete hadn't called on him to help sell tickets during the evening rush.

Seemingly every fairgoer had decided to spend suppertime on the Pike. The restaurant at Hagenbeck's Animal Paradise offered some light food, but also, in the arena, family entertainment and a place to sit and rest for a spell. He could understand why the crowds would want to come their way, but Max grumbled when Pete insisted he join him at the entrance to help hawk tickets.

"Suckers, every one of them, easily parted with their money," Pete said behind his hand as if he had bothered lowering his volume. He demonstrated for Max the process of selling separate tickets for admission to the concession, as well as seats in the arena for the next available animal show, and the experience of riding on a turtle, elephant, camel, or ostrich. Each ticket sold for a separate price and each opportunity came with different limitations. All sales had to be meticulously recorded and all visitors' questions answered in a timely manner in English.

"I had one ticket-taker walk off the job already today—on opening day! Another asked Carl if he could take a supper break and the old man was foolish enough to let him go. Haven't seen him since. I won't be sad to see the geezer go back to Hamburg in a few days." Pete spun a large gold ring on one of his manicured fingers and looked up at the ceiling of the tiny ticket booth. "So, you'll have to do."

That Carl Hagenbeck would be leaving St. Louis so soon was news to Max, but he didn't have time to let his thoughts linger on it. He would have rather taken care of the snakes than been stuck inside the ticket booth. The reptile exhibit had grown that very week to include, in addition to the giant tortoises and two American alligators, four twenty-foot-long pythons, a rattlesnake, a bright green viper, and two king cobras that took turns being charmed by Inesh. Any of these creatures might have resembled a big-eyed bunny rabbit compared to the red rage that stiffened Pete's jaw when Max struggled to keep the ticket sales straight.

"You stupid German." Pete sighed and pushed his hand out of the way to scribble a correction in the book. "You have to learn to do this. I can't stand here all day."

Max threw up his hands in frustration and yelled, "Das ist nicht meine Auggabe!" A small girl, perhaps four or five years old, standing in line with her parents, began to cry. At the sight of her distress, Max's chest tightened, his vision blackening around the edges. Pete's response to his outburst became a buzzing swarm in his ears.

Max tried to pull in a long breath, to calm his frayed nerves but could only do so when he saw the child's father kneel to comfort her. He focused on the two of them, the girl in a pale blue dress, her chestnut hair falling in curls down her back. The father wore a crisp brown suit, the knees of his trousers ruined now with the dust of the Pike. He hugged his child and whispered in her ear until she brightened. He stood then and grabbed her by the hand. The mother took the girl's other hand and the family of three, good moods restored, stepped out of line and crossed the Pike to stand in line for the Mysterious Asia concession.

Max exhaled and, as the buzzing began to lift, he realized Pete continued speaking to him. "And now your incompetence has driven off customers."

There were many things Max would have liked to say to Pete in response. He would like to have explained, in English this time, that ticket sales had never been part of his job, that he'd been hired to care for animals and that his shaky language skills made customer interactions difficult for him. He'd have liked to tell the horrible man that his own impatience with an innocent employee who was trying his best is what had driven the family away, but the angry man would not have seen reason and so Max said, "I am sorry. You are right. I am slow, but I understand what I need to do, and I will manage."

Pete, red-faced, shook his head. "Again," he said, exaggerating the enunciation of each word. "Adult admission to the concession is ten cents. For the arena shows, it's twenty-five cents for children, fifty cents for adults. Track rides are ten cents, and those need to be recorded here. Make sure you present them with the correct tickets for their purchases. Think maybe you can handle that?"

"I understand. I can do it," Max said.

Pete hovered for several minutes, scrutinizing Max as he sold tickets to the next four sets of fairgoers in line. It was a laborious process, and

Max could see, in the expressions of American visitors full of questions he found difficult to understand well enough to answer, frustration equal to his own. At last, Pete slid out the back side of the ticket booth and made his way to the hexagonal kiosk in front of the main gate. Once there he spread his arms, his manicured hands to the sky and began to extol the wholesomeness and educational value of the Animal Paradise on the Pike. He left Hagenebeck out of the name, but from this perch, Pete fielded questions about the many delights inside the concession and removed some of the pressure from Max.

By the time the streetlights came up on the Pike, and the crowd at last began to thin, Max could almost appreciate the man. They had, in the end, formed an effective team.

As Max recorded his final ticket sale, Pete stepped down from the kiosk, knocked on the door to the ticket booth, opened it a crack, and leaned in. "That was hopeless, Max."

Max slumped in his chair and rubbed a hand across his weary brow before answering. "I thought it went well once you started answering the questions."

"That's not sustainable. Clearly, you're not competent enough be working in ticket sales."

"No," Max agreed. "I think I should take care of the animals, which is what I was hired to do."

Pete grunted. "I'll find you something more suitable."

Max was about to explain that Reuben already kept him busy with tasks and that there was no need for Pete to add to his list when Pete began to talk again, this time about a subject Max had not anticipated.

"Shehani sure was pretty on top of that elephant this morning." The loathsome man wiggled his eyebrows at Max. It made his insides slither. "Sat up nice and straight, a real exotic princess ready to conquer the world."

Max agreed with the apt description. Shehani was an exotic princess in his mind, regal and elegant.

"Couldn't even tell how nervous she was," Pete continued.

Max clenched his jaw until it hurt. Pete couldn't have known Shehani was nervous about riding the elephant in the parade unless she herself had told him or if he had somehow eavesdropped on their conversation. Neither was a comfortable notion for Max.

"How did you know she was nervous?" Max asked in what he hoped was a casual tone.

Pete shrugged. "She told me. I talked to her this morning before the parade. You'd never have known it, though. She rode like a champion."

"An elephant rider champion?" Max's lip twitched in puzzlement when he thought of the trophy one might receive for such an effort.

"Well, could have been a professional anyway. Like she was born to it, which I guess she was."

"I suppose she was."

Shehani came from a whole country of animal trainers as far as he knew. Max didn't know anything about the land called Ceylon except that it had spawned an angel who'd been inexplicably delivered to the same place at the same time as him, in a place neither were likely to be. When he thought of her dark skin, her flowing pink dress, her intrepid handling of an animal so large it could easily crush him, Max didn't miss Stellingen so much. He could imagine wanting to be an American in St. Louis where everything was possible, even that a German potato farmer might admire a beautiful, dark-skinned girl from Ceylon.

Chapter 12

Max survived the first two weeks of the fair in a blur of exhaustion. The animals needed constant care, particularly those performing in the shows. Reuben had designed five unique performances with various combinations of animals so that no creature performed more often than once every three hours. The people were not as lucky.

Shehani performed in all but the arctic animal show, not only dancing with elephants and cobras but also whirling, whip in hand, amidst lions and tigers perched atop chairs, their eyes tracking her every flutter, awaiting their chance to snap at a limb. The electric lights that nightly illuminated the palaces did not shine as brightly as she did.

Max watched when he could, but coordinating feedings and cleanings around animal movements proved a constant and rigorous task that kept him busy throughout the long days. The Hagenbeck crew worked well together. Each man had his list of tasks, some assigned to managing the various animal rides the concession offered, a job Max was grateful not to have received. Instead, he'd become the floating employee who stepped in to do whatever needed to be done, and once two new ticket booth employees had been hired, it was a role he filled well. The demands on his time were a steady stream, but as long as he made himself indispensable to Reuben, Pete left him alone.

In this crucial role, Max waited from the sides of the arena as Reuben handled Flick and Flock, his daring and charming goats, the control of which looked like magic to Max and, judging by the calls of delight, to the audience as well. As had been planned, the goats butted at Reuben and stomped their hooves, their behavior precisely what would be expected of goats. Their high-pitched bleating teased and dared him to command them until the instant he did. At little more than a pointed look, each stubborn animal fell into line. Flick bent his front legs, dropping into a kneeling position. Flock circled him and settled into a mirrored kneel, curly horns touching without the slightest hint of aggression. That's when a small terrier named Flossie, that had been gleefully taking in the proceedings, gave a happy yap to the crowd and climbed up Flick's back to perch on the platform created by the goats' kissing horns.

Reuben scratched the pooch behind his ear and the little dog stood on his hind legs, his tail flapping happily behind him. Then he dropped his front paws to one side, marched down the back of Flock's neck, and turned so that he was standing tall, balanced in the middle of the goat's back. At a word from Reuben, Flock stood and pranced about the arena, with Flossie playing the part of a furry jockey. The laughter of the crowd roared in Max's ears as Flick got in on the action. He lined up behind the other goat and the dog walked off the back of the one over the head and neck of the other to perch atop Flick's back.

The animal trainer raised a hand and Flick, now with Flossie on his back, walked toward the big empty cage in the middle of the arena. Beside it stood a series of steps the goat did not hesitate to climb, Flossie still wobbling on his back. The two made it to the top without incident and, as they did, a large horse-like creature pranced through the large gate at the back of the arena floor.

The zebroid was the result of one of Carl Hagenbeck's experimental cross breedings, this between a horse and a zebra, resulting in an attractive tawny coat with faint stripes that caused the audience to gasp. The animal looked to Reuben who called her forward with a series of clicks to stand beside the stairs, even with the goat that had a terrier on its back. Flick didn't hesitate. As soon as the zebroid stopped, the goat stepped, sure-footed, onto her strong back, creating a stack of animals that caused a stir of excitement in the crowd. The striped creature trotted a lap around the outer edge of the arena to cheers of appreciation and then stopped in front of Reuben.

The trainer held out his arms to catch Flossie, who jumped from Flick's back. Then Reuben gave the mare a pat on the flank that sent her toward the gate where Max waited to receive the animals and lead them from the arena to their enclosures. Flock followed, bleating, behind them.

Max held tight to the zebroid's bridle and whispered a prayer that the other goat would follow him back to the enclosures. From the arena came the gasp of the crowd, and he knew the lion and tigers had been released into the center cage where Reuben would soon invite Shehani to step inside with them, impressing the audience with an image of savage bravery and power over even the most dangerous of beasts. Reuben could convince all manner of animals to do things it was simply not in their natures to do, a skill Max was coming to realize this beautiful woman also possessed. Each spoke the language of animals, but he also listened to them and often followed their lead. They observed the minute body language of each animal and carefully calculated the risks with each encounter.

Max did not have such an uncanny ability. A shriek in the arena startled the mare which shook its head, rattling Max's bones as he held on tightly to the bridle. Flick slipped and tumbled to the ground. The goat regained his footing with a distressed bleat while the zebroid huffed her general disapproval of the situation. Max didn't blame her. The tiny hooves of a goat digging into one's back couldn't be very comfortable.

Clearly no happier with this turn of events, Flick steadied himself and, without so much as a backward glance, the ornery animal trotted in the wrong direction, away from the zebroid and Max, and toward the front gate past two ticket sellers, a sign announcing the time of the next show, and a line of fairgoers too surprised to stop him. Max reached out just in time to grab the second highly offended goat by a horn.

"Wait!" Max yelled, delighted he'd spoken in English without so much as a thought, until he realized the goat might understand German better. "Warten!" he yelled. The goat did not listen to this command either but continued without hesitation out onto the Pike.

Max didn't know what to do. He couldn't leave the zebroid and the other goat unsecured. He reasoned that Flick would surely return on his own to eat, but then Max thought of all the tasty offerings up and down the length of the Pike and the echo of Reuben's voice telling him goats would eat nearly anything. Max called once again in frustration, and though the goat continued to ignore him, someone else responded.

Shehani came into view around the corner of the arena and sprung into action the instant she took in the problem. "I will get him," she said, running for the exit, the bells of the costume she'd donned for the show tinkling with each step.

Max hated that she'd come to his rescue, but with the incessant bleating of the other goat still caught by its horn, and the impatient stamping of the horse, he made himself turn away from the vision of her running, skirt swirling behind her to proceed to the enclosure and secure the remaining animals in his care.

"Shehani!" He heard the call as he secured the gate behind the last goat and saw Lorenz Hagenbeck himself rushing from the arena, his head on a swivel. "Shehani! The lions! Rube needs you in the arena!"

"She is on the Pike," Max called. "She'll be back in a minute." Then Max ran past his boss, through the front gate, and out onto the crowded brick road.

Pedestrians jammed the street, stopping in front of the intricately decorated buildings, reading signs featuring parade times, and lining up outside the Mysterious Asia concession. That's where he finally spotted her in an even larger collection of swirling skirts as a line of dancers from that concession demonstrated their skills there on the street. Her bright dress and glistening brown skin fit right in with them, and she might have been a part of the demonstration had it not been for her tight grip on the horn of a goat who would not budge.

Max rushed toward her, pushing past angry fairgoers who grabbed for their wallets when he brushed up against them, assuring themselves they had not been pickpocketed.

"Shehani," he gasped, reaching out to grab hold of the other goat horn.

"Max." She looked at him as if it were the most natural thing in the world to be standing at the end of a line of Indian dancing girls holding onto a wayward goat. Then again, perhaps that was the kind of thing that passed for normal in Ceylon. He had no way of knowing, but he appreciated her calm.

"Lorenz is looking for you. You're needed in the arena. The lions."

Panic dropped like a veil over her face and she ran before he was finished speaking.

"Thank you!" he called after her, sure she did not hear him as she leapt over the chain in front of the Animal Paradise, leaving him with a death grip on a goat horn, enveloped into an Indian dance before an astonished crowd. Merriment buzzed at his predicament. One of the dancers swirled a scarf around her body and subtly bumped him out of her way with her hip. He took the hint and, to his relief, so did Flick. The animal had once again become docile and perfectly willing to move in whatever direction Max urged him. This time, the crowd parted for him to proceed back to his own exhibit, many of them focusing on him rather than on the dancing in front of them.

He wished they would ignore him, but as they would not, he decided to make the best of it, and summoning the clearest English he could muster, he waved a hand toward the ticket booth across the street and said, "Come see the trained goats at Hagenbeck's Animal Paradise on the Pike. Next show at six o'clock."

Max wrangled Flick into his enclosure, scattered feed for the waterfowl on the banks of the pond in the middle of the yard, and greeted the few animals that approached him. Most did not. The schedule was a grueling one for them as well, and Max couldn't blame them for being tired. He'd have liked to sit and rest on the rocks for a bit, but he needed to see to the monkeys before their next showtime.

⁂

Gasps and cheers drifted behind him as he made his way around the back side of the arena from the primate enclosure and as he rounded the corner he spotted the reason why. Five elephants, handled by mahouts with bejeweled hooks, bowed and paraded up a ramp toward a platform connected to an enormous chute that emptied into the pool in their enclosure next to the arena.

The giants stood, each waiting for its turn to join Reuben on the platform, and as they waited, Lorenz spoke into a megaphone, his voice carrying over the crowd who were enthralled not by both the elephants and his words.

"What you are about to witness, believe it or not, is a natural behavior of the elephants of India and Ceylon who slide down muddy river banks into the water where they spend most of their time escaping the equatorial heat."

As he said this, the first elephant walked toward Reuben, squatted on its haunches and stretched back so that it slid down the chute and landed with an enormous splash to the delighted squeals of the gathered and newly soaked crowd.

The next animal moved into position and Lorenz continued his speech on elephant behavior, weaving together details of herds making as much as twenty-two miles of a journey from the interior of India to the coast, crossing the sacred Ganges River, babies on the backs of mothers who stopped to rest on a sandbar halfway through their swim.

Splash! A third animal followed without prompting to join the first two playing and splashing happily in the water, their trumpets competing with Lorenz for the attention of the crowd. Max had seen the routine, thrilled most by the reaction of the crowd. He scanned the shocked and delighted faces of the children perched on fathers' shoulders, ladies' dimpled cheeks rosy with glee. One scarred and shabbily dressed man's rough appearance was entirely overtaken by the euphoria of standing in the whimsical world of the fair. He gaped at impossibly large creatures shooting the chutes much the way fairgoers could for a small fee at on the other end of the Pike.

An eager but sometimes clumsy bull named Monte became the next to take position on the chute and begin the descent, bumping Reuben's hip on the way. The animal trainer lost his footing and, to gasps from the audience, slid down the shoot, entering the pool right behind Monte's tidal wave.

Silence draped the crowd. Shehani stopped dancing, her hand at her mouth. The three empty-handed mahouts ran to the water's edge, shouting foreign words at the elephants. Max did not move for many seconds. Lorenz lowered the megaphone. The fifth elephant plunged down the shoot.

A second later, Reuben's head broke the surface of the water near the far edge of the pool, and the elephant nearest him scooped him up with her trunk to boost him toward the reaching hands of the mahouts. With their help, he clamored out of the pool, shook the water from his hair, and waved to the crowd, attempting to mask a grimace with a reassuring smile.

Lorenz lifted the megaphone and yelled, "Looks like our head animal trainer couldn't resist the idea of a swim!"

The audience exploded with applause and whistled calls for an encore performance. Only the members of the Hagenbeck team knew the event hadn't been part of the act, and neither Lorenz nor Reuben, who each took an extravagant bow, were about to let them know how unexpected and dangerous the swim had really been.

Chapter 13

"This, my friends, was a day worth remembering." Lorenz raised his glass first to Reuben, and then to Carl Hagenbeck. "Not without its struggles, mind you, but everyone is whole, the animals are well, the audience left happy, and my father can return to his tierpark trusting us all to embrace the circus mantra, 'the show must go on.' Whiskey for all!" Lorenz's voice rose above the din of the room with most of the crew of the Animal Paradise packed into Cheyenne Joe's cowboy saloon at the end of the night.

The saloon formed a part of the Congress of Nations and Rough Riders of the World concession to the north of the Pike and the fairgrounds, making it an easy walk for the men of Hagenbeck's Animal Paradise. Joe was as lively as his establishment with a broad, friendly grin and a wide-brimmed hat perfectly contoured to fit his head. He and Reuben and Lorenz had become fast friends during the early days of their arrival in St. Louis and Joe had offered to keep the lights on any night the Hagenbeck boys, as he called them, wished to drink away the day.

Max carried no such desire, but when Reuben threw a damp arm around him and invited him along "to drink to our success at overcoming the worst, and to Carl's health before he heads home to Hamburg," Max couldn't say no.

The day had been a long one, and not exactly what Max would call a success, first with the escaping goats and then Rube's surprise swim. Mutti would worry when he didn't arrive home as expected, which was not an excuse a grown man could give to his supervisor. Max didn't know how to explain that he disliked spending time in the company of drinkers, a byproduct of being the son Felix Eyer, a man who'd been drunk more than sober for most of Max's life, for most of his own miserable life as far as Max knew. He'd never asked Mutti about his father's drinking before Max had become old enough to understand it. He would never ask her, just as he would never explain to Reuben and Lorenz and the handful of others from the Animal Paradise why he didn't wish to go out drinking with them.

Instead, he slid onto a bench seat at a corner table and accepted from Reuben a glass of whiskey along with a sloshing mug of dark beer. Already several drinks into the night, his supervisor said, "Goats are assholes, Max." His S's slurred so the word he said sounded like ash-holes, a metaphor Max didn't immediately understand. "But I bet chasing Flick and Flock is still better than getting conscripted into ticket sales."

The slight slur of his words served as the lone indicator of Reuben's inebriation, a realization that astonished Max. Neither angry nor stupid as Felix would have been under similar circumstances, Reuben maintained clear eyes and managed to be well put together, his hair combed neatly, parted straight down the middle as always.

"Yes," Max admitted. "I avoid Mr. Williamson when I can."

"Good idea, Max!" Reuben clicked his mug against the full one that sat in front of Max, sending beer sloshing down the side. "Pete's an ash-hole, too. But he said our pretty dancing girl grabbed Flick for you and bailed you out." Reuben's eyebrows popped up and his voice dropped into a teasing, conspiratorial whisper. "You could do worse, you know. She's a lovely girl. There'd be some who might give you a hard time, but Carl Hagenbeck's own brother settled in Ceylon and married himself a local. Happy as can be."

Max looked down at his beer and pretended to sip, unwilling to look Reuben in the eye after the suggestion Max hadn't yet been brave enough to entertain. Shehani had retired for the evening. Her brother, however, had joined the crew at the saloon and sat in a corner talking with Carl Hagenbeck, the two men deep in conversation. The snake charmer spared not a glance for Max, but he sensed the intensity of the glare he deserved for the inappropriate thoughts that had already flitted unbidden through his head.

"You're quite the hero, Max, letting that sweet girl fight your battles for you." Reuben slapped the table and hooted. Perhaps the drinking was beginning to affect him after all. "Ah, don't worry about it. You'll get him next time."

With that, Reuben turned away, raising his glass to the men at the next table, which included Cheyenne Joe himself, before throwing back the last swallow of the frothy beer. Max stared at the back of him, and at Joe who stood to reach over the bar and retrieve a whiskey glass and bottle with which he replaced Rube's drink. Max ignored his mug and swirled the contents of the smaller glass. He gave it a sniff. The familiar burn of alcohol singed his nose. As far as he could tell, the cowboy whiskey was as foul as Felix's vodka had been. He put the glass back down on the table without taking a drink.

He'd have liked to be the kind of man who could stay out socializing with his friends after a long, hard day of work, but the more they drank and the more he listened to them recount the myriad of difficulties they'd encountered since the opening of the fair, and the wonders they'd seen as this magical event they'd all been dreaming of materialized before them, the more Max wished he could be at home tucked into bed.

He pushed his chair back and stood, deftly sliding his untouched whiskey glass onto the next table past Rube. Several more men shuffled through the door, including Pete Williamson, an entrance that resulted in Lorenz excusing himself from the table nearest the door and move to join the crowd in front of Max, and farthest away from Pete. Max saw his opportunity to escape as the newcomer regaled the table with some story about Reuben getting himself kicked out of a German pub for attempting to bring an elephant inside with him.

"It was a little elephant, young, barely more than five hundred pounds."

"You brought a baby into a pub?" Joe asked him, his words too loud and significantly slurred. "That's why you got kicked out."

"Wait." Rube touched the side of his nose and leaned toward Joe. "You're telling me that if I had tried to bring an adult elephant into the pub with me, that would have been fine?"

"I don't see why not," Joe replied. "I'd serve him."

A hearty chuckle burst out of Reuben who said, "I'll remember that the next time I want to show one of my elephants a night on the town. I'll bring him to see Cheyenne Joe!"

The last thing Max saw before he walked out of the saloon and into the dark, empty fairgrounds were Joe's widening eyes, round with disbelief.

Max caught one of the last, nearly empty streetcars that would deliver him to his uncle's neighborhood. The city's swollen fleet of trolleys ran late during the fair to both empty the crowd from the grounds to hotels throughout the city and to carry weary workers home after long days.

Despite Max's fatigue, not all parts of the city had yet settled into the night. Streetlights blazed and each revealed remnants of activity—patrons emerging from drinking establishments, the ruder citizens of St. Louis, the rebel-rousers and drunkards, their manners loud and inconsiderate.

PARADISE ON THE PIKE

Max hugged himself tight and withdrew into the safety of his coat and the center of the streetcar, careful to avoid the scrutiny of any of the city's less desirables. He'd heard the rumors of gangsters who allegedly ran the seedy underbelly of city politics. This, Max suspected, was the time for them to shine, when all the decent people were tucked safely into their beds.

By the time he stepped off the streetcar, Max's head swam with images of them, lurking in every shadow, guns at the ready. His teeth chattered as he hurried down the street and up the stairs into his uncle's house, neither pausing to be thankful for the flickering porchlight and the unlocked door, nor thinking to use care when pushing open the door, an action that led to a shriek.

Max stumbled backward onto the front step, a heaviness settling in his stomach at the realization that Freida stood there holding her nose with both hands.

"Max!" Tears shined on the edges of her eyelids. One hand dropped and she reached out to steady the door.

"Damn!" Max recovered his balance and stepped forward to take the door from her. "'schuldigung!"

"No," she said, gently prodding her nose which didn't appear permanently damaged. She took two steps back giving him room to cross the threshold and close the door behind him. "Not at all. The fault is as much mine. I was checking the door lock and wasn't thinking that anyone would try to come through."

Max reached back and slid the bolt. "Locked."

"Thank you."

"But I really am sorry if I hurt you."

"You didn't, Max, but I appreciate your concern." She tapped her hand against her nose and sniffed, a bright smile forming. "And did you notice that your first response was in English?"

He screwed his mouth and thought back. "Was it?"

"It was." Frieda giggled. "They say the best sign that you really know a language is if you curse in it."

"I didn't." He grew unnaturally warm under her scrutiny and he shook his head. "Oh, no. I did."

"A word you probably picked up from the worksite, maybe even from Ernst. You owe no apology for that, either, but I wouldn't let Matilda hear you use it if I were you."

He opened his mouth to assure her he would not be so careless when it occurred to him that this might be his best opportunity to truly express regret for his previous behavior. He touched her lightly on her arm. "Frieda," he said. "Please let me apologize."

She pulled from his grasp, but not in the hurried way she might were she cross with him. "You already did that, Max."

"Not for the cursing, though I will be careful of that. I meant for my behavior. I know I said it at the time, but I think you are still angry with me. I was stupid. I know that. I knew it then, too, I was only—" He trailed off, seeking the right words. She did not offer any suggestions, and the silence stretched for several uncomfortable seconds as he searched his brain. "I was homesick. And you were kind. Are kind, I mean."

"It's not a problem, Max. I'm not angry with you. Whatever awkwardness there has been between us, let's put an end to it. It's done."

From up the stairs came the low babble of a restless babe which drew Frieda's attention and the conversation appeared to have come to an end, but when the noise subsided without erupting into a cry of distress, she surprised him by sitting on the steps and releasing a breath of relief. That's when he noticed her wan complexion and the dark circles under her eyes.

"Are you unwell?"

She cupped her cheeks and sagged forward to prop her elbows on her knees. "Tired is all. Motherhood is a lot."

He supposed it was, but didn't know what to say to such a statement. She didn't give him the chance to respond anyway before she changed the subject.

"Ernst misses having you on his crew. They're working on a building project by the river now. He's been complaining about some of the workers and mentioned how good you had been. You do appear very happy at the animal concession. Are you happy?"

"I am," he said. "Construction is good work, but I enjoy the animals and the trainers I work with."

"Does it remind you of home?"

"Maybe a little bit. The Hagenbecks are from the same region of Germany that Mutti and I came from, though I work most closely with an Englishman, Reuben Castang. He's a wonder with the animals and he is a patient teacher, like you."

"Well, I don't know that I was very patient when I slapped you and ended our lessons. That was unkind."

"I deserved it."

She brought her hand to her chest. "Yes. Perhaps. But your English certainly has gotten better."

"Thank you. I've been working on it." He had, in fact, been working hard on it, intentionally engaging American staff in conversation and spending time mingling with the crowds at the fair, eavesdropping on their conversations and attempting to piece together meaning from whatever scraps he picked up. He'd even asked Reuben if they could speak English when working together. The animal trainer happily obliged, pleased to see Max working so hard to fit into his new homeland, though if he were honest, even with himself, Max might admit his motivations extended in a much more specific direction.

"There's something else different about you, too," Frieda said. "You were so melancholy when you arrived, like a cloak of sadness settled on you and you couldn't shake it off. I wasn't convinced you wanted to, but now it's gone. Something turned on the sunlight in your life. If I didn't know how much time you spent working, I'd think maybe it was a woman."

She smirked and rose from the stairs. "I'll not pry, though. Not tonight anyway. I'd better get to bed before the baby wakes me up again. Good night, Max."

"Good night," he answered, but his mind buzzed with her accusation. He didn't know if his happiness had exactly come from a woman, but his thoughts drifted to Shehani during quiet moments, the shape of her popping into his mind as he drifted off to sleep. The memory of her open, friendly beauty accompanied him to the Animal Paradise each day and wove its way into his thoughts as he went about his work. Now every time he escorted the goats from the arena to their enclosure, he would now see Shehani in his mind, a goat horn gripped in her fist, her knuckles pale with the effort of keeping the beast under control amid the flurry of the dancers of Mysterious Asia and their swirling, colorful skirts. The image made him laugh and it made him warm, and it made him very, very happy.

Chapter 14

Max's coworkers bore no visible signs of their late-night revelry the next morning. Trainers and maintenance crew shuffled around one another in an industrious dance that approximated efficiency as they cleaned enclosures and saw to the animals' needs. Even Reuben, who'd been drunk enough to suggest bringing one of the elephants into the bar, looked no worse for wear the next day.

Rube helped Max with the camels, zebus, and the mischievous goats, cleaning away their droppings and pitching them fresh hay while their trainer spoke to Flick and Flock as one might speak to cherished sons, a habit Max teased him about.

"In some ways that's exactly what they are," Reuben said, embracing the parallel with surprising nonchalance.

Max leaned on the handle of his pitchfork, ready to listen to a story. The animal trainer didn't disappoint. "When I was a young man first arrived in Germany to study under the great Carl Hagenbeck, I begged for the opportunity to make a show with the goats. He was gracious enough to let me try, though I doubt he expected much from my efforts. How surprised he was when I had them stacking themselves into pyramids and jumping through hoops.

"They understand me, you see. And I them. They have a stubborn streak, goats, but also delightful senses of humor. They're highly intelligent. And, I think you'd be hard pressed to identify a more obstinate animal. If you can convince a goat to work with you, you can train any creature."

Max might have questioned that last statement, but after chasing Flick through the carnival atmosphere of the Pike, discovering the goat mesmerized by the colorful skirts of the Sinhalese dancers across the way, he supposed he'd developed a kind of kinship with the creatures. Rube had, of course, moved on to bigger, more dangerous, and much more impressive animals, but there was no question the man had a way with goats.

They finished up there and Max headed next to arctic tableau where sea lions and penguins dove out of the way of the stream as he hosed down their enclosure before they recovered their footing and rushed toward him, anticipating their morning fish.

Because of the cumbersome logistics of providing these sea animals with salt water in their enclosure, their pools contained fresh water. In order to keep the animals healthy, each had to be daily hand-fed a fish stuffed with a salt pellet, the difficulty being in isolating the individuals in order to accomplish the task when all were anxious for food.

The sea lions proved simple enough as long as Max's aim remained true, but the penguins presented more of a challenge. The tuxedo-clad horde waddled around his feet, trilling and honking at him, each as indistinguishable to Max as the identical lampposts stretching down the center of the Pike.

Ten frenetic minutes passed before he'd devised a system that finally worked and had him leading each bird with a fish in hand around to one side of his body, painfully contorted to block those impatiently awaiting their turn, and then shoving the tablet-laced fish into the clutches of a knife-edged beak. In this way nine penguins ingested their medicine and Max stood, stiff-legged, hand bleeding, to toss the rest of the morning's feast into the water where the chattering colony happily retrieved it.

PARADISE ON THE PIKE

"Hello there, Max. Quite the bumbling performance." Pete stood on the front edge of a crowd that had gathered to witness Max's graceless penguin feeding routine and which finally began to disperse. Unfortunately, Pete made no effort to move along the path with the other fairgoers. "If the birds are finished with you, come on out here. I want your help with something."

Max offered no more than a shrug in response, wondering whether he could pretend he'd not heard the man. He decided he could not, picked up the empty fish bucket, and let himself through the back door in the fake rocks white with painted snow and wound his way out to the path.

Pete's drawn complexion, perhaps even a touch green, suggested he'd not weathered the night of drinking as well as his colleagues. He pulled his hat down low as if to hide his shame from the strengthening sunshine. Max knew a hangover when he saw one and wondered how late the night had gone.

"Okay, Mr. Willimson?" Max asked when he reached him.

"Ah, you Germans sure can hold your liquor. Look at you, fresh as the morning after a night like that." Pete tossed a hand in mock disgust, and the motion elicited a cascade of giggling chatter from the penguins on the other side of the divide.

"Simmer down, you ugly birds," Pete grumbled and brought his hand to his chest. "I don't know how you can stand it."

"I—" Max started to explain that he'd left early the previous night and had drunk not so much as a sip, but he thought better of it. He enjoyed holding this mysterious kind of German power over the man and was pleased to let him think he could drink him under the table, even though he almost certainly could not. "It is the German constitution, I suppose."

"Yeah, well, I said I'd find a better job for you and I have. Carl is on his way to Hamburg this morning and he left me a little project. I'll need your help with it."

123

Max's stomach flipped. "What kind of project?"

Pete moved down the path with his lengthy stride, leaving Max no choice but to keep up with the man who addressed him without so much as looking back. "Do you take care of the reptiles?"

"Most of the time that's Oscar," Max said. This information drew a scowl from Pete, and so Max added, "I've fed the tortoises."

Other than delivering trays of chopped greens from the prep kitchen to the tortoise yard, Max had largely avoided the reptile swamp since his initial concession tour with Lorenz. He'd appreciated that on the daily list of task assignments, the reptiles had generally fallen to a more experienced zookeeper named Oscar who'd worked with Lorenz and Reuben when they traveled as a circus. The enclosure, not yet open to the public, had received more inhabitants since Max's first visit.

Along one edge of the grassy pen that held the giant tortoises, allegedly hundreds of years old and large enough to offer rides to brave children, stood the boardwalk that formed a sort of bridge above a swamp-like pool of now alligator-infested water, and led visitors to the wall of glass-fronted vivaria that held all manner of frogs, salamander, lizards, and snakes. Most of these creatures had been recently acquired and because they ate infrequently had been left largely unmolested to acclimatize to their new homes before opening this portion of the concession to the public.

As much as he enjoyed caring for most of the animals, Max had to fight his nerves at the thought of snapping alligators and enormous snakes that coiled and squeezed the life from their prey. He'd have rather focused on the tortoises, whose slow movements lent them the appearance of harmlessness, but the second Pete pushed aside a flap in the canvas that temporarily cordoned off the entrance to the swamp walk, the gators absorbed all of Max's attention.

Pete slithered through the opening, his lanky body resembling the animals that waited on the other side of the canvas. Max swallowed hard and followed past a pair of protruding eyes and the toothy snout of a prehistoric beast. A second gator clung halfway onto land on the far side of the water, its snout in a sunny patch, its tail lazily drifting back and forth.

The two scaly reptiles were small but dangerous enough that the water did not continue under the walkway, which was built up about three feet on each side. Like the rest of Hagenbeck's Animal Paradise, it had been designed for both maximum freedom for the animals and optimal view for visitors. While the concession contained few fences, or tight animal quarters, with trenches and clever landscape design making up the largest portion of barriers and minimal railings to protect guests from falling into the gully separating them from hungry lions and bears, the vivaria were an exception to the rule.

Max assumed nobody wished to chance an unprotected encounter with a snake. He certainly didn't care to, but Pete gave no indication of concern, clomping as he did across the boardwalk and straight up to the wall of contained reptiles. Beneath the vivaria stretched a stack of two steps which would allow the littlest fairgoers to climb close and lean against the glass to come eye to eye with a large lizard or snake.

"They are safe?" Max asked, pointing to the glass containers and embarrassed at the warble that had worked its way into his voice.

Pete sneered and pointed to the dried blood Max's hand. "Safer than shoving your fingers in a penguin's beak, I'd wager."

Max glanced down to his sliced-up digits and then back to the alligators.

Beads of cold sweat gathered on Max's forehead. Correctly reading his anxiety, Pete added, "By the way, I wouldn't stick a bloody hand too close to the snappers back there."

Max balled his hand in a fist that caused his cuts to sting.

A smirk played on the businessman's lips. "But you can settle down. The job I have in mind for you has nothing to do with the gators. It's the snakes you'll be working with today."

That didn't comfort Max in the slightest, and the sneer Pete wore told him the shock had been an intentional one.

"I know little about snakes," Max offered as a plea. "I killed them sometimes on the farm in my homeland."

"I'm not asking you to kill them, but it's good you have had *some* experience." Pete tapped on the glass front of a vivarium containing a coiled snake with dark brown scales accentuated by speckled rings. The creature responded with a flick of its long tail, causing Max to involuntarily shudder. Pete tapped again and said, "Ever worked with any venomous ones?"

Max shrank from the question, his heart pounding so loudly in his ears that he heard nothing else for several seconds. Pete cleared his throat and Max did the same.

"In Germany, we have the viper and the Addier. They are dangerous but not deadly to men."

"Makes you the perfect man for the job." Pete slid open the lid on the container holding the snake he'd been molesting and the creature began to uncoil, giving Max a closer look at its dark brown scales and of lighter beige bands running across its back that matched the shade of its belly when it lifted its head to investigate the sound of the shifting lid. Sharp black orbs looked up out of a scaly face dwarfed by comparison to wide flaps that stretched out like wings beneath it. Max stepped back from the terrifying serpent he'd spied dancing to the sound of the snake charmer's flute. His stomach lurched, threatening to release its contents as the creature raised into the shape of a question mark, a forked tongue flicking the air.

Gas lights built into the side walls of the vivaria warmed the same cool spring air that kept the alligators relatively docile, and the snake took full advantage of it now, studying the large mammals that had awakened it from its slumber.

"This," Pete said, his words slick, "is an Indian King Cobra. Deadly. And hostile."

Max wiped sweaty palms on his pants, the stinging slices on his fingers forgotten. "And what are you expecting me to do with it?"

"You need to milk it."

"What?" Max pictured the cow back home that he'd had to milk twice a day and could make no sense of how one would do that to a snake.

"It means to express the venom. Get it to expel all of it and then it will be as safe as a kitten for a while, which our snake charmer will appreciate I'm sure, though he's immune anyway."

"If Inesh is immune to the venom, then why not have him do it?"

"He's busy."

"I'm busy," Max said, too quickly. Pete's complexion reddened. Max regretted his petulance.

"Our Sinhalese set the stage for our animals. Fairgoers don't just want to see the elephants and snakes of India. They want to experience the animals and people of another part of the world. You, Max, are a German grunt worker on the Pike. There are hundreds of you. And I promised you a job you were suited to." Pete stood easily a foot taller than Max and the man used that to his full advantage as he spoke. Max shrunk beneath the belittlement as Pete seemed to uncoil and lengthen until he loomed over his victim like a serpent with fangs full of venom.

Max's stomach twisted into a painful knot. "Why is the venom collected?"

"Well, Max, it makes a fine deadly weapon, of course." Pete held Max's gaze for a silent beat, then winked. "Nah, I'm kidding. It's valuable stuff. And it's a special project of old man Hagenbeck's. When it's dried it's sold to scientists working on anti-venoms. That's why our snake charmer is immune to the cobra venom, because he's been exposed to small amounts of it since he was a child. Of course, only cobra. They're all different, and we've got three types of venomous snakes in our collection."

"How deadly is it?" Max's voice cracked. He wished Pete hadn't noticed, but the man's eyes crinkled in cruel delight.

"Depends on the species, and on the concentration. Most of them, if you milk frequently, won't have enough ready to go in a single bite to kill a man. Some of them would make him wish he were dead anyway. I imagine that's similar to your German adder and viper." He pointed to the cobra now engaged in prodding the top edge of the vivarium with its snout. Pete casually slid the lid back into place. "A single bite from this guy, however, can produce enough venomous punch to kill up to twenty people."

Max tasted bile.

Pete brought his hands together with a clap. "Okay then, I'll talk you through the process. Hand me that tool over there."

He pointed to a long pole with a small Y shaped hook at the end. It looked like the large tongs that sat beside the fireplace in Uncle Reinhardt's parlor, useful for grabbing and maneuvering smoldering logs.

Pete wiggled his head in the same direction. "There's a thick pair of leather gloves on the step here. You're going to want to put those on."

Max didn't question that. He shoved his hands inside the gloves, his injured fingers protesting the roughness of the leather, as Pete moved the lid once again and reached the long tool into the cobra case. The snake pulled back its head in response, stretching up to the top of the case and presenting the perfect opportunity for Pete to grab the creature by the neck, directly behind the head with the over-sized tongs. He swept the flailing snake from the case and dropped it onto the top step, still in a firm grasp of the tongs as it writhed to get at him with no success.

"There," said Pete, smiling. "Now, you take a gloved hand and clamp down hard right behind the tongs. He won't be able to get at you, as long as you keep hold of him, which you will do."

This command from Pete was stern and certain, and Max understood that failure in this part of the operation could spell disaster for both of them. He took a deep breath and did as he was told, applying as much pressure as he could behind the head of the angry snake.

"Got it," he said.

Pete removed the tool then and donned a second pair of gloves that had been hanging from his belt. The snake calmed somewhat when it realized it could not get its fangs into the enemy that held it, though this did nothing to soothe the nervous quiver in Max's muscles.

Pete pulled an object from his coat pocket—half of a mussel shell, which he covered with a thick pad of green leaves also from his pocket. "All right, Max? You take this with your free hand, but make sure you hold steady pressure on the head."

Max did as he was told, though the muscles that held down the cobra had begun to shake. Some of the fight had gone out of the snake and its body, nearly five feet in length, lay limp on the step.

"Now, place the shell with the leaves on top even with the snake's mouth and let him strike it." Max mentally steadied himself, clasped the shell with the tips of his fingers in order to keep his own leather-clad flesh as far from the fangs as possible, and slid it beneath the cobra's jaws. The neck stretched beneath his gloved hand and then came the sickening pulse of tiny muscles as venom began to flow from the snake fangs into the leaves to be collected in the shell.

The entire process took only moments, though it might have been an eternity to Max. Pete picked up the shell, brushed the leaves aside and carefully tipped the contents into a flask he'd taken from a storage cabinet built into the wall at the side of the glass-fronted cases.

He smirked his grudging approval. "Well done."

Max failed to respond from the midst of this unnerving predicament—with a firm grip on the neck of a highly venomous snake and no idea what to do next.

Pete secured a small piece of waxed paper over the jar and took his time labeling the specimen before placing it back into the cabinet. Then he said, "Well, you better put him away. You've already got your hand in the right place. Pick him up and stuff him in, his head first. His backside will follow. Be quick about it and close the lid. He'll be mad for a little bit, but remember, you just milked all of his venom. If he gets you now, you won't get more than a stomachache and a bruise from it."

Cold sweat slicked the back of Max's neck, but the reminder did help. With one uneasy exhale, he blew out as much anxiety as he could, lifted the snake in a tight fist, and flung it through the opening. The animal's head hit the inside of the glass with a forceful thump, and Max took advantage of its temporary stunning to slide the lid back into place.

He collapsed onto the top step, wiped the sweat from his brow, and attempted to recover his breath.

"That went very well, Max. You're a natural!" Pete, unruffled by the experience, took another muscle shell from his pocket, picked up the snake pole, and thrust both toward Max. "Three more snakes to go."

Max barely stopped himself from crying out that he couldn't do it. The man had picked him out for special torture, but if not Max, it would be someone else, and he reasoned that the process was simple enough as long as he was careful. Slowly, he rose from the step and took the pole from Pete. "How often does this have to be done?"

"We'll do it every two weeks. That will give the snakes plenty of time to recover their full store of venom."

Pete smirked and slid open the lid on the next case, which held a snake less frightening in appearance with a pattern of thick bands in subtly different shades of beige down its back. What terror it lacked in appearance, however, it made up for in sound as it rose up and vibrated the end of its tail to make a sharp rattling sound. Max didn't give himself any time to focus on this development and jabbed the tongs into the vivarium, clasping the thing behind its head.

"This is the job you wanted, kid," offered Pete. "It's not all goats and elephants."

Chapter 15

The warming May air still blew cold across Max's shoulders and he shivered beneath his perspiration-soaked shirt. Though his nerves had begun to settle, Pete's insistence that the snakes would need milking again in two weeks formed a shadow at the edge of his thoughts. His experience with the reptiles had put Max behind schedule, and he hurried toward the kitchen to prepare the fruits and vegetable he would serve to the monkeys.

On his way he glanced into the arena where Trieste, stare trained on Reuben, had laid to rest beside a bleating lamb in a crowd-pleasing Biblical tableau. Max keyed his way into the animal kitchen, grabbed a bucket from a lower shelf, and began sorting spring berries and lettuce leaves onto the food scale.

"Are you unwell? You look as if you might be sick." A feminine, accented voice floated through the open window in front of him. A moment later, Shehani pushed in through the door of the small room. "Has something terrible happened?"

"I'm okay." Max's heart beat faster at her nearness, the woodsy, spicy scent of her skin tickling his nose. He scooped fruits and vegetables from the scale and dropped them into the bucket. "It has been a strange morning."

"What has been strange about it?" The dancer placed her forearms on the countertop and leaned forward, resting much of her weight on the surface. She let her head hang and yawned. In addition to taking part in almost every arena show, Shehani frequently balanced on the back of Lizzie the elephant in either a parade or promotional stunt on the Pike. As much as Max might have liked to believe she'd come to see him, the kitchen was one of a few quiet places in the Animal Paradise. It was a good place to steal a restful minute.

"Mr. Williamson assigned me the task of milking the venom glands of the snakes."

She raised her head to look at him, her brow furrowed. "Had you ever done that before?"

He shook his head. "Never. I've killed a few snakes on the farm, never handled live ones."

Shehani bit her lower lip. "Snakes can be tricky. You are very brave."

"Thank you for that," he said, still trembling slightly from the ordeal. "I don't think it is true, but thank you. How have the shows been going?"

"Well, I think. The stands have been filled and the cats have not decided to eat me yet." Amusement twinkled in her eyes. "Have you not had a chance to see?"

He thought of replying that he had not both because he wanted to hear her tell him about it in her voice that hit his ears like melodic foreign waves, but he didn't want to lie to her. "I have caught glimpses," he admitted.

"I know," she said with a giggle, and he wanted more than anything to know what that giggle meant. "I see you peeking at me around the edge of the seats sometimes. I look for you. It makes me more comfortable to know you are there."

"Is it uncomfortable for you?" he asked. "To dance in front of people?"

A dimple deepened on her pretty round cheek. "It's the lions and tigers that make me more nervous than the people. The audience loves it when I dance in the cage with the big cats. Mr. Castang is teaching me to use the whip to divert their attention so I will soon perform alone with them—an idea I don't relish. But I don't mind dancing. That I have done since I was a little girl, and it allowed my brother to bring me here to America." She placed a hand on him and his muscles stopped quivering. "I am grateful for that."

"Do you not have family back home?"

She shook her head. "It is only Inesh and me. My mother died when I was young, my father a few years ago. He once traveled across Europe with Mr. Carl Hagenbeck, as part of a touring ethnographic exhibit, part of seventy Sinhalese including Mr. Pamu."

"And so now you dance so that you can see the world." Max swallowed his nerves and added, "And you do it beautifully."

"You're kind. Practice is making me better, but have you seen the dancers in Mysterious Asia across the Pike?"

"I have," he admitted. "The one time with the goat. And they were not exactly graceful when he joined them."

She laughed. "I remember. How is our friend Flick?"

"No less ornery. He likes to attempt new and ingenious ways to escape. But he is well behaved when he's sleeping."

"In his dreams I bet he is with the dancers again."

"Maybe so. Are they Sinhalese like you?"

"Yes, but also no. They are from a different part of Ceylon, and they are Buddhist. They have danced a more traditional version of the Kandyan dance probably since they were very small. It's the national dance of our country, based on the Ramayana, a poem that tells the story of Lord Rama."

"That is not the same dance you do?"

"I dance a version of it, too, but in Ceylon I am unusual. I'm Christian because when my father traveled through Europe, he became Christian.

Like you."

Max wasn't sure if he could really claim to be Christian. He supposed he was, though the closest he'd come to the Church that he could recall was a brief visit paid to them by the local minister after Felix's death. It had not been a cordial one and resulted in Mutti angrily ordering the man to leave. After that, Max had constructed a flimsy coffin himself and the two of them had held their own private sort of memorial, burying Felix beside the barn with a bottle of the swill that proved his undoing. The memory made his head hurt.

"I think you dance more beautifully than the ladies of Mysterious Asia." She studied him in a long stretch of silence, and he feared he had come on too strongly.

At last she smiled. "You're a kind man. But what about you? What brought you to America? You have not been here long, I assume?"

"No. Not much longer than you." He rubbed the back of his neck, thinking about how to answer her question. "I came because my father died."

"I am sorry. He wanted you to see the world?"

"No," Max said. "I think that for my father the world was a very small place, and it is better without him in it."

Shehani slid her hand down his arm and grabbed his hand to squeeze. She said nothing at first, but simply studied him, her soft brown eyes wide with concern. At last she said, "For whatever sorrow has brought you here I am sorry, but I am glad to know you."

"Thank you," he said, the words tripping over his tongue.

"Do you miss your home?" she asked.

"I did," Max answered after a beat during which he relished the sensation of his hand in hers. "But I am beginning to think home can be in a different place. How about you? Do you miss your home?"

"Not yet. Perhaps before the fair is over, I will, but for now I am glad to have met wonderful new friends."

Max felt his chest puff, his shoulders lifting of their own accord as a pleasant warmth climbed the back of his neck.

"Friends like Lizzie," Shehani teased, and his heart did cartwheels inside his chest. "And you, of course." She squeezed his hand once again, dropped it, and gazed out the kitchen window toward the arena.

Shehani sighed and stretched elegantly. "It's nearly showtime again. I need to get back."

"How can you stand having all those people gawking at you?" Max thought back to the intrusive stares he received on the Pike as he held onto Flick, how he wished he could hide from all those curious gawkers.

"I can stand it," she said, leaning in to give him a kiss on his cheek. "Because I know that you are beside the bleachers watching me."

Chapter 16

Henry the detective asked Mutti to the fair. That was the talk buzzing among the family when Max returned home one evening about a month into the fair. It was one of the rare days he made it home in time for supper. Lorenz had given each of his men one half day during the week so they could enjoy the fair or take care of other business. The show was running more or less smoothly now, six times a day, and the team worked well enough together that when one was gone, others could fill the void.

Max did want to explore the fair, but he didn't particularly want to do it alone. He'd thought about asking some of his uncle's family, perhaps Frieda and some of the older children, but he feared that the awkwardness might reemerge between them. She had also visited the fair already with Ernst. He'd used connections from his days on the construction crews and managed to secure them free tickets. To hear her talk about it, though, she'd missed the best parts, focusing on the grand exhibit buildings Ernst had helped construct and entirely skipping the Pike with all its peculiarities and wonders.

He'd have gladly taken his mother as well, but Mutti already had a date.

"Why don't you come with us, Maxie?" she asked.

"I'm not coming on your romantic outing with some man."

"Henry is not *some man*," she said. "He's a detective and a lovely gentleman."

"That does not make it better, Mutti." He was too harsh. He regretted it as soon as the words flew from his mouth but he didn't know how to soften them.

"When is your next half day?" she asked, persistent in that way only mothers can be, both infuriatingly stubborn and inexplicably endearing.

"Tuesday," he admitted. "I will have to help clean and help prepare for the ten o'clock animals show, but then I will be free to do as I like."

"Excellent," she said. "I'll see if Henry can move our outing to Tuesday and we'll come to the Animal Paradise for the early show. Then the three of us can spend some time together. He really is a wonderful man. I'd like you to get to know him."

The last thing in the world Max wanted to do was to get to know a man who was interested in his mother. A detective, too. He didn't particularly care how nice the non-German-of-German-heritage Detective Duncan was. He didn't belong with Mutti.

"Fine," was all he managed to say. He hadn't seen her so genuinely happy since Felix died and it did buoy his spirits. What dimmed his enthusiasm was the realization that the last time he had seen the lightness in her step was actually on the day itself, when his father had dropped dead. When he reflected back on the day, he could not see it, but there it was in an uninvited flash of something lurking at the edge of his memories, threatening to crack the image of his mother.

With great effort he pushed it aside, willing instead the image he knew of her, that of a fresh widow whose entire world had begun to crumble.

∞

Tuesday arrived with bright sunshine and the promise of one of those truly gorgeous May days that brought with it the hope of life and renewal and all things lovely. The scent of spring flowers filled the air and mingled with the enticing aroma of fried delicacies from all over the world, designed to offer the fairgoer anything his heart desired.

Max missed the entrance of his mother and her escort as they made their way into the arena bleachers, but he spotted them as he retrieved the goats from Reuben. Mutti wore her blonde hair swept up beneath a stylish straw hat that was remarkably American. Her dress, too, was a new one that the nieces had recently helped her fashion. He'd not yet seen her wear it and it looked all wrong. He searched in vain for the faded woman who haunted his childhood.

This Mutti stood and clapped gloved hands for the bear now standing on hind legs atop a small platform in the middle of the performance cage. Beside her stood the detective, now fully visible. He was a tall man, solid but not fat, in a lightly colored summer suit. His dark hair had been neatly trimmed, his face shaven clean, and he possessed the serious kind of demeanor one would expect to see in a detective. Max liked the man better when he was nothing more than a pair of scuffed shoes emerging from shadows.

Henry Duncan's gaze wandered from the bear and lit on Max. The detective nudged Mutti's shoulder and pointed. Her smile brightened when she saw him and she waved, which pleased Max, though he did not return her greeting, concentrating instead on Flick, the ringleader and troublemaker of the two goats growing antsy beside him. He wanted his mother to see him working hard, and he wanted her friend the detective to see it, too. If this relationship turned into some kind of romance for his mother, he didn't want to give this detective the impression that he was a vulnerable, fatherless child in need of protection.

Max settled the goats and made his way back into the stands. There was no space for him to climb up next to Mutti, but that was okay with him. It was time for him to focus his attention on Shehani anyway, and he wasn't sure he wanted Mutti's eyes on him when his were on the Sinhalese beauty.

She was striking this day, in her colorful, flowing dress. She'd changed to a light green skirt, more sheer than the pink she'd been wearing, he assumed because the weather had warmed. With it she wore a darker green blouse that hugged her breasts and revealed a patch of smooth brown skin at her waist. A flowing scarf-like piece that matched the skirt swooped up over her one shoulder and tucked back into the skirt. Shehani had never been so beautiful, and she mesmerized as she danced and swayed among the elephants, tiny bells on her dress ringing softly with every swish of her hips.

Guilt burned at him over the pleasure he took in ogling her while knowing how she didn't particularly enjoy dancing among the animals. No matter what she said, he couldn't believe she hadn't been performing in this way her entire life.

The audience, too, was entranced until the elephants began to move again at Reuben's command. One of the mahouts used his jeweled hook to spur them on, but the beasts neither needed the encouragement. He had to scramble out of the way of one of the giants so as not to be trampled underfoot. The elephants now looked only to Reuben who led them in their finale up onto the platform above the shoot, as Lorenz narrated above them. By now Reuben had become well practiced at avoiding a plunge himself and the crowd cheered furiously as, one at a time, the elephants slid into the water with a gigantic splash that left the spectators in the front wet and squealing.

―――

"What a lovely girl," Mutti commented as the three of them walked out of the concession and onto the Pike.

"Who is that?" Detective Duncan asked. He'd insisted Max call him

Henry as his mother did, and though he'd obliged, Max struggled to think of him that way. He preferred the distance of formality, at least in his head.

"The Indian dancer, with the elephants," Mutti said.

"I didn't see her." The detective's—Henry's—comment sounded disingenuous to Max's ear, as though any man would fail to notice the ethereal Shehani. "I wonder, Max, did you happen to spot the man standing closest to the baby elephant? Dark hair, scarred face, shabbily dressed?"

Max shook his head, then to his mother said, "She's Sinhalese."

Mutti slipped her hand through Duncan's crooked elbow, the two of them together making an alarming picture of a couple as they strolled beside Max heading east along the Pike.

"What on earth is that?" Mutti asked.

"The dancer. She's Sinhalese, from Ceylon," Max said.

Mutti stared at him blankly, but Henry jumped in.

"It's an island off the coast of India." He turned his head and looked directly at Max, his brow furrowed. "Had you ever seen that man before? The one with the scar?"

Max cleared his throat. "I didn't see the man today, so I couldn't say."

"It makes me wonder. . ." Henry began, then paused and changed directions. "Is that where the elephants are from as well? Ceylon, I mean?"

Max wasn't actually sure, though he was grateful the conversation had returned to a subject he could at least comment upon. "They are Asian elephants, I know, but I suppose they could have come from somewhere else. They were trained in Hamburg."

"Who ever heard of German elephants?" Mutti asked, and Max scowled at whatever stupid persona his mother was playing at. He couldn't stand the thought that she would downplay her intelligence in order to impress this man. She'd done enough of that when she lived under Felix's thumb, only recently emerging after nearly vanishing in his father's dark shadow.

"The Hagenbeck family has been training animals in Hamburg for several decades," Max explained. "That's why they needed more space to grow. It's why they wanted our farm."

"Ah, that's right. You sold your farm to Carl Hagenbeck." Henry Duncan stopped walking and looked straight at Mutti as if his words contained a question. Max walked several paces ahead of them before he realized they were no longer moving and turned back toward them.

"Had I told you that?" Mutti asked the detective.

Henry responded with an odd silence until Max reached them again. Then the detective shrugged a shoulder and said, "Well, I guess you must have. You haven't told me much about your life before coming to St. Louis."

Mutti flicked a hand in the air. "It was a small life." She stopped then and looked to the ground as if she'd dropped something before she raised her narrowed-eye gaze to study Henry. "You don't remember whether I mentioned that we sold our farm to Herr Hagenbeck, but you remember that it's true. Do you know him?"

"Oh," Henry said as if he'd been caught in a lie. "No. He seems like an interesting fellow, though. It's an amazing coincidence, isn't it? It's the kind of detail that sticks in this detective trap of mine." He tapped the side of his head with one finger and started walking again. "I was surprised at the connection, is all. Did Max know he was going to be able to get a job working for the same family in St. Louis?"

"Oh, no." Mutti might have been breezily nonchalant had her busy fingers not worried at the cuff of her sleeves. "Max discovered the Hagenbeck concession by accident. He began working on a construction crew before the fair opened with his cousin Ernst."

"Oh, yes, the one who doesn't work at the restaurant."

Max chewed his lip. The detective sure did know a lot about his family.

PARADISE ON THE PIKE

It made him wonder if this Henry had gotten closer to Mutti than Max realized and whether there might be a subtle way he could ask.

Mutti reached her hand out to Max and threaded her arm beneath his so that now the three of them strode arm-in-arm straight for the end of the Pike. "Maxie is as talented with construction as he is with animals."

"Is that so?" Henry asked. "What buildings did you work on?"

Max pointed to the right where a wide path veered off of the Pike and toward the Plaza of St. Louis. "Festival Hall primarily."

"Should we take a look?" Henry asked.

Max buried his hands in his pcokets. "It's an amphitheater, though the organ might be worth seeing." He hadn't actually been inside the building since its completion. The last time he had really looked at it at all, it wasn't yet entirely covered with the white plaster that made it look as if it were a permanent marble structure and the dome wasn't yet finished. He admitted that, from a distance, it did look pretty impressive, as did all the main buildings around the Grand Basin, stretching out like great tentacles from Festival Hall. It was in these buildings where fairgoers would browse products of industry, new innovations, and exhibits celebrating the various states and nations who contributed.

"Let's go see the Palace of Manufactures," Henry suggested. "Then we can work our way around."

Mutti and Max readily agreed and the three strolled past a large statue of King Louis IX, scepter in hand, atop a galloping horse, then veered left toward the massive palace building.

Max had not been inside the manufacturing building. If possible, the spacc appeared larger inside than out and contained representations of the textiles industry, equipment used for ventilation and heating, lighting fixtures, plumbing demonstrations, and varied displays from many countries including Japan, France, and Germany. Max hardly knew where to look and couldn't begin to take it all in.

"It's amazing," Mutti said, agog.

Henry took her hand in his. "What's amazing to me is how quickly this all came together—all these buildings and all the coordination between nations. It was an enormous undertaking and it has worked. And," he turned to look at Max, "you have had a part to play in it. These buildings, the look of them, like they are straight out of the ancient world. I'm very impressed."

"It's an illusion," Max replied, using a word of which he was particularly proud. Shehani had taught it to him after he'd been perplexed at her description of her dance.

"I know," Henry said. "Nothing but an intricate magic trick. I saw a lot of the process, patrolled the grounds occasionally during construction, and talked to the people in charge. But isn't it wonderful that we are here to witness this kind of magic?"

It wasn't a question, exactly, but Max couldn't get it out of his mind as they walked into the building and through the many displays. Magical was the word he'd have used to describe the wonders it housed.

∞

The Palace of Manufactures was only their first stop of the day, which soon took them, again at Henry's suggestion, to the Palace of Education where the St. Louis Police Department had partnered with several law enforcement agencies to showcase innovations in the science of policing.

The three of them wandered together through the exhibition, Henry enthusiastically pointing out first a trunk in which a body had once been discovered in some famous case and both the diary of a known murderer, and the rope once used to hang him. Mutti wore a forced mask of interest that Max made no attempt to imitate. Henry, fortunately, steered them away from the photographs of lynchings and of a bloated body washed up on a lake shore, though Max did not fail to notice them.

With a dull ache in his stomach, Max nearly asked if they might leave to visit a different display, when a narrow table caught his eye. The table held a mahogany box that contained a dozen pots of ink and a rubber roller, as well as a sheet of clear glass and a stack of blank white cards. Beside the table stood a uniformed officer of the London Police and in front of the table several people stood in line.

"What is this?" Max asked Henry, pointing.

Henry's whole aspect lit with delight. "Oh, it's Scotland Yard's fingerprint demonstration! I was hoping we'd get to see it. We've always used a method of identifying criminals by their physical features, but it's been based on head shape and facial measurements and the like. The problem with that is that different people can be extremely similar. Take siblings, for example. Even those that aren't twins may have identical or nearly identical features."

"So, this fingerprinting means you can differentiate them?" Mutti asked, causing Henry to beam at her.

"That's what they say. I haven't seen it yet, though. Let's see if we can learn more."

Mutti shrugged her consent, and they lined up to wait for about five minutes before getting to the front to pepper a friendly British police officer with their questions. Henry identified himself as a detective with the St. Louis Police Department, and the officer became even friendlier.

"It's a pleasure to meet you, Detective. I'm John Ferrier with the London Police. Would you like a demonstration?" The two shook hands.

Henry replied enthusiastically that he would and bounced into the seat meant for a suspect at the officer's desk, above which pictures and descriptions of various fingerprint patterns hung on the wall.

While Max and Mutti looked on with interest, the officer took each one of Henry's fingers one at a time, pressed them onto a pad of dark ink, and carefully rolled each onto a white card. He repeated the procedure with a second card. After he was finished, he offered a wetted cloth to Henry to wipe off the ink, which he did with little success.

He held up one card to hand to Henry. "That one is for you to keep if you wish. The second will be filed away in our records."

Henry slapped his knee with his palm. "And there's no one else in the world who has identical prints to these?"

"No," the foreign detective said. "Not a soul. And the best part is that once we have a set of fingerprints on record, we can discover matching prints from crime scenes. Prints are left everywhere."

He pointed to the clear glass, slid open a drawer on the back of the table, and withdrew a stack of clear, flexible pieces of film.

The officer continued, "Everything anyone touches will have traces of them left behind by the oils on their skin. If the surface is smooth enough, we can study them under magnification, determine distinct markings and, with complete accuracy, pin a specific criminal to the crime."

"Astounding! Of course, it will take some time to build up a record."

"Yes," the man agreed. "We are working on it in London, all over England actually, and in Ireland and India and other parts of the Commonwealth as well. We fingerprint anyone who comes into our custody as a matter of course. Often it helps us determine that a suspect was not present at a crime scene as well."

"And has this met with resistance?" Henry asked. "I know several of our detectives are leery of it. They prefer the Bertillon method of measuring features."

"There is some incredulity, as you might expect. It's a new science and not everyone trusts it yet, but we've been using it with a great deal of success now for a few years, and our detectives are getting better at collecting fingerprints as part of their evidence gathering procedures. Frankly, I don't see why we have to use one or the other. I view them as having entirely different applications. Yes, fingerprints are used to distinguish people from one another, as Bertillon measurements do, but that's not all they're good for. Bertillon is helpful in crime scene identification if there is witness testimony that may be either corroborated or dismissed. Fingerprints require no witness. They are themselves the silent witness no criminal realizes he is leaving behind at the scene of his crime."

"Max," Henry said, startling Max from his thoughts. "Why don't you give it a try?"

Max couldn't think of a good reason to say no, but his every muscle resisted moving toward the seat as Henry vacated it for him.

"Is that really necessary?" Mutti asked, her manners stiff.

Henry frowned but recovered quickly. "Well, no, I suppose it's not necessary. I just thought it might be fun." He lifted his ink-splotched card. "A nice keepsake of the day. We could do yours as well."

Mutti scrunched her nose. "No, thank you. I would rather not cover myself in ink. Max shouldn't either. He returns to work tomorrow. What would Herr Hagenbeck think if he were to show up with his fingers stained?"

Henry tilted his head and chuckled. "I expect the goats wouldn't mind too much."

Max couldn't help it. He tried not to laugh and ended up snorting, which earned him a stern look from his mother and an appreciative smirk from Henry which slid from his lips when Mutti did not relent.

"You're right, of course," Henry finally said. "I can explain away my dirty fingers as professional curiosity and continuing education. Max should present a more professional front."

Mutti celebrated her victory with a stiff nod. "Well," she said. "This has been fascinating, but let's go see something else. I hear the Philippine Village is not to be missed."

Chapter 17

"It's like we've walked into another world," Mutti said as they crossed a stone bridge toward the Philippine Village and took in the sights of thatch-roof huts hovering on stilts above a lake. Natives piloted rough made boats across the surface of the water as if living a typical day.

Though the area did contain some larger buildings that featured information about the hunting, fishing, and agricultural activities of the Filipino people, a series of culturally diverse villages constituted the bulk of the exhibit. Each bend of the path brought them to another primitive collection of handmade huts, a far cry from the glistening white palaces elsewhere on the fairgrounds. The women appeared respectably covered, but many of the children wore little, and some of the men were clad in nothing more than a loincloth.

"They must be cold." Mutti hugged herself and looked at the ground as though shocked. The day had been a bright one, but as the evening approached and the spring sun began to drop in the sky, a noticeable chill descended. Detective Duncan offered Mutti his long coat, which she readily accepted. Max scowled but, grateful for his own coat, he was glad he'd not had to make the gesture himself.

Henry, tall and well-built and evidently untouched by the cold, pointed to a small group of the Filipinos circling a campfire and commented, "These people are probably much more comfortable in less clothing than they would be in the heavy garments of America."

"Perhaps," Max said, "but immodest people get cold, too." Shehani danced through his mind shivering in her flowing gown of sheer fabric until warmed by exertion. Even in the warmer clothes in which she had first arrived at the fair, the St. Louis spring had been exceptionally chilly for her.

"These people don't look as if they mind too much," came Henry's dismissive reply.

In truth, they didn't look to Max like they were thinking about much of anything. The people of the villages stared hollow-eyed at the white fairgoers while simultaneously performing the daily tasks of their strange lives.

The women wove baskets and prepared food. Children shrieked as they chased one another and played, performing for the crowd who laughed at their antics. Occasionally a child approached a particularly attentive visitor with a hand outstretched to receive a coin to squirrel away somewhere. Max averted his gaze before he could be identified as a potential income source.

About halfway through the village, Max, Mutti, and Henry discovered a group of men smoking and speaking rapidly in a foreign tongue. They, too, sat around a fire above which hung a spit that contained a roasting animal. Max's stomach rumbled at the scent of the cooking meat. He'd not eaten since before their venture across the fairgrounds, and hunger clawed at him. When they got closer, he stretched his neck to see what they were cooking. His stomach clinched again, this time in distress at his recognition of the clear shape.

"Savages." Henry had clearly seen it, too, and he tugged on Mutti's sleeve to guide her away from the view that she might be spared the indecency he and Max had already suffered.

"What's the matter?" she demanded, pulling from Henry's grasp.

"It's a dog, Mutti," said Max. "They are cooking a dog." He'd heard the whispers of this daily practice on the lips of fairgoers who delighted in feigning shock, expressing unearned disgust for the Filipinos who'd been brought to the fair by organizers intent on creating a sensation.

"Ach du meine Güte!" Mutti's cheeks drained of color, but she recovered her wits with grace. "I suppose if it's what you've got, it's what you eat."

"I think we have a greater variety of choices than that at the fair," Henry pointed out.

"Well, then," Mutti said. "We'd better get out of here and explore some of those options. I don't wish to be asked to stay for dinner here."

It was one of those rare moments, becoming more frequent in recent weeks, when Max was incredibly proud to call Emmi Eyer his mother. For all the weakness he'd seen in her in the years they lived with his father, she was a remarkably confident woman, one who wouldn't be taken in by the likes of Detective Henry Duncan.

After visiting the Philippine Exhibit their party of three grew particularly quiet, each evidently trapped inside personal reflections. For Max, the experience stirred a strange sympathy, even a sense of kinship. Not long ago, he himself had been an outsider, unable to speak the language of his new home which was crowded and smelly and loud compared to the tiny corner of the world he'd inhabited in Stellingen. He didn't feel that as keenly anymore, but the sharp memory of it persisted and the blank expressions worn by many of the Filipinos had felt familiar.

They had traveled from their homeland to become objects of curiosity on display, even encouraged to emphasize their cultural differences. He thought of Shehani's insistence that in Ceylon she did not dance with wild animals, but that here she did in order to please the crowds. He wondered to what extent he had observed life in the Philippines and how much had been simply a show—a show put on for gawkers whose perceptions of the lives lived in foreign lands served primarily to feed their sense of superiority.

The notion didn't sit well in Max's stomach. By the time they'd strolled past the large floral clock and Henry suggested they stop at a restaurant across from the now newly opened Observation Wheel, Max no longer had an appetite.

"I think I'll say goodbye for now. Thank you for the day. It was good to meet you, Henry." Max stretched out a hand that the detective shook, while Mutti looked on smiling. Much to Max's surprise, he hadn't disliked the man as he'd thought he would. Henry Duncan was considerate and kind, and clearly interested in Mutti's opinions in a way the monstrous Felix had certainly never been. The very thought of his father provoked shivers entirely unrelated to the chilly night air. The detective elicited no such reaction from Max but instead exuded a sense of calm and comfort.

"We'd be happy to have you eat with us and take in the colorful lights at the cascades after." Henry dropped his chin, giving such an impression of genuine disappointment Max nearly changed his mind.

"Thank you but no. You two go ahead. I have some tasks I want to see to back at the Animal Paradise, a few odd jobs that will make my morning easier tomorrow."

"Well, Max, it was a pleasure to meet you, too."

Mutti stepped toward him and reached up to smooth the lapels of his jacket. "Don't stay out too late. The morning comes early and you don't get many days off. Use the time well."

"Of course," Max said. She was entirely correct but didn't generally give him such motherly advice. It took him aback, and he wondered briefly if this show of concern was for the benefit of Henry. His mother had been more apt to give him advice in the last several months since they'd left Stellingen, but she remained Mutti, largely emotionally closed off to him.

PARADISE ON THE PIKE

This night had been different. She was relaxed, happy even, when he kissed her cheek. "I'll be home at a reasonable hour.

"I promise."

Chapter 18

Mutti hadn't pressed for further explanation before disappearing with her gallant detective into the Lemp Restaurant. With relief, Max watched them walk away arm-in-arm. In truth, nothing he could do tonight at the Animal Paradise would make the day flow more smoothly in the morning. The other keepers, most of whom stayed on the grounds through the night, would have handled any of the tasks left behind on his half day.

Reuben himself would certainly double check that everything was in order before he vacated the fairgrounds for the temporary apartments he and Lorenz had constructed nearby or, more likely, for Cheyenne Joe's Cowboy Saloon.

Max had not joined them again since the night of Carl Hagenbeck's sendoff and had no intention of doing so this night, either. He'd planned to follow his mother's advice and call it an early evening, but after seeing the Philippine Exhibit and the curiously exploited people in it, he had an overwhelming urge to find Shehani.

Her people did not wear loincloths or eat dogs. They spoke fluent English, at least more fluent than Max, and carried themselves with dignity as they shared their culture with the visitors at the concession. His darker thoughts whispered, however, that they often did so from within a cage in the center of an arena, designed to protect its audience from the animals within—a collection that included both wild beasts and brown-skinned people whose features were not so different from the natives in the Philippine village.

Max reached the Animal Paradise minutes after the closing of the final show of the day and had to fight against the flow of a large outbound crowd to enter the concession. Large lights blazed, spilling pools of light onto the otherwise shadowy pathways. Some visitors milled about, exploring the enclosures around the perimeter of the concession. The tortoises on which fairgoers could ride had been put away for the night, their energy levels not conducive to their purpose once the sun went down, but the ostriches could still be heard barking out in dismay as riders tried to hold onto their backs. Most of the animals Max passed rooted through their pens for morsels of supper, spread throughout the yards to occupy their minds. The Hagenbecks insisted upon this extra step, always concerned that the animals' habitats be as stimulating as possible to encourage natural behaviors. Happy animals, they said, were busy animals. That was the great secret to the effective, gentler training that made Hagenbeck stand out in the captive animal trade. The creatures trusted and worked with their trainers because they derived enjoyment from the process, not because they would be punished if they didn't follow commands.

This had been a major philosophical difference between Reuben and the Sinhalese mahouts when they'd first arrived, another way in which the mahouts were categorized as foreign and inferior. Eventually, Reuben persuaded them, and the jeweled bull hooks they carried became mere cultural accessories rather than tools of persuasion.

Max passed the large enclosure of grazers. Those not engaged in eating had settled down to sleep after a long day of work. Next, he passed the predators, the tigers pacing as always, following his progress past them with slinking steps. He scanned the milling guests along his way, and he spotted several of the mahouts. He waved to them as he went, recognizing

Shehani's brother mingling among them. The snake charmer frowned and did not return the wave, though Max sensed the man's scrutiny long after he'd passed by.

Max didn't locate Shehani herself until he reached the far edge of the animal park, next to the entrance to the reptile swamp. He might not have seen her at all, as the lights in this part of the park were scarce enough to discourage the congregation of visitors in the back of the concession. Instead, the light placement formed a strategic design meant to guide the guests toward the front gate and out onto the Pike once the evening grew dark. He only knew she was there, covered in a dark cloak that hid her bright dress, because he heard her.

There could be no mistaking her feminine voice, tinged in anger.

"I want no part of that."

"I just offered to show you my snake." This second voice he recognized immediately. The oily, venomous syllables belonged to Pete Williamson. "I thought you were a charmer like your brother. You certainly look comfortable dancing around them with all that bare skin."

"I've never charmed a snake in my life."

"I doubt that," he said, his words slow and stretched and dripping in unpleasantness like an overpowering cologne. "You've charmed me."

"I need to go. My brother is expecting me."

"I've got all the time in the world. If you ever change your mind and want a peek at a snake that's worth your time, you just let me know."

Not wishing to slow her escape, Max hesitated before revealing himself, but did so then, unable to endure the man's disrespectful taunting.

"Leave her alone, Pete."

"Well," he said, turning toward the sound of Max's voice as he stepped out of the shadow and into the single light that illuminated the entrance to the reptile swamp. The lanky man placed his bejeweled hand on Shehani's arm and a wave of indignation welled up inside Max, ready to crest. "Last I checked we weren't on a first name basis. I thought you had the afternoon off. Weren't you going to the fair with your mother and father?"

"*Detective* Duncan is not my father," Max said, his jaws aching with the tension it took to hold back the stream of angry words he held for the man standing in front of him, brazenly clutching to the arm of the woman Max wanted more than anything to protect. He wasn't sure when it had begun, but the emotion was strong and undeniable, and more powerful than any crush he'd mistakenly developed on Frieda. He thought of the women in the Philippine Exhibit, ogled by leering fairgoers in the name of education. He'd sensed a kinship with them and an overwhelming sorrow on their behalf. He felt that now for Shehani as well, this beautiful, vulnerable woman subjected to the whims of a jackass. He hoped Pete might find the identification of Henry as a detective intimidating. Perhaps it worked because he let go of Shehani before replying.

"Oh, that's right. Your mother has a gentleman friend," Pete mocked.

"Yes," Max said, refusing to give the man the satisfaction of appearing rattled. "She's been a widow for more than a year, and she has begun a friendship with one of the lead detectives in the St. Louis Police Department. What business is it of yours?"

Pete didn't respond, but Shehani did, stepping away from him and closer to Max.

"How was your day at the fair, Max? Did you see anything wonderful?"

"I did," he said, glad of a change in subject. Pete leaned against the archway at the entrance to the swamp and crossed his legs.

"We toured the Palace of Manufactures and the Palace of Education, then took a car ride across the fairgrounds to the Philippine Village. Have you been able to tour the grounds much?"

She shook her head. "I don't venture far. Mr. Lorenz and Mr. Reuben would not mind, of course, but my brother worries. I would need an escort." She ducked her head with the last words as if embarrassed to speak them, or perhaps embarrassed by what they might imply.

Max nearly seized the opportunity to invite her to visit some of the exhibits with him but thought better of doing so within earshot of Pete Williamson. Instead, he said, "I don't think your brother likes me very much."

Shehani glanced over her shoulder toward Pete and shook her head. "It's not you. He's protective. Since my father died, it is the two of us. He's afraid he can't protect me well here, but I have told him that you are a good friend to me." She leaned in to whisper, "And that Mr. Williamson is not."

"Are you in danger?" Max asked, his heart in his throat.

After a pause she whispered, "I don't think so. He is one rude man." She stood straight and resumed their conversation once again in a normal volume. "I'm too busy here anyway to get into trouble, with all the shows and demonstrations advertising for the concession. Many people have questions about the elephants and about my culture. I endeavor to answer what I can, to be an ambassador for my people."

Pete slow clapped, the sound sharp in the growing night. "That's very noble, dear, but you can't imagine any of these people care about your culture? They're here to see a pretty woman in a strange dress who entertains them in ways it isn't proper for white women to do. They want to watch your hips wiggle because it's sexy, and all these stiff and proper people need a little sexy in their lives."

"That's enough," Max said. Shehani examined her feet, but he could see from the corner of his eye the glimmer of a tear on her smooth cheek.

Pete held up his hands, palms out. "I just don't want her to get the wrong idea about what all these people are after. You take those Filippinos for example, and yes, I have been to the village to see it. Some of those men are barely dressed. Say what you will about proper white ladies, but wave a loin cloth in their direction and I bet they won't turn away. I'm sure your mother enjoyed her education in the Philippine Village."

Since the death of his father, Max hadn't wanted to hit anyone so much as he did in that moment. He didn't need to know the word to know that this man had made a very crude statement in front of Shehani, and whereas Max never would have raised a hand against Felix, he had no hesitation about hitting Pete Williamson. He balled his fist, drew a deep breath, and felt first Shehani's light touch and then her firm grip.

"Mr. Williamson has work to do with the snakes. We should leave him to it. I wonder if you could escort me to my brother. I do not care for the paths when it is this dark. I'm afraid I might lose my footing."

"Him you want to be alone with—the filthy immigrant who can barely speak English. I guess there's no accounting for taste," Pete snarled. "The savage is picky."

Max clenched his fists and stepped toward Pete, but Shehani tugged on his arm and pulled him away toward the darkness without giving him the chance at a retort.

"He is a small-minded man," she said. "And small-minded men are not worth the effort."

She did not let go of him until they were well beyond the spot of light illuminating the reptile walk entrance. Before he followed her around the curve of the arena toward the entrance, Max looked back one more time and was surprised to see two figures standing together. There had been no fairgoers in that darkened corner of the concession, but Pete appeared engrossed in conversation with this shorter individual that had to have come from somewhere.

"Who is that?" Max asked Shehani, causing her to stop and return several paces toward him.

"I don't know." She pulled her wrap more tightly around herself. "And I don't want to know anything to do with that man."

"He bothers you often?"

"Often enough. I don't want to talk anymore about it." She continued to walk and rounded the arena. Max took a few steps behind her but paused to peer back toward Pete, and as he did, the second man turned his craggy visage toward the light, which illuminated a vertical scar running down his forehead. Max saw Pete hand something small to the man who stuck the object into his coat pocket before slipping out of the light and heading in the opposite direction around the arena. As the dark filled in behind him, Pete's attention remained fixed on his withdrawing companion.

Max couldn't imagine what nefarious business the two might have needed to conduct at the swamp during the darkest part of the day, but something about the faded figure niggled at the edge of Max's thoughts. It might have been recognition, but the fleeting thought faded rapidly when it found no purchase in his memories. If he wished to see Shehani safely delivered to her brother, his speculating would have to wait. Max hurried to catch up with her and did so inside the front gate.

The scrape of wood against wood greeted them when they reached the front gate—the sound of a window sliding closed. The doors to the concession had been already been secured against the now mostly empty Pike, and Reuben Castang emerged from the front concession office followed by three of the Sinhalese men—Inesh and two of the younger mahouts whose name Max couldn't remember.

A vein throbbed in Reuben's neck as he spoke to them through gritted teeth. "Tell that son of a—" His gaze shifted to Shehani and Max and he paused, evidently rethinking what he wanted to say. He jabbed two fingers, one at each of the mahouts. "Remind Mr. Williamson, should he try to give you instructions again regarding the elephants, that these animals are my responsibility, not his, and that in the future, directions regarding their care will come only from me."

Next, Reuben turned to Inesh in a softer tone. "If you have any more problems with that scoundrel, you let me know. I have friends in the County Sheriff's office I can call on to make a problem disappear if necessary."

He dropped his hand then, his pointed finger melting in with the rest of his fingers to make a fist that he shook as he spoke. "And tell all your cohorts, I don't care who says what, or how you all break wild elephants halfway across the world. If I see or hear that any of your number is abusive toward these animals, he'll be on the next boat back to Ceylon."

The two mahouts hung their heads and whispered apologies, which seemed to satisfy Reuben who transformed into his normal jovial self as he addressed the newcomers. "Max, did you and your mother enjoy the fair this afternoon? What brings you back here on your evening off?"

Max glanced at Inesh now standing silently beside his sister and couldn't confess he'd returned to the concession in hopes of seeing Shehani. "We had a nice time. Just making sure all is ready for tomorrow."

"Oh, how conscientious." He gave Max a friendly thump on the arm. "It wouldn't hurt to have someone sort the tack behind the herbivores, if you don't mind. Things got a bit jumbled between this afternoon's shows."

Despite his exhaustion at the end of a long day, Max didn't care to disappoint the now smiling animal trainer. He swallowed a sigh. "I can do that."

"Excellent! Thank you." Reuben looked at the two mahouts and raised his eyebrows as if to suggest that Max's easy compliance should be the standard for behavior among the Hagenbeck crew. "Good night to all of you."

Reuben flipped off the light in the front office and sauntered off in the direction of his workroom, half of a small shed built into the side of the dark arena.

Shehani said to her brother, "We should be going."

Inesh responded with a rapid, angry string of foreign syllables. Shehani replied, less angrily to Max's ear, though he could not understand her meaning, nor was he comfortable asking once Inesh barked a few short words to the mahout and the two of them stormed off, following the same path Reuben had taken minutes earlier, leaving Shehani winded and with a deep frown on her pretty face.

"Can I help?" he offered.

The hard lines around her mouth softened when she looked at him. "You are kind, Max. Inesh is being Inesh. He'll be back shortly and we'll leave together." Her sad smile did not reach her beautiful eyes and in the shadows of the closed concession, it was as if a dark cloud had settled over her. "Thank you for being my friend, Max."

The words melted into Max's heart, warmth spreading to his toes. For the second time this evening she had called him her friend, and while he hoped he could be much more than that, he cherished her trust in him.

"You don't think Reuben would really send any of you away, do you?"

"No, I don't think he would. It is sometimes difficult to understand the way things work here. The Hagenbecks handle elephants much differently than they do in Ceylon. The mahouts are used to treating the animals more harshly because they are asked to do more important things. Elephants there help clear forests and haul wood. Sometimes they are called on to perform water rescues. By night they live in the forest and then are captured each day by the same mahout to be put to work. The gentle training methods Mr. Castang uses are unfamiliar, and to some extent mistrusted by the young mahouts, but they are learning. Mr. Castang, despite his blubbering, is a patient man."

Max agreed, but he also had one more burning question if he could be brave enough to ask it. "Would you want to go home, if you could?"

"I told you," she said, her answer immediate. "I would be happy to make a home in a country that can make a fair as wondrous as this."

"Even if it means putting up with a man like Pete Williamson?"

"The world, I think, is filled with Mr. Williamsons. We have them in Ceylon, too." She grabbed his hand and squeezed. "But there are decent men in the world, too. Men who defend women against villains and volunteer to sort tack on their nights off."

Chapter 19

Max's dreams, once haunted by the image of his father's broken corpse, consisted now of swirling skirts, jingling bells, and Shehani, smiling and giggling at him with full red lips, a portrait he sketched over and over in his mind. He'd slept better than he had in months with this dream so sweet he dreaded wading through the dark fog of twilight sleep to the troubling hours of daylight, even when Frieda's voice cut into his bliss.

"Max." She gently shook his shoulder, and he popped open one eye to discover her fresh and perky, the now squirming toddler Marguerite perched on her hip. "I think you will be late to work if you don't get up."

He shook off his dream and sat up, unsettled at the prospect of the day, as if some unknown foreboding niggled at him only to be pushed aside by the embarrassment of seeing his cousin's wife in his attic bedroom.

"I'd have woken you sooner, but I assumed you'd already gone. Ernst left an hour ago. I thought you were roughly on the same schedule."

"What time is it?" he asked, pulling fingers through his tangled, greasy hair.

"Nearly eight o'clock."

Max sighed. "Okay, it will be okay. Sorry, I had a late night."

"You certainly did," she said, wrinkling her nose. She was cross, he could see, but he wasn't sure why.

"Your mother returned by 8:30 last evening with her detective. I quite like him," she added. "She said you'd made an excuse not to eat supper with them and went to work to clean up some loose ends. I left a plate of food for you in the icebox and never heard you come in, even though I was up past eleven with the baby." She gave the little girl a squeeze.

"I got caught up. There were complications at the concession. But it has all worked out now. Thank you for the supper. I'm sorry I didn't manage to eat it."

"How are you doing, Max?" Frieda lowered herself onto an old wingback chair Matilda had deposited in the corner by the door. Max's room contained a hodgepodge of castoff furnishings. A wardrobe with broken hinges stood against the wall opposite the bed and held his small collection of rough work clothes and the one nice travel suit he'd purchased before making the trek to America. A washbasin stood next to his bed, and the corner now held the unfortunate chair with lumpy stuffing and worn upholstery that featured several holes. It was adequate for only short sits.

Max sat up against his headboard, surprised at the informality of Frieda sitting in his bedroom like this. She did have the baby with her, and nothing dangerous or difficult could happen between them. For the first time since they'd met, Max didn't even want it to. Not even the small, devilish side of him experienced the least bit of discomfort in the presence of his cousin's wife.

She remained pretty. That much had not changed. But he had. Before he noticed it happen, his devotion had landed on another object. When he settled into bed at night, it wasn't Frieda he saw; it was the big dark eyes and wavy black hair of Shehani, her skirt swishing around her legs as she danced among the hulking gray elephants and the majestic lions, adding color and beauty to their impressive presence.

"I'm doing well," he said simply.

"Your English has certainly improved," she said, a light blush rising on her cheeks.

"Because of you."

"I doubt that, though I appreciate it. I suspect you've found proper motivation to learn is all."

He shrugged in his undershirt. That and a pair of briefs was all he wore beneath the bedcovers, the realization causing a rush of self-consciousness. He glanced down at his legs extended in front of him beneath the blanket and then at Frieda who gave no indication she noticed his discomfort.

"Is it the children?" she asked. "You are very sweet with them, so patient. I know they can be a lot."

"No." Max shook his head and inched up the edge of the blanket. "I enjoy them. And yes, being around them does help with the language."

"They are brutal judges and they talk fast."

"So does everyone at the fairgrounds," Max said.

"I suppose that's true. But trust me, the children really do adore you, especially Claude. You two have a special bond. None of the rest of us are able to get through to him lately."

"Claude is a good boy. His good nature is sometimes hidden by his sadness. He lost a parent, you know."

She studied him with sad eyes. "Like you."

"Yes." Max's voice broke over the simple syllable.

Frieda pushed on, undeterred by the rawness of his emotion. "I wonder, too, if perhaps you've met someone special?"

Max's cheeks burned at this shift in the conversation. He attempted and failed to hide the pleasure her question stirred in him. "What would make you think that?"

"I'm sorry. It's not any of my business. I thought maybe if you wanted to confide in anyone, or ask for advice, I was under the impression that we were," she hesitated, and Max's breath caught in his chest as he mulled over how she might end the sentence. What were they? They hadn't been anything, except that maybe when he kissed her and earned a well-deserved slap for it, just maybe she had also kissed him back. At the time, he thought he might have imagined that spark between them, but looking at her now, he wasn't as sure.

"...friends." She looked down at her lap as if embarrassed by her own words. "Good friends."

"We are," Max assured her. "The best of friends. I don't know how I would have made it when I first arrived without your help. And Ernst." He added her husband, both because he meant it and in order to lessen the intimacy of the moment.

"Well, it was Ernst who said something, actually. He mentioned that you appeared very happy at Hagenbecks and he speculated that you'd met a special someone at the fairgrounds—someone to put a certain gleam in your eye."

"Is there a gleam in my eye?"

"I think there is," she said as she stood. The baby squealed. "I also think you'd better get ready to go to the fairgrounds so you can see whatever charming young lady put it there."

Chapter 20

Max's growing admiration for Shehani had lifted one of the burdens of his heart and healed the bruise left behind by his schoolboy crush on his cousin's wife. It hadn't entirely calmed his soul, but perhaps this latest conversation with Frieda finally had. He played it over in his head on the way to the fairgrounds, and by the time he flashed his employee identification badge and entered at the main Lindell entrance, his thoughts had once again returned to Shehani.

Like him, the Sinhalese woman was an outsider, trying to make her way in a new world, a new foreign life. He admired her ability to stand up for herself, to battle her demons, something he hadn't yet been able to do. His demons still lurked a shade beyond his reach, prowling lions poised to pounce. He hoped that Shehani, the tamer of lions and charmer of snakes, could help shine a light on them.

These thoughts turned with him past the Tyrolean Alps and the Streets of Seville where he shuffled into the dense crowd piling up outside of Hagenbeck's Animal Paradise. The strangeness of his stalled progress pulled him from his private reflections to the unusual chaos at hand.

"Excuse me," he said to a tall man in front of him, made taller by the act of standing on tiptoes and craning his long neck in the direction of the concession. "Do you know what's going on? Why are we delayed?"

It wasn't time yet for one of the several daily parades down the Pike, and Max couldn't imagine a reason for the holdup.

The man lowered his heels and rubbed a hand across his whiskered chin. "There's a crowd in front of one of the concessions it looks like. A long line of people who can't get where they're wanting to go. Like us."

"Is it the animal show?" Max asked, adjusting his weight back and forth, unable to locate a clear line of sight.

"I don't know what's what, but there's police in front of one of them."

"On the right or the left?" Max asked, his anxiety growing.

"On the right."

Max's mouth filled with a sour taste. It had to be the Animal Paradise. Nothing else made sense, but he couldn't think what would bring so much police attention to the concession's doorstep. In a panic he began to push, apologies falling from his lips as he shoved his way into and between the small spaces around bodies, as if he were nothing more than a curl of smoke.

Ignoring the grumble of the men and the indignation of the ladies, Max continued to slink his way for the next several minutes to the gates of the Hagenbeck Animal Paradise and Circus Show where uniformed members of the fair's Jefferson Guard formed a solid line to keep curious Pike visitors at bay.

"Move along," one of them said through a drooping mustache. Like the others, he carried a sword and a commanding air that suggested to Max he might draw it if pressed, a message evidently also received by some in the crowd as those nearest began to move out further down the Pike. Other curious fairgoers pushed up into place, some lamenting the closure.

"I want to see the elephants shoot the chute!" yelled one little boy. When his mother explained to him that he could not, the boy screamed in protest. Several other children in the crowd joined the complaint, prompting angry fathers to approach the guardsmen in an attempt to glean information and, in one case, offer a bribe.

"The concession is closed," the officer said. He sneered at the man and made no move to take the money thrust toward him. "I can't change that. It's a police matter."

The disgruntled fairgoer closed his fist, wadding up the offered bribe before he turned on his heel and forced his way through the crowd.

Max stepped up to the mustached guardsman.

"Sir, please step back," the officer said more loudly than necessary, his hand on the hilt of his sword.

"I am sorry, officer." Max held up his palms and put on the best, most elegant airs that Frieda's patient tutoring had taught him. "I work here in the concession. I take care of the animals. I am needed inside to see to their welfare."

The officer wouldn't look Max directly in the eye, but he removed his tight hold on his sword hilt, smoothed the front of his uniform, and pointed to his right, to the guardsman at the end of the row who held a clipboard. "Go tell that man there your name. He has the list of workmen. If what you say is true, he'll let you through."

Max thought to be insulted by the man's implication that he might be lying and about to get called out, but he was too eager to get through the gate and figure out what exactly was going on.

"Thank you," he said, and then added, "May I ask what is going on?"

Another scowl and a sharp jerk of the man's head in the direction of the clipboard was all the answer Max got. Frustrated to be so unceremoniously dismissed, he moved toward the other officer with the clipboard and gave him his name.

"Um, yes, Mr. Eyer, here you are. You're on the list," the man with the clipboard said, with a much more cheerful disposition than his colleague. Clipboard man stepped aside and indicated that Max could proceed through the gate. "I imagine you can find all the information you need in there. Afraid I can't tell you much, anyway. We're the gatekeepers. The detectives are inside."

Max thanked the man and pushed open the gate to the seemingly abandoned concession. The arena in front of him stood empty, the door of its great, vacant cage hanging open. Beyond the murmur of the crowd outside the barrier, no human noises met his ears. The animals, too, unworked and resting in their enclosures, struck him as unusually still. Elephants did not trumpet. Goats did not bleat. Lions did not roar. Only the eerie song of the territorial monkeys rose up to echo through the solemn atmosphere.

Max looked around, unsure where to go, and decided at last to simply follow his morning routine until he discovered a reason to vary it. He started toward the grassland enclosure and fished the keys from his pocket to open the backstage door. Inside, he grabbed the bucket, broom, and rake, and let himself into the outdoor pen. His presence, or perhaps the scrape of the rake against dirt, stirred some of the animals into action, and a few of the more curious beasts sidled up beside him. Flock butted him gently with small, blunt horns, and Max scratched the goat behind the ears.

"Max!" He looked up from his work when he heard his name. Reuben stood on the other side of the trench with another law officer, this one in a uniform that did not belong to the Jefferson Guard. Reuben waved for him to approach them, and Max put down his tools to exit the enclosure, walking up to the two men, his hands shaking at his sides.

"Mr. Castang," he said. "What has happened?"

Much to Max's surprise, Reuben laughed. The police officer beside him did not. "Leave it to Max to go straight to work without first discovering the source of all the disruption of the morning. Mr. Eyer here is one of our best employees. He thinks of nothing but the welfare of the animals in his charge. I have the utmost confidence in him."

Max swelled with pride at the compliment, then deflated again when the officer's unfriendly scrutiny fell over Max. He withered beneath it. "Mr. Eyer," the officer said. "My name is Detective Cullen. I'm an investigator with the St. Louis Police Department, assigned by Chief of Detectives William Desmond to consult on a case with fair security. I am going to need to ask you some questions."

Max attempted to swallow his unease, but his dry tongue made it difficult. "Ja, that is fine."

"You can use my office." Reuben pointed behind him to the divided storage shed that served as the animal trainer's office. His portion of the space featured little more than a desk at which Reuben filled out detailed training charts and did whatever other paperwork he couldn't pawn off on someone else.

"Thank you," Cullen said and walked toward the shed with no more invitation than a quick "Mr. Eyer," over his shoulder. Max hesitated but followed at a subtle nod of encouragement from Reuben.

The detective opened the door and indicated that Max should walk in before him. Max hadn't been inside the office much. Reuben rarely spent time there himself, preferring to be with the animals. The dingy space did have one large window that let in the morning light. One wall contained a shelf of haphazardly placed books—a few bound copies of animal husbandry guides and a handful of training journals. Behind the desk hung clipped newspaper articles tacked to the wall. Some of them displayed German headlines that Max could make out. Others were in English or other languages he could not decipher. Most featured pictures of one of the Hagenbecks with one or more animals. Reuben appeared in some.

Cullen pushed inside and sat in the chair behind the desk, leaving Max to settle on a stool on the opposite side. As a rule, Reuben had no use for meeting with anyone in his office and the space had not been designed for such a situation. As the head animal trainer, he conducted little of the business end of things. That aspect of the concession had been handled by either Carl or Lorenz Hagenbeck, with the largely unwelcome assistance of Pete Williamson.

Max placed his hands on nervously bouncing knees and waited while the police detective shuffled through a stack of papers on the desk before fixing his concentration on Max, pen poised above a new, blank sheet of paper, ready and expectant.

"Mr. Eyer, could you please tell me where you were last night?"

Max sat straighter on the stool and furrowed his brow. "I'm sorry, but what is this regarding?" he asked.

"I merely asked you a question. What were your whereabouts yesterday evening and into the night?"

"Yesterday was my half day. I worked here until the one o'clock animal show ended in the arena. Then I accompanied my mother and a friend of hers to visit other parts of the fair. That's where I spent the largest portion of my afternoon and evening."

Cullen scribbled notes as Max talked, rarely looking up at him, which somehow made Max want to give him more information, and even wanted the follow-up question.

"Who was this friend of your mother's?"

This Max was anxious to share, hopeful that dropping the name of a detective might grant him some benefit in whatever the investigation entailed. "Detective Henry Duncan," he replied.

At the mention of this name, the man stopped writing and sharply looked up at him. "Duncan, you say? I'll have a word with him. But you mentioned that this was the largest portion of your afternoon and evening. Were you with the detective the entire night?"

"No sir," he admitted. "Detective Duncan and Mutti—eh, my mother—went to eat around seven and I returned here briefly to see if I might help prepare for work the next day before heading home for the night. I don't stay on the grounds like some of the crew. My mother would never allow that."

"And where is home?"

Max gave him his uncle's address, and the man added another scribbled note.

"What did you do when you arrived here?"

"I checked on the animals normally in my charge to ensure they'd been appropriately fed and watered in my absence, which I'm relieved to say they had been. Mr. Castang asked me to reorganize the necessary equipment for the next morning's shows and so I did that." Max fidgeted on the stool. "I really do need to get to work."

The officer flicked his wrist as if to waved off Max's concerns. "Your duties are being covered by others while we talk. None of your animals will go hungry, I promise you."

Max mumbled his thanks for this reassurance, though truthfully, he would never have doubted it. Reuben would sooner light his hair on fire than let the animals suffer, and with the concession closed to the public and no shows to perform, he and the other keepers and trainers had plenty of time and staffing resources to cover Max's temporary absence.

"Which animals are in your charge, Mr. Eyer?"

"Ähm, most of them fall under my duties from time to time, but primarily I care for the grassland animals, the ostriches, and the arctic animals, as well as the carnivores."

"Lions and tigers?" Cullen asked.

"Yes, and sometimes bears. I also help with elephant care, as they require so much, and Reuben wants to make sure they are used to my presence coming in and out of the arena as I do."

"Mr. Castang is quite skilled with the elephants, isn't he?"

Max rearranged himself on his perch, increasingly uncomfortable. "He's skilled with all the animals. I don't think he's ever met one he couldn't train."

"Yes, I get that impression. Reptiles, too, do you think?"

"I don't see why not."

"And what about you, Max? May I call you Max?"

"Max is fine. What do you mean, what about me?"

"Do you ever care for the reptiles? Are you good with them?"

"Me? No. Mhhh, yes, sometimes I have to care for them." The detective's writing paused and as he raised his gaze to Max, his left eyebrow quirked upward toward his wrinkled brow. "I avoid that part of the concession when I can. The reptiles make me uncomfortable."

"But you have cared for them?"

"A little," Max admitted. "I have assisted with them. Mr. Williamson has asked me to perform some of the reptile tasks, but he is more familiar with them than I am. If you have questions about them, he'd be the one to ask."

The officer stared hard at Max for another uncomfortable pause before leaning back in the desk chair and stroking his imaginary beard.

"I would do that, Mr. Eyer. But I guess no one told you that Mr. Williamson is deceased."

The blood drained from Max's cheeks and his stomach churned as he absorbed the information. "Pete?" he said, stumbling over the name, even as simple as it was. "Is dead?"

"I'm sorry, son." Max leaned into his forearms on the desk. "Was he a good friend?"

Max fought the desire to explain that Pete had not been a friend at all, had in fact been the one supervisor Max despised—a man with no sense of decency or care for others, who treated Max as a dispensable immigrant most useful for sacrificing to the venom of a snake, and who insulted a foreign beauty with lascivious contempt. But Max could not say these things. He did not wish to speak ill of the dead, and more than that, the physical sensation of bile clawing its way into his throat precluded any response at all. Max had no choice but to let his silence become his answer, which seemed to satisfy the detective.

"You have my sincere sympathy, Mr. Eyer."

"Thank you," Max choked out through the fire that had overtaken his vocal cords. A hot tear rolled down his cheek and his limbs grew cold. He shivered. "What happened?"

Detective Cullen leaned back again in the chair and sighed. "That's what I'm trying to determine. There was a terrible accident. At least that's what we'd assumed, but Mr. Hagebenbeck insists it couldn't have been."

Max licked his lips, gathered his strength, and asked, "Why would he think that?"

"Honestly, I suspect it's wishful thinking. If the death was an accident and one of his animals to blame, he's probably afraid we'd have to shut him down. Businessmen of any stripe are protective of their interests. Mr. Williamson was a partner in Mr. Hagenbeck's American business, correct?"

"Äh...hm," Max said, unsure of his qualification to answer this line of questioning. The detective's manner toward him had transformed, as if Max had somehow become more informant, or even confidante, than suspect or witness. "Yes, I think that is correct."

"He was authorized to give you orders," Cullen prompted, gesturing with a waved hand for Max to continue.

"He gave some orders," Max admitted. Sweat pooled on the back of his neck and the walls of the small room threatened to entomb him.

"And you were obligated to follow these orders?" The detective's mannerisms had shifted again to something new that Max had a hard time understanding.

"Mr. Castang is the one I report to." Max's attempt to explain spilled out too quickly, but he could not slow it once he'd begun. "Sometimes Mr. Hagenbeck—Lorenz, not his father, who has gone back to Germany to build his tierpark, his zoo—will have a task for me, and sometimes Mr. Williamson will, too. He had me sell tickets one time, but I am better at caring for the animals."

"Which is why Mr. Williamson asked you to take care of the reptiles."

Max nodded, relieved to have been interrupted, but more comfortable now that his words had begun once again to flow. "Detective Cullen," he ventured, "would you close the concession if Mr. Williamson died because of an accident with the animals?"

"It's not my call, but yes, I think we would have to, at least for a time. It's a public relations problem if word leaks out that a man-eating alligator is killing people at the World's Fair. It would mean panic, not to mention the grief the city would get from the press, especially the boys in Chicago. There'd be no end to it."

"That can't be what happened," Max snapped, but then thought about it. Other than perhaps the snakes, safely contained inside thick glass vivaria, the alligators scared Max more than any other animal in the concession. Their monstrous maws haunted him. He'd thought of them emerging from the murky water of their swamp to snap at him with their long snouts full of jagged teeth. "The alligators really killed him?"

"That's what I'm trying to determine, Mr. Eyer. Hagenbeck's Animal Paradise on the Pike is a popular concession. No one wants to see it shut down, but that may be what we have to do until we get some answers."

"So, Pete was found in the alligator swamp, then?" Max's thoughts filled with the image of those long, jagged teeth now dripping in blood—Pete

Williamson's blood.

Cullen rubbed his lightly whiskered jaw. "Parts of him were."

"Where were his other parts?" Max asked, shocked.

"Well, I expect inside the alligator."

Max couldn't comprehend the man's calm demeanor in that instance. His own skin itched, his limbs had grown heavy, and the edges of his vision began to fill in with darkness. He might pass out, right here in front of the detective. Like a woman. In a desperate attempt to prevent this, Max stood from the stool and lunged for the door.

"I need air."

The detective followed him out and patted his back as Max bent over a nearby bush to heave.

"Mr. Eyer, I understand why you're upset. But I really do need you to reconstruct the evening for us. You were here in the concession after dark, you said?"

Max straightened and wiped spittle gathered at corners of his mouth with the back of his hand.

"Ja," he said. "Ja, I was here just as the sun was going down. I checked on the animals and walked the concession to encourage visitors to begin to clear out."

"And did you see other staff at that time?"

"I saw Shehani, the Sinhalese dancer." Max wasn't about to volunteer that he'd done his rounds specifically to look for her.

"Where did you see her?"

"She was in the back of the concession, near the reptiles." Immediately he felt the urge to heave again but fought back the reaction. Shehani had been near the reptiles. She could have been the one taken by the gators.

"Not inside the reptile walk?"

"No." Max shook his head. "On the path outside, standing in the pool of light from one of the lamps.

"Alone?"

"She was talking to Pete, to Mr. Williamson, alive at the time."

"Anyone else?"

"I think only Pete. And then me when I got to them."

"What were they talking about?" the detective asked.

"I don't know what they were saying before I got there. The conversation ended as I approached." Max experienced not the slightest twinge of guilt at omitting the contents of the conversation. If Pete had died after speaking to Shehani in the manner he did, Max couldn't summon much sympathy for the man, and he would not give the detective any reason to think the slim and graceful Shehani could have committed violence. The notion might have made him laugh under less grave circumstances. "I said goodnight to Mr. Williamson and then Shehani and I walked to the front of the concession so she could meet up with her brother."

"What time was that?"

"Around nine o'clock, I think."

"And then you went home?"

"No," Max said. "Well, yes, not long after, but I had to straighten the equipment first. Mr. Castang was at the front gate in the main office. Inesh and two of the mahouts were with him. I think they'd been arguing."

Cullen consulted the notes in his hand. "Inesh is the snake charmer. And which of the mahouts were with him?"

Max hesitated. "I don't know them all very well. The lighting was poor."

Cullen jotted a note. "So, you got instructions from Mr. Castang, finished up your work, and then made your way home. Did you see anything else that might be important?"

"I saw someone else by the swamp walk. I looked back as as Shehani and I walked away, and there was another man talking with Mr. Williamson, who gave him something small that the man put in his pocket."

"Was this man one of the workers?"

Max considered that and shook his head. "I don't think so, but I've seen him here before. He comes to see the elephants."

"Can you describe him?" The detective's pen twitched in his hand.

Max closed his eyes and conjured the image of the unknown figure from the previous night. "He was a white man, not too tall or short, similar me, with a scar running down the middle of his face."

"A scar, you say?"

"Yes." Max ran a finger down the middle of his forehead from his hairline to the top of his nose. "Like this."

For the first time since Max had met him, Cullen broke into a grin so crooked it appeared as if half of it had melted. "I have an idea who that could have been." He stuffed his notes into his coat pocket and at the same time removed a card that he handed to Max. "Thank you for your time, Mr. Eyer. You've been very helpful. If you think of anything else that might be important, let me know."

Max studied the card in his hand, printed with the name Jerome Cullen and an address for the St. Louis Metropolitan Police Department.

The detective placed a hand on Max's shoulder then. "I'm sorry for the loss of your friend."

As Max watched the man walk down the pathway toward Reuben and his next interview victim, he couldn't help but reflect on Pete's untimely end and on how very sorry for the loss Max was not.

Chapter 21

The instant Reuben and the detective disappeared around the edge of the arena, Max rushed in the other direction to the swamp walk where he discovered most of the animal keepers and trainers, including Shehani, the elder Pamu, and the rest of the Sinhalese—all except Inesh whose turn it must have been to stand before the inquisitor.

"Max!"

He scanned the gathered crowd to find Lorenz Hagenbeck holding a hand up to him in greeting. Looking as fresh as he always did, and very much like his father in a pressed linen suit, Lorenz jogged toward Max.

"I assume you took your turn with the good detective? How did it go?"

"It went well, I think," answered Max.

Lorenz guided him to the shade of a fence along the backside of the arena and opposite the now gated off swamp walk. "What did he want to know?"

Lorenz had slipped into an easy German with the question, a switch performed so seamlessly, Max didn't notice the transition, though he answered in the same. The majority of those around them spoke primarily English, and some had no German language knowledge at all. It was the code, then, of the concession, for those members who could speak it when they didn't want anyone else to listen, and it filled Max with pride to be among the elite.

"He wanted to know my schedule yesterday, where I was and who I saw."

"You weren't here, correct? Rube said it was your half day and that you spent the afternoon exploring the fair."

"Correct, but I did come back later in the evening. I spoke with…" Max paused. The name Pete almost tripped from his lips, but when it came time to pronounce that simplest syllable, his mouth resisted forming the name.

"Mr. Williamson?" Lorenz guessed in a whisper. "You spoke with Pete?"

"Yes, I did."

"How did he behave? Was there anyone else there with him?"

"He was the same as he always is." Max shrugged. "He was a difficult man to get along with. He was giving Shehani a hard time, as he always does."

"He gives Shehani a hard time?"

Max stared at Lorenz, who struck him as exceedingly obtuse. "He always has, from the moment she arrived."

Lorenz removed his hat and wiped his brow with a handkerchief that he then returned to his pocket, a crease deepening across his forehead. At the same time, the frown he'd been wearing began to break loose, his hard demeanor beginning to ease.

"Thank you, Max. That's helpful information."

"We argued," Max continued, not sure what to make of his boss's reaction. "Nothing unusual, a reminder to maintain some manners around the lady."

"How chivalrous of you."

"The interaction didn't last long, and then I escorted Shehani to the front office behind the gate where her brother and another Sinhalese man waited for her. When I looked back, Pete was talking to someone else."

"Who?"

"Have you noticed a man with a long scar running down the middle of his forehead who likes to come see the elephants?"

"You mean a fairgoer?" Lorenz asked. "I'm afraid they all blend together in my mind. Pete was probably giving the man some directions and encouraging him to leave the concession."

"Maybe," Max said, the word dripping in skepticism.

"And you told all of this to Detective Cullen?"

"Yes, all of it," Max said and then revised his answer. "Well, I didn't mention that Pete and I argued."

"Was it you and Pete who argued, or was it Shehani and Pete?"

Max's pride swelled with a fierce protective spirit. "It was me and Pete." This time it wasn't hard to say the man's name. What was difficult was not to spit on the path when he said it. Max could see the wheels turning behind Lorenz's calm façade. The animal trader needed a scapegoat, and if he could pin a murder on a foreign girl, no one would look too closely at it. The concession would be saved.

"What exactly happened?" Max asked, more to distract the other man from the possibility of this nefarious plot than to satisfy his curiosity. "I mean, with the body?"

"Reuben found it early this morning. I came in right behind him and he alerted me immediately. The body was not in good shape."

"I assumed as much."

"But it was not entirely consumed, either. I don't believe the gators are responsible for his death. I don't think they would be so bold as to attack a person that large."

Max didn't care for the implication that the creatures would not hesitate to attack a smaller person.

"And Pete has always had somewhat of an affinity for them. He often took it upon himself to feed them." Lorenz sighed and massaged his temples before continuing, "None of our animals would attack someone who feeds them. Why would they see him as a threat?"

Privately, Max had a hard time understanding how anyone or anything would view Pete Williamson as anything other than a threat. A better defense might have been that perhaps scaly, cold-blooded monsters tended to recognize one of their own kind. The thought was a terrible one—irreverent and dismissive of the recently deceased. Max would not entertain it. He would *try* not to entertain it. But he would also not mourn the loss of Mr. Williamson.

"If it's not too much to ask, what parts of him were missing?" Max cringed to know he'd even formulated the question and couldn't be sure how Lorenz would take it, but to his surprise, the man didn't even pause before answering the question.

"Most of his bottom half. His upper torso, head, and one arm were found intact. A ghastly thing to see."

Max's breakfast threatened to make a reappearance and his head began to pound. Even more disturbing to him than the bloody pictures formed by Lorenz's vivid description was the ease with which his boss rattled them off, like he was describing a sunset and not a grisly scene of death.

"The coroner has taken the remaining pieces away at this point and there's some cleanup to do, but I think we can open by noon and maybe get in a one o'clock show, if the police will let us reopen."

"You think they will?" Max doubted he could go about his day at this point, as if nothing had happened, and it shocked him that Lorenz might think any of them could or should.

"I don't know," Lorenz admitted. "Maybe not, but if I can give them a solid lead on their investigation, and remove the animals themselves from their primary suspicion, then perhaps."

"Do you think it might be a little disrespectful of Mr. Williamson's memory to go on with the day as if everything were completely normal?"

Lorenz paled and cleared his throat. "Of course. I know. A man is dead, and that is a terrible tragedy. But Max, you know as well as I do Pete wasn't a great man. We can mourn him while carrying on the work of the concession he was so proud of."

Max couldn't argue with the sentiment that Pete hadn't been a great man, but still, he himself was a little traumatized by the events of the morning. It was going to be a terrible day for all of them and he said as much to Lorenz, who frowned and sighed at the suggestion.

"Do you really think so? The animals have to be cared for regardless. We aren't a collection of weak men. We see life and death all the time, when we feed the carnivores, when we lose an animal."

"I suspect people will view this death differently than that."

"You might be right. Actually, Reuben said something similar when I suggested we might open back up. I still have to give the investigators something or they'll consult with the fair directors and have us shut down permanently before we know it."

"Maybe at least the reptile swamp should remain closed."

"Oh," Lorenz said, his thoughts clearly wandering in new directions. "That would be a shame. We only recently opened it up. I can't imagine the gators would cause a problem, especially now."

Max shook his head. "I'm sure they wouldn't, but the public would probably object to seeing them when they have been involved in the death of a man, even if they weren't responsible for it."

"Or it could be an opportunity. Some people love the macabre. The rumor of man-eating gators might pull more people into the concession."

"I don't think you can have it both ways. If word gets out, the crowds may come running, but the fair directors are more likely to close our gates."

"Of course, you're right." Lorenz appraised him. "You've a mind for business, I think. And yes, we must keep in mind that no matter what happened, this was a terrible tragedy. That is how the public will see it."

"Yes," Max said, with as much sincerity as he could muster, because of course everyone should see it that way, and it troubled him that he considered that Pete becoming gator food might not have been such a terrible thing, a thought so disgusting it drowned out the fact that Lorenz had continued speaking.

"...and as soon as the police will allow it, we'll need to get our people in here to put the exhibit back together. In the meantime, the animals will need care. The alligators of course won't need to eat again for a little while at least." He paused and inappropriate amusement played across his lips, gone almost as soon as it materialized.

"Lorenz," Max said, disrupting the terrible conversation. "It's about time to milk the snakes, isn't it? Who is going to do that?"

Lorenz's head jerked in response to this question. "Why would anyone need to do that?"

"Venom collection?" Max said, embarrassed by Lorenz's response to his question.

Lorenz furrowed and then relaxed his brow. "Oh, there's no need for that. There are researchers in Europe that want it and Father's done some collections for them, but there's no market for such a thing here. It wouldn't be worth our time. What even would make you think of it?"

Max hesitated. "Curious, I suppose," he said at last. "I think someone mentioned the possibility one time. I didn't know if it was something we do."

Lorenz glanced back toward the curtained off swamp from which two police officers emerged. "Not that I'm aware of," he said as he stepped toward the men, leaving Max alone to wonder what Pete had been up to with the snake venom.

Max couldn't solve that puzzle, but he did very much want to locate Shehani. He asked around, but no one at the swamp knew where to find her, and so he made his way back to the grassland enclosure. There he spotted Reuben, free now of Detective Cullen, carrying on an enthusiastic conversation with a camel slowly munching hay and looking remarkably disinterested.

"Reuben," Max called, before he could make out the words. He didn't wish to startle the man, nor did he wish to invade his privacy.

Reuben looked up toward him and patted the camel on the neck. "Hello, Max. I finished up in here after you went back to your interview. Everyone is fed and happy."

"Great! What else needs to be done?"

"I think all the animals have been seen to at this point. How did the interview go?"

Max gave Reuben the same vague answers he'd given Lorenz, but this time he asked where he might find Shehani.

"She returned to the barracks. She was terribly upset." He put his hand up to the side of his mouth and pretended to lean in, though the trench separated him from Max. "I mean, well, of course she was. I was told she and Pete were close."

A hot coal burned in Max's chest at this assertion. "They were not," he said.

Reuben squinted. "I got the impression from Pete that they'd been closer than I'd have liked. She's a talented young lady, and much too good for the likes of him."

"There was no relationship." Max could not verify this claim exactly, but he didn't doubt the truth of it. Pete had thought her attractive. Max agreed. He couldn't blame the man for that, but he'd also witnessed Pete tormenting her with his lewd comments and overtures. Max hoped that was all it had been. If anything untoward had sprung up between them, Shehani could not be blamed.

Reuben's eyebrows drew together. "If you say so, Max. I believe you, and

I'm glad to hear it. I was beginning to think the two of you might make a handsome couple. You probably know both of them better than I do. Er, *knew* them better. Or him, is what I mean, of course." At the correction, he averted his gaze and altered his stance, uncomfortable it seemed with the conventions of speaking of the deceased.

"Anyway, the herbivores have been seen to. The reptiles won't be available to access for some time, and I'm headed to the big cats and the bears now. If you wouldn't mind checking on the arctic enclosure, I'd appreciate it. I sent Oscar there earlier but I'm afraid he may have been waylaid by the detective."

Max said that he would and asked, "The elephants?"

"The mahouts took care of them this morning before they departed. I'll make sure they get some training work in after I'm done with the carnivores so they don't go too stir crazy. I'm thinking maybe we can open again tomorrow. It might be too much to hope that we could be able to do so today."

"Yes, I think so, too."

"Well, if you'll see to those couple of things, then you might as well call it an early day." He turned back to his work, sweeping up soiled hay on the other side of the trench, then said more quietly, "That is, if the police are finished with you."

"I hope they are," Max said in answer, though Reuben's focus remained on his work, the conversation at an end.

Chapter 22

His conversation with Lorenz darkened Max's emotional state, but it was nothing compared to the dour mood of the ostriches who rewarded his attention by hissing and snapping at him. One might think they'd find it a relief not to be carrying rambunctious fairgoers on their backs, knocking them this way and that as they laughed and held on for dear life, but evidently the exercise had a soothing effect on the birds because without the activity, they were even more cantankerous than usual.

The tortoises, however, despite living in close proximity to the grisly scene of Williamson's death, maintained their demeanors of constant calm. One could never know for certain what the animals might be thinking, as they always moved slowly and gave off the general impression of thoughtful intelligence, but if they were concerned about the curtained off backdrop once again blocking the view of the boardwalk that separated them from their crocodilian neighbors, the tortoises gave no indication. Max knew them to be the oldest animals in the concession, far older than any of the men who cared for them, and he suspected them of greater wisdom, too.

Or perhaps the ancient creatures found themselves as melancholy as Max, whose slow steps across the fairgrounds, past the barracks where most of the concession workers stayed, and onto the streetcar caused more than one stranger to take notice of him, their expressions full of sympathy.

No one greeted him at the door when he entered his uncle's house, though he could hear the evidence of the youngest children coming from some distant room. No one expected him at this hour, which made him stealthy and grateful for the clear path to his attic bedroom with no need for deflecting uncomfortable questions.

The single shuttered window disallowed the bright sunlight and cast the room into darkness unnatural for the time of day. Max opened it, sat down on the bed, and moaned softly as his head dropped into his hands and he closed his eyes.

He didn't keep them shut for long. Images drifted unbidden through his mind. First came the image of Shehani, cold and angry, arguing with Pete, though he knew that wasn't right. She'd been brave and strong, throwing off the rude overtures, her behavior under the circumstances justifiable. Next came the vision of Pete himself, bloodied and torn to pieces in the snapping jaws of two alligators fighting over his devastated remains—this he conjured as easily as he would a memory.

He shook his head to clear a persistent buzz in his ears and dropped backwards onto the quilt-covered mattress, flopping with a thud. New pictures pushed their ways into the corners of his thoughts. This time it was Felix's face he saw, ashen and lifeless against the hard packed dirt of the barn. Max had blocked out so much of that moment and all that led up to it. He'd discovered the body and had delivered the news to Mutti, afraid the smallest hint of relief might taint his dutiful display of grief.

But then Mutti hadn't been as shocked as he'd expected, initially giving him a great sense of calm and later offering up nothing but worry. Beyond the drunkards who missed their favorite swill before moving on to seek their poison elsewhere, no one would be expected to inconsolably mourn the passing of Felix Eyer. Similar to Pete in that regard, Felix did not inspire warmth from others. Still, some sort of emotional response, an indication of complicated grief he might have reasonably expected from the man's wife, or even from the man's son.

Max couldn't think about it anymore. The silence he'd appreciated when he first arrived home now sat like a lead weight on his breast, vibrating with the relentless pounding of his heart, mirrored by the drumming of a dull ache in his head.

He sat up, rubbed his palms against his thighs, and stood, lightly stretching the tension from his back and neck. He needed the company of others, the distraction from all his terrible, swirling thoughts.

He descended the stairs to discover the children now sitting in the parlor with their grandmother busy reading to them all from a children's book. She spotted him and waved. He waved back at her, pretending to misunderstand her invitation to join them, threw on his coat, and let himself out the front door, ignoring the little voice of Claude calling after him.

The sun still provided relentless daylight, but the afternoon had grown long as he'd wallowed by himself. Probably all of the other seasonal Hagenbecks employees with commitments lasting only the duration of the fair had all worked themselves out of the job for the day. If he returned to the fairgrounds, he might discover some of them at Cheyenne Joe's, and he considered joining them. For once he could have used a drink, but in the end, he decided against spending the money to once again catch the streetcar, only to surround himself with conversation that would inevitably turn to the grisly death at the concession. As much as he might want to hear theories and insights, his curiosity proved insufficient to overcome his sense of dread and convince him to take part. There were other places he could get a drink.

At the left turn toward the streetcar stop, Max turned right instead, toward the river and toward his uncle's biergarten. The place was already busy by the time he arrived, clogged by an older clientele that preferred to have a light dinner before the sun set. A warm May breeze blew off the Mississippi, carrying the scent of spring daffodils along with the riverfront's ever-present undercurrent of dead fish. A few blocks from the water, Max thought it might be nice to sit at one of the outdoor tables and catch glimpses of barges and riverboats drifting along the busy riverway.

He claimed a small table next to the fence that surrounded the biergarten, tucked behind a pillar wrapped in blossoms from a dogwood tree, and enjoyed a minute of peace, shattered when a waitress cleared her throat beside him.

Startled from his blessedly empty thoughts, he looked up to see his cousin Hugh's wife Annmarie, her hair tied back in braids, mimicking the costumes worn by German workers at the Tyrolean Alps concession on the Pike—what he assumed every American must think every German waitress should look like. He fidgeted, reflecting that the fantasy designed wasn't so different than that constructed with the ethnographic exhibits on the fairgrounds, though of course, most of the customers at Winkler's Biergarten were at least partly German themselves.

"What are you doing here, Max?" she asked, without the slightest hint of accent, her pencil poised above a notepad ready to take his order as if he were any customer and not her cousin. Her impatient scowl she wore, not visible to the rest of the tables, betrayed her frustration with his presence. He supposed she was concerned she might not receive a tip from him, and he vowed to himself to give her one. He also didn't answer her question.

Instead, he asked, "Is my mother here?"

She twirled her pencil until it pointed in the direction of the door leading to the indoor seating space. "She's in there."

He intended to thank her and order a beer, but she didn't give him the opportunity, spinning instead on her heel, leaving him the option to speak to her back and communicating a clear message—she saved service for those more likely to tip.

PARADISE ON THE PIKE

Max reluctantly stood, crumpled his cap in his hands, and made his way to the door. A soft bell tinkled overhead when he pushed it open, and there Mutti stood, at a counter filled with older men all dining alone. He watched as she refilled cups of coffee and mugs of beer, and slid plates piled high with steaming traditional German foods toward eager customers. He waited for her to raise her head from her work.

When at last she did, she saw him immediately and she lit up with adoration as mothers often do when they see their children at unexpected times.

"Max," she said. A warm glow spread across her cheeks. "What brings you here this time of day? Is everything okay?" Her smile faltered as tragic possibilities drifted across her features. He hoped she wasn't imagining anything as terrible as the truth.

"I was given the afternoon and evening off."

She rounded the counter and motioned for him to grab a seat at an empty table. She slid into the chair across from him. "I don't understand. You had your afternoon off yesterday."

"Yes, but something happened."

She reached across the table to brush a lock of hair from his forehead. "What happened, Maxie? Do you…did you get fired?"

"No, no nothing like that." That she reached such a conclusion so effortlessly disturbed him. It bothered him that she thought him the kind of worker to get himself fired from a job where he was actually needed. "The concession is closed for the rest of today." He didn't add that fear for the very fate of the concession niggled at him. Financially, he could absorb the lost wages for a while. He had few expenses, living as he did in the attic of his uncle's house. His mother, too, earned money and could help keep herself. But if he were to lose the opportunity for this job, if it became more lucrative for Hagenbeck to take his animal show on the road, as he had done in the past, then Max would find himself lost in this new city without much sense of what might come next for him. Perhaps he would don lederhosen and wait tables.

"Is there a problem with the animals?" Mutti asked, the tension in her brow releasing. Though Max would view problems with the animals as devastating, apparently his mother had a different perspective on the matter. He doubted her relief would extend to animals feeding on humans.

"There was an incident." She frowned and waited for him to continue, but he had difficulty forming the right words. She waited him out, again in that way she always did when she was certain a confession would escape if she left enough space for it.

"It's the alligators. They got hold of something they shouldn't have."

"Oh," she said and sat up tall in her seat. "Were they hurt?"

"Eh, no," he said, careful to regulate his tone so as not to raise any alarm bells in her head. "The animals will be fine. Everything will be fine. The shutdown is a precaution and should be resolved soon."

"They couldn't just take the things somewhere else for a while? They had to shut down the entire concession?"

"It seemed best under the circumstances."

Her brow furrowed, the desire to challenge his story written in the stiffening of her muscles, but the tinkling of the bells above the door rescued him from having to expand his explanation. Mutti looked up at the entrance and her expression lightened.

"Oh, Henry! I wasn't expecting to see you today. How lovely!"

Mutti's suitor walked into the restaurant with a commanding air, his presence somehow filling more space than it had when Max had first met him. His jaw pulled tighter, the thin lines of his face deepened. He was altogether more intimidating and serious in appearance than the somewhat happy-go-lucky man of the previous day. That man was giddy with excitement as he shuffled around the criminology exhibit and pointed out peculiar and wonderful sights at the fair. Max quite liked that man, despite his wariness of anyone who might show interest in his mother. This version of Henry, however, Max wasn't sure about.

The stern detective reached them in two long strides. "Emmi," he said as she stood to greet him. Max did not stand at his approach, but Henry placed a fatherly hand on Max's shoulder. "I'm relieved to see you here, Max. How are you holding up?"

Dread seeped into him followed by embarrassment at appreciating the comfort this man offered as a father might—a better father than Felix Eyer ever had been. Max might have allowed himself to appreciate it had suspicion not darkened his mother's complexion.

"I'm fine," Max grumbled, and then the dam broke loose and his mother's worry spewed forth in a way that made him increasingly uncomfortable and small as if he were a young boy, bearing the burden of a guilty conscience he hadn't entirely earned.

"Henry, why are you asking after Max?" The fire of her accusatory glare burned him. "Max, what are you not telling me? What exactly has happened? And don't give me some rubbish about alligators."

"Actually—" Henry attempted to interject, but Mutti would not allow it, her tirade not yet finished. The entire atmosphere of the restaurant heightened with her outburst to one of awkward agitation. The other waitresses stopped what they were doing, and Uncle Reinardt poked his head out from the kitchen to glare over the counter at his unhinged sister. She paid him no mind and kept right on going.

"You come in here in the middle of the day when you should be working to tell me some tale about animals getting into something they shouldn't and shutting down an entire concession? If there's something wrong, Max, you tell me. You don't make the police come to do it." She flung her hand angrily in the direction of Henry who shrank beneath her outburst.

"Mutti," Max infused his voice with as much calm as he could manage. "I hadn't finished telling you all yet. There were alligators involved. Tell her, Henry."

Henry rose to the appeal, hands held in front of him as though in surrender. "Yes, he is telling the truth. It's only that to tell more of it should be done with care." He looked around at the restaurant in which no one spoke a word, their ears trained to the situation unfolding in front of them. "Perhaps we should take this conversation to somewhere a little more private."

Out of the corner of his eye, Max saw his uncle nod his consent from behind the counter. Henry ushered Mutti out the door, Max trailing them beyond the gate of the biergarten to the walkway on the edge of the street. There the three of them sat on a bench, Max dreading the coming conversation and the fear he knew Mutti would soon possess.

"What is going on?" She practically spit the words at both of them. Henry held her hand and Max sat on the other side of him, wishing that didn't bother him.

"Emmi," Henry began. She slid her hand out from his and looked past him to Max.

"If my son has been hiding something from me, I'd prefer to hear it from him."

Henry turned toward Max, who chilled under the scrutiny of his mother and her detective suitor.

"Okay," he said finally. "When I went to work this morning, a line of Jefferson Guard officers stood in front of Hagenbeck's Animal Paradise, closing the concession off from the public."

"By order of the St. Louis police stationed at the fair," Henry added. "The guard helped with security. They didn't touch the scene. They just called the police in."

"You were there?" Mutti asked.

"No. Not early in the day. I'm not assigned to the fairgrounds, though our chief of detectives called in one of my colleagues to head up an investigation, and so I heard about it. I went by the site before coming here, hoping to talk to Max and offer what assistance I could."

"Why would Max need assistance? What happened?" Mutti's volume ran away from her again, her voice high and tight, making her impatience palpable.

"There was a death of one of the staff members," Max said. "Herr Hagenbeck's American business partner, Pete Williamson. His body, or what was left of it, floated in the alligator swamp."

"What was left of it?" Mutti's hand flew to her heart. "Oh, how terrible. You saw this?"

Max shook his head. "Not really. The police had the scene blocked off by the time I got there. I think maybe I saw a hint of blood when I took care of the tortoises next to it, but that is all."

"I'm glad to hear that," Henry said. "I saw more than that and it was..." He paused and his gaze shifted toward Mutti before he finished, probably not with the words he would have chosen had she not been present. "Difficult to see. As any crime scene is, of course."

"Crime scene? Are you going to arrest the alligators?" Mutti asked.

A nervous chuckle burst out of Henry, and then stopped abruptly. "No. I don't think that would make a lot of sense. The alligators, even if they had the wherewithal to be held accountable for such a crime, are fairly innocent in all of this. They did not attack the man. Someone else did. Then probably tried to dispose of the body by dumping it in the alligator swamp. It might have worked if these had been bigger animals, but we think they got too full to finish the job."

Mutti stood up and walked several paces away from the bench with her arms curled around her stomach. "Oh, no, this is too much."

"Der Mord?" Max asked, the words sticky on his tongue. "You think? Why would you think it was—"

"Murder?" Henry supplied the English word Max couldn't produce. "I'm not the detective in charge, but my colleague has consulted with the head animal trainer, and the two of them have been unable to come up with a scenario in which the animals would have attacked so viciously and so successfully in their current environment."

"An accident, then?" Max offered. "Is it possible Mr. Williamson fell in while working and the gators tore into him?"

"That was the initial assumption." Henry rested his arm up on the back of the bench, snaking it behind Max as he spoke, which struck him as both too casual and much too fatherly for his comfort. Max leaned forward. Mutti stared at them both, her mouth ajar.

"But there's the question of what the man would even be doing on the swamp walk at all. It wasn't as if he looked after these animals."

Max said nothing to this, choosing instead to ignore Pete's now unexplained obsession with the venomous snakes contained in the vivaria at the far end of the boardwalk across the swamp, and allow Henry to continue his explanation uninterrupted.

"There's no evidence of an accident," he said. "The railing along the boardwalk isn't broken. There are no scuffling boot marks that might suggest a person tripped over and fell off, even if he could have casually fit between the railings, which I can't imagine happening. And there's a lot of blood."

"What does that have to do with anything? Gators are frenzied feeders." Max had seen this for himself. It was why he didn't particularly relish being near the beasts. They weren't exactly polite about their table manners.

"They thrash about with their food. It's a distressing thing to see. That's why we don't feed them when there are visitors at the concession. Most people can't handle the sight."

"Yes, Mr. Castang explained that, but he also mentioned he's never seen so much blood on the boardwalk itself."

"Was there really that much?"

"It wasn't so much the volume of blood as it was the placement of it. There was no evidence of blood at all on the walkway portion of the boardwalk, where you might expect to find some in the case of a furious feeding situation. Where the investigators did discover blood was on the handrails. That baffled Castang as well. He couldn't say how it might have splashed up that far. And even if it had, it would have appeared as drops, and not the way it did, as more of a smear."

"What does that tell you?" Max was still leaned forward, away from Henry's outstretched arm, and didn't necessarily want to encourage closeness from the man, but his curiosity demanded answers. The whole idea of what the blood might tell investigators fascinated him.

"Well," Henry looked at Mutti as if to seek permission to continue this line of discussion. Paler than ever, she turned her back on them both. Henry's eyes remained fixed on her back, and he chewed the inside of his cheek before continuing. "It tells us that this Pete fella was dying before he ever went into that water."

"But how do you know he was bleeding badly enough for that to have been the cause of death? Could he have cut himself or something, bled on the railing and then fallen in the water and been killed by the alligators?"

"That is quite enough, I think." Mutti turned back toward them sharply, her features stern, her lips tightened into a thin line. "This is all so morbid. Is this why you came here, Henry, so you could shock us with these awful details?"

"No, not at all," he assured her and stood, sliding his arm from the back of the bench and weaving it behind her instead. Max's stomach churned. "I never meant to upset you. I thought of Max when I heard about the incident, and then when I saw he wasn't at the concession, I only wanted to know he was okay. Was this Pete a friend of yours?"

"He was one of the bosses," Max said. "Nothing more than that."

"Did you like him? Was he a friendly man?"

"Are you interrogating him?" Mutti asked. "Is he a suspect?"

Henry held up his hands in surrender, yielding to the anger now directed at him. "I'm not even an investigator officially on the case. If Detective Cullen didn't ask any of these questions already, then they don't need to be asked with any connection to the crime. I'm trying to ascertain, as a friendly, concerned, and vaguely connected party, whether or not Max is okay."

"I am," Max said quickly. "I really am, Mutti. Mr. Williamson was not an overly pleasant man. I won't miss him much, but I doubt anyone will. My biggest concern is what will happen with my job. Henry, do you know if the police will allow the concession to reopen?"

"I am not privy to that information, and so I can't make any promises, but what I do know is that Mr. Hagenbeck and Mr. Castang have been doing everything they can to cooperate with the investigation. I suspect they will be allowed to reopen. I'm sure they will at least receive leave to do so from the city police department. It may be a day or two yet. A man has died, and we need to make sure the concession is safe, that the public is safe. You have to understand that."

Of course Max understood, and he said as much, but the thought they might not reopen made him uneasy. He wondered if Hagenbeck and Castang might consider hiring him to come along if they decided to cut their losses and take their show on the road, and whether or not Shehani might be a part of that as well. The notion held a certain appeal.

"Besides, I think they are close to making an arrest, and if that should happen, then I think it very likely the concession will be up and going again soon. But I wouldn't be surprised if they are required to remove the alligators."

"I certainly wouldn't mind," said Mutti. "I hate the idea of you working around man-eating beasts."

"I wouldn't be too disappointed, either," Max assured her. "To be honest I've always thought them frightening." But this concern was not the one currently worming its way into Max's brain and beginning to burn there. "You said they are close to an arrest? Who are they arresting?"

Henry shook his head. "It hasn't happened yet and since this is not my case, I don't know all the details. Even if I did, I couldn't discuss them with you. As I'm sure you're aware, they interviewed all the workers today. All I know is that Cullen dug up something suspicious."

"The man with the scar?" Max asked, desperate to keep Henry sharing.

Henry's head tilted. "What's this about a man with a scar?"

"I saw him outside the swamp walk last night, talking with Pete. He's the man you were asking about, isn't he? The one who comes to see the baby elephant? Who is he?"

Henry squinted at. "Did you tell all of this to Detective Cullen?"

"Yes," Max said, and repeated his question. "Who is the man with the scar?"

"If it's the same man," said Henry, his words drawn and careful, "he's a known gangster, name of Tom Egan. Owns a shady saloon on the corner of Broadway and Carr. Rough crowd. And yes, I saw him when your mother and I visited the concession."

"A gangster! In the tierpark?" Mutti looked up to the sky and stretched out her hands, palms up. "A gangster who can't get enough of a baby elephant."

"Unlikely." Henry released a chuckle he swiftly swallowed back. "I suppose a gangster, like anyone else, might make an innocent visit to a zoological exhibit once, but more than that and we begin to wonder if there's some nefarious connection."

Max didn't hesitate to encourage this conjecture. "I'd seen him before, but I didn't know who he was at the time. And if there's a connection from organized crime to the concession, it would be Pete."

Chapter 23

Max never managed to get the drink he'd been after, unwilling as he was to linger at the biergarten beneath the curious glances of the patrons and open disdain of Annmarie. In Max's opinion, not all his cousins had made good marriages. More generous, Mutti excused the woman's behavior as protectiveness over the family business, which Max couldn't deny his presence had disrupted.

Mutti hadn't wished to stay either, and after she offered Reinhardt a brief explanation of all that had transpired on the fairgrounds, her brother readily agreed that she should allow Henry and Max to escort her home.

Unfortunately, home proved no more comfortable for Max. His mind played over the unbidden apparition of Pete Williamson's mangled body gripped in a deadly tug-of-war between the blood red teeth of two grotesque monsters, a working of his disturbed imagination that would not let go of the terrible thoughts.

Max couldn't handle the questions his family would surely direct at him. How he could explain the demise of Pete Williamson to the children or, for that matter, to Frieda or Aunt Matilda, without causing them all a great deal of distress, he couldn't fathom. And so, he wound his way back to the fairgrounds.

"The fair is about to close, you know," said a burly man sitting on the curb beside the entrance. Max responded by lifting his workman's badge toward the man who flicked a careless hand toward the opening next to the recently added entrance turnstiles. Once inside, he turned right down Administration Avenue and headed straight for the Pike.

Hagenbeck's Animal Paradise stood dark and quiet. No lines of excited people or barkers advertising trained animal shows and camel rides announced its presence. A scarlet rope stretched between shuttered ticket windows across the entrance, taking the place of the line of Jefferson Guardsmen from the morning. One officer remained, shiny brass buttons gleaming in the glow of the tall streetlamps that cut down the middle of the Pike, his surveillance directed at the swirling skirts of the dancing girls of Mysterious Asia across the street.

Max approached him, straining to listen for sounds of life, either human or animal, within the eerily silent concession.

"Sorry, buddy, this one is closed." Max nearly jumped when the officer spoke to him. "I'm going to need you to move along."

"I didn't mean..." Max began, then realized he didn't know quite what to say. "I work here. I was here earlier and talked with the detective."

"So why are you back?" the man asked.

Max hesitated. Explaining to the officer that he wished to view the crime scene, that he hoped doing so might settle his poisoned psyche, presented as an unappealing option that could even elicit suspicion. Instead, he decided to tell a partial truth. "I didn't want to be alone with my thoughts and was hoping some of the other workers might not have left."

The officer stepped toward him, the sword conspicuous on his belt. "It's been a rough day, I realize. For all of you." His tone might have contained genuine sympathy. The man pointed a hooked thumb over his shoulder. "It's been pretty quiet in there for a while. I think most of the workers have gone already, but a few left not too long ago. I heard one say something about heading to the cowboy bar to blow off some steam. I imagine most were too keyed up to hit the bunks. Didn't relish the idea of being around the scene of a grisly death. It's a good night to stick together."

"Danke," Max said, touched by the man's concern and too exhausted to dream up another excuse to offer the guardsman for entering the concession. Max turned to exit around the left of the Animal Paradise and follow the railroad tracks to the Congress of Nations and Rough Riders Show where Cheyenne Joe's Cowboy Saloon would still be in full swing.

Normally a lively tavern filled with hearty laughter, staged gunfights, and plenty of the kind of bawdy choruses men sing outside the hearing of decent women, the cowboy bar was a noticeably subdued place that night. As always, the air hung heavy with smoke, but the men inside shared little cheer with one another. Most of the day's fairgoers had gone, and almost to a man the place had been populated with weary grounds workers. The Hagenbeck crew took up its usual corner, and Max walked up to several tables of sullen-faced zookeepers, animal trainers, and maintenance workers. Lorenz sat by himself in the very corner and lifted a hand in greeting to Max, who'd never seen his boss so solemn.

He pulled back a chair that scraped on the rough wooden floor and sat with his elbows on the table. "Any news from the detectives? Can we stay open?" His stomach churned in anticipation of the answer to the question. The potential closure of the concession weighed as heavily on Max, as did the notion of murder at his place of employment. If the Paradise on the Pike could not continue, he feared his only option would be to work in a mind-numbing construction job with Ernst.

Lorenz took a long swig from the beer mug in front of him and signaled for a waiter to bring both another for him and one for Max. "Well," he said, his countenance drawn and sorrowful, "we can reopen."

"I'm confused," Max said. He accepted the mug the bartender brought to the table and took a long-anticipated swallow of the brew. He grimaced as bitterness coated his tongue. "Shouldn't that be good news?"

"Yes, but the police think it was murder. A murder at the Hagenbeck Animal Show. Can you believe that?"

"Someone murdered Pete?" Max pretended surprise, though his earlier conversation with Henry Duncan had indicated as much.

"Apparently so," Lorenz said. "Which is good news for the alligators, of course, though the fair wants us to take them off exhibit. I plan to appeal that decision. I don't think the poor beasts should be punished for eating available food. It's not as if they themselves killed Pete."

"But they would, wouldn't they?"

"Ach! That's what the fair directors say. They assume once the animals have a taste for human flesh, they'll not accept plain old fish and chicken like they would normally get. Personally, I can't think Pete tasted as good those other highly palatable options."

Max nearly chuckled at this statement but thought better of it when he saw the heaviness weighing down Lorenz's countenance.

"But the problem isn't that the alligators are innocent," Lorenz said. "It's that someone else is guilty. Someone on our staff, it seems."

"It's not someone on staff," Max blurted.

Lorenz lifted his chin and pointed a finger at Max's nose. "What do you mean by that?"

"I only meant——" Unsure how to continue, Max paused. He didn't want to betray Henry's confidence, but loyalty to Lorenz and to the concession demanded that he share reassurance where there may be some to lend. He leaned across the table and whispered, "I am not supposed to know this."

Lorenz brought a finger to his lips and winked.

Max fired glances to his right and left to verify their conversation would continue unnoticed by anyone at nearby tables.

"My mother knows a detective with the St. Louis police. He's not investigating this case, but he said they were close to making an arrest of a known gangster in the area."

"No." Lorenz took another drink from his beer. "I don't know anything about this gangster of yours, but they did make an arrest."

Max sat up straight. He reached for his drink determined to get past the unpleasant taste and reach the sweet release of drunkenness. "Who did they arrest?"

"The snake charmer."

Max coughed, sending his swallow of beer down the wrong way, which made him cough more. Lorenz pounded him on the back and asked after his health, but Max dismissed the concern with a wave. When at last he could form words, he asked, "They arrested Inesh? Why?"

"As a matter of fact, it was something you said." Lorenz raised his stein in a mock toast to Max. "When you asked me whether we needed to collect the venom from the snakes it didn't make any sense at the time, but then the police discovered vials of venom stored behind the vivaria, in various stages of drying. They think it might have something to do with how he died."

Max took another gulp from his mug. The beer burned down his esophagus to land uneasily in his otherwise empty stomach. The sharp-edged liquid brought him no great warmth as it was rumored to do but abandoned him to a shiver as the edges of his vision grew dark. He would not panic, could not, in front of the hardworking men of the show, men whose jobs consisted of piling up dung and risking their lives alongside beasts that in lightly altered circumstance would not hesitate to either trample or make dinner of them. Max bit down hard on his tongue, allowing the pain to bring him back into the moment.

"Why would that prove Inesh did it?" he asked.

Lorenz threw up a hand, nearly knocking into his own beer stein. "It doesn't prove anything, of course, but he's immune to the cobra venom, which means he could have handled it without fear for his own life."

"Does he have a motive?" The slight Sinhalese man would be a surprising source of violence.

"I don't know," Lorenz said. "But the police needed to arrest someone if the show was going to reopen. The public needs a villain, and who better than a funny little man with brown skin and a penchant for snakes, eh?"

Max leaned across the table and looked Lorenz directly in the eye. "You don't think he did it."

"No, Maxie boy, I don't think our peace-loving snake charmer friend did it." Lorenz, who'd clearly drunk more than he ought, let a burp bubble out. "But nine times out of ten the police are going to look at the foreigner first, and I can run an animal circus without a snake charmer, but I can't run one without elephants, and I can't run an elephant show without my mahouts."

Max didn't know how to respond. An innocent man, Shehani's brother, had been locked up in jail for a crime he most certainly did not commit, and Lorenz's primary concern was the preservation of his elephant show?

"I imagine Reuben can handle the elephants if it comes to it," Max said, his caustic tone as sour as his stomach.

"Of course Rube can handle the elephants. He trained them. That isn't the point. He's a white Englishman, for God's sake. No one wants to see a white Englishman lead an elephant through its paces in the ring. It takes away the mystery, the ambiance. A young, strong Sinhalese mahout with a bejeweled hook, gliding around the elephants, commanding them and captivating the audience, now that's what they want to see."

"And no one would think a white Englishman, skilled with handling animals of all varieties, might murder the business partner he disliked." Max hadn't realized what he was saying until the words floated into the air around him and it was too late to pull them back. The tables closest to them fell silent, and many of Max's coworkers turned toward him.

He didn't suspect Reuben any more than Max suspected Inesh or that the alligators had acted with malice on their own, even if there could be a horrible logic to his accidental assertion. An apology half formed on his tongue, stopped only by the simultaneous shift of every saloon patron's attention toward the wide swinging doors as a large, gray elephant stepped inside Cheyenne Joe's.

Max joined the others in turning toward the door where Lizzie struggled to slide her bulk through a doorway constructed with room enough for a cowboy to enter on horseback, but evidently designed without the consideration of an elephant's requirements. From behind her boomed a sharp command from Reuben Castang. "Lizzie, crouch!"

With remarkable coordination, the elephant pushed her head forward and stretched her thick legs, dropping her back so she could inch her way through the frame as a cat might slink under the bottom edge of a fence. The cowboys sitting closest to the door whooped and jumped up to pull tables and chairs out of the way. At another word from her trainer, Lizzie settled on her belly in the empty space. Walking in behind her, Reuben carried a large piece of red and white checkered cloth that he luffed like a great sail over the top of the animal's back, doing his best to smooth it over her as it fell.

"Joe!" Reuben called, stretching out a hand to indicate the recently displaced cowboys. "Drinks and sandwiches for the gentlemen at the elephant table. It's all on Lizzie."

Cheers and guffaws filled the saloon as the cowboys slid chairs back up to their unusually gracious hostess and attempted to balance their drinks on her back. Reuben took a bow, in complete command of an audience with much lifted spirits.

Max chortled along with them, glad for his comment to be so amusingly overshadowed. He turned to Lorenz and said, "Not a bad elephant show for a white Englishman."

Lorenz shook his head and stood. With mirth on his lips, he lifted his mug in a toast to Reuben. "Never underestimate Reuben Castang. I should know that better than anyone."

Lorenz reclaimed his seat and drained the last swallow of beer from his mug, before saying, "Look, Max, I wouldn't worry too much about this murder business. The police have less evidence against Inesh than they have even against his tiny sister. And maybe there's something to this gangster theory. They'll be free again before you know it."

"What do you mean *they'll* be free?" Max asked, his question nearly swallowed by the noise of the boisterous crowd as Lizzie, apparently tired of playing the role of picnic table, stood to send food and drinks spilling to the floor.

Fearing the distraction would prove too great, Max repeated his question. Lorenz shrugged and ran his fingers through his thinning hair. "I'm sure there's nothing to it at all, but they arrested Shehani, too."

Chapter 24

Max couldn't speak. The muscles of his neck clinched, forcing waves of pain through the back of his head where the information he'd just received should be processed but instead was being violently rejected.

"Why?" It was the one word he could manage at last.

Lorenz failed to notice the question, absorbed as he was in Lizzie's antics. The elephant shook off the last remnants of sandwich stuck to her hide and turned to squeeze her way out the door.

"Oh, God in heaven." Lorenz pushed back his chair and slithered out from behind the table. "There she goes."

Lizzie had managed to wiggle outside and bellowed a loud trumpet that faded as she ran farther away, Reuben scrambling behind her into the night.

"I better go after them," Lorenz called, already halfway through the door himself.

Max barely took in the chaotic scene unfolding around him, trapped by a persistent disbelief that anyone could think Shehani capable of murder. "I'll prove it," he said to himself, and then he said it again louder than before so that had anyone in the saloon not been distracted by Lizzie's abrupt departure, they'd have heard him.

Determined, Max swallowed what remained of his beer. He ordered two more at the bar and set one of them down in front of the closest Hagenbeck employee, the Irish maintenance man Finn. Max shoved the drink toward him and said, "What can you tell me about the night Mr. Williamson was murdered?"

Finn squinted at him and then at the fresh beer. "You a detective now, Max?"

Max sat in the chair opposite the redhead. "I'm trying to help. I think they've arrested the wrong people."

"Maybe they have, but I don't know anything. I wasn't in the concession that late, and I stay the hell away from the crocs whenever I can."

Max slid back his chair and attempted to catch the eye of one of the keepers at the next table, an older German named Oscar, but before he could, Finn added one more thought. "Look, I know it don't seem likely that little Indian woman could have killed him, but with her brother's help?" Finn shook his head. "The way Williamson tormented her? Who would blame her if she did it?"

Silently, Max agreed, but he wouldn't believe her capable of violence. He called Oscar's name and the old zookeeper turned to look at him.

"Don't usually see you here, Max," the old man said. "What brings you out tonight?"

Max raised his full beer to his lips and took a swallow. "Needed a drink."

"I understand that," Oscar said.

Two other men sat at the table with him and both grunted their agreement, one of them saying softly, "Hell of a day."

"To Pete!" Oscar raised his glass high in the air and everyone in the bar, Hagenbeck employees and cowboys alike, mimicked him. "Bastard though he was, may he rest in pieces."

The man chortled at his own joke, a jubilant sound bubbling up from his beer belly, which danced gleefully to his tasteless irreverence. The saloon erupted with similar amusement that dropped off as sluggish, inebriated brains grabbed hold of the punchline's reference to the terrible state in which Pete's body had lain.

Max had failed to laugh at all, and Oscar tugged at his shirt collar. To Max he said, "I meant no disrespect, of course. A man is dead."

"It's okay," Max assured him. "You're right about Pete Williamson. He was a bastard. I'm only asking around to try to understand what happened to him."

"The dancer had enough is what the police say happened, and her brother, the snake man, helped her kill him." Around the table heads nodded.

Max drew his hand over his chin. "I can't accept that she could be that brutal."

"You'd be surprised, son, at the brutality people are capable of." Oscar softened. "Look, she could be innocent, but she's a foreigner in a foreign land and suspicion falls heavily on such."

"I'm a foreigner in a foreign land," Max said with indignation. "So are you."

"Yes, well, you know it's different. You and I are Germans. We're Europeans, from the land of this nation's ancestors. We are looked at with suspicion, of course, but it is not the same suspicion as those whose backgrounds are more exotic, more foreign. Here in St. Louis, there is a German mayor, there are German schools, German language newspapers. Have you had a difficult time getting around the city with limited English at your disposal?"

"No," Max admitted. "But exotic does not mean murderer."

"I agree with you, but the police will do their jobs. If she's innocent, they'll figure it out."

Max wished he could be so confident. "I mean to help if I can. God, he really was a bastard, wasn't he?"

"Hmm?" Oscar said. "Oh, yeah, he really was. You know it was his idea to put in the reptiles in the first place. A fitting end, I suppose."

"Hagenbeck didn't choose them?" Max asked.

"Nah. Old man Hagenbeck sent the snakes, but the gators were Williamson's idea. They don't make great exhibit animals, but they're cheap and they're American, so easy to get here. At the same time, unless people live near swampland, they aren't familiar with them. Pete wanted as many cheap animals as he could get. Hagenbeck never cared about that. He'd have rather had flashy animals. He never thought much of the damn goats, either. If Rube weren't so attached, we'd never have had them here."

Thinking of chasing Flick out onto the Pike and into the line of dancing girls at Mysterious Asia, Max said, "I wish he'd won that argument."

"Ha! I bet you do. Can't make Rube understand they're nothing but trouble. He loves those things. They keep Finn there in a job, though. The damn things keep breaking their way out and he has to figure out ways to stop them. And you know, at least they never killed anybody."

"Neither did the gators," Max pointed out.

Oscar pulled his hand across his mouth, drying his beer-soaked mustache on his sleeve. "Nah, I suppose not. Someone sure wished it would look like they did, though."

"You think that was intentional?"

Oscar stared long and hard at Max. One eyebrow quirked, and he took a deep drink from his beer. "What I think is that whoever killed Pete didn't want there to be any evidence at all, wanted to wipe the slate clean so nobody would have to think about the man again. Probably was hoping the gators would ingest every last bit, which just goes to show that whoever killed him probably wasn't a reptile expert. If he was, he'd have known those gators weren't big enough to take care of the body in one night."

Max's head swam with this information. He'd not been involved in the care of the alligators, but most of the concession's keepers would have been at some point. There weren't very many of them and they cross-trained to better ensure the smooth running of the concession. Almost any of them should have known the approximate amount of flesh the two alligators could consume at one time, making it less likely the murderer was one of the staff. That was information he could use.

Max thanked Oscar and his companions for their time, finished his beer, ordered another, and continued his investigation at the next table, his spirits lifting even as his brain began to fog.

Chapter 25

The next morning, Max remembered why he didn't care to drink. He'd awakened to the hammering of a fist on his bedroom door and an unsympathetic greeting from his infuriated mother. Max sifted through the ache in his head and recalled making the decision to leave the cowboy bar in time to catch a ride home rather than stumbling to the shantytown the Hagenbeck crew had constructed two blocks away. Already sick from his overindulgence, Max hadn't relished bedding down on an uncomfortable cot surrounded by the sounds and odors of too many unwashed bodies in too little space. Now he questioned his choice.

"Maximilian Eyer! Get up!" This shrill roar recalled childhood mischief and well-deserved discipline meted out by his mother, too often followed by his father's more severe version of punishment. Max shuddered in his bed before dragging himself upright, attempting to stretch stiff muscles while fighting a throbbing head and trying to hold onto the contents of a distressed stomach.

One final thump on the door preceded the pounding of fading footsteps accompanied by unintelligible grumbling. Max groaned and pulled himself upright to splash his face with water from the basin beside his bed before throwing on clothes to descend the stairs and accept his inevitable penance.

"How could you do that to me?" Mutti plopped down a plate with a louder than necessary clatter on the wooden table as Max sat down. "There was a murder, Max. A murder! And then you were missing. Do you have any idea what you put me through, staying out half the night like that?"

Max's breakfast consisted of a thick slice of dark bread and two under-cooked eggs, their running yolks even more unappetizing than the spittle flying from his mother's angry lips. He slid the plate away. Mutti shoved it back toward him.

"You need to put something in your stomach." She rolled her eyes, speaking to the heavens as she said, "Lord knows I understand how to take care of a drunk."

Thoroughly chastised, Max picked up the bread and nibbled a corner, forcing himself to swallow. His body did not immediately reject the offering, but in no hurry to try it again, he set the slice back on the plate. The attempt caused his mother's tight jaws to relax. Max ventured an apology.

"Es tut mir leid. I was drinking with the Hagenbeck employees for a good cause. I was trying to gather information to clear the name of a friend."

"That is the job of the police."

"Yes it is, but they arrested someone I know is innocent."

Mutti scowled, but she sat in the chair at the end of the table, attentive at least.

Max, careful to avoid the egg yolk, took another bite of his bread. "I always thought beer was an easier drink to handle."

"You'll want to eat those. Trust me." Mutti pointed to eggs. "Beer is not as unpleasant as vodka, but if you drink all the beer, you will be sick as a dog all the same. A dog that needs to eat."

"Yes, Mutti." He forked a small amount of egg white into his mouth.

"You think you'd know better," Mutti mumbled.

Max didn't have the strength to respond to her mutterings, a manifestation of her justifiable disappointment in him.

"Eat!" she ordered, louder this time. "And get to work. The animals need you, I would think."

"Yes, Mutti, they do. And I'm going." He managed one more bite of bread and several swallows of strong black coffee. Then stood and donned his hat. "Mutti," he said before he could change his mind about what he wished to say. "Will you see Detective Duncan today?"

"I might." She blushed. His gut lurched. "Why?"

"I want to talk with him about the investigation at the concession."

"He can't talk about that. He's a good man, Max. If he can't talk about it, he won't."

"I wouldn't expect him to. I just wanted to share an idea with him."

She glared at him with suspicion. "It's not his crime to solve. And it's not yours, either."

"I know. He was clear about that, but the detective in charge is looking in the wrong direction. I need Henry's advice on how to encourage the man to redirect his attention."

"No." She stood and swiped his breakfast plate to place it into the kitchen sink. The determination in her voice shocked him. "You will not ask Henry to second-guess his colleague. You are not a detective, Max. They are doing their jobs and if they have arrested someone, then that is that. The murder is solved, and everyone can be safe and go back to their regular lives."

"Except they have the wrong person," Max said.

"How do you know?"

"Because Shehani wouldn't have done it. And more importantly, I don't think she could have done it."

"Who is this woman to you?"

"It's not who she is to me, Mutti. It's that she's innocent."

"She's a savage. They probably kill people for fun in her country."

"You don't mean that. You don't know anything about her country."

"And you do?"

"Not really," he admitted. "But I do know her."

"How well do you know this savage woman, Max?"

"It's not like that, Mutti."

"Nichts da. I'm sure it's not." Hands on hips, she studied him a second before shooing him toward the door. "Get to work, now," she said. "Don't come home drunk again. And don't even think about bothering Henry with your foolish theories. I don't want you talking with him about this or any other murder."

His foot hit the top step as he processed her words and before he could stop himself, he snickered, turning back to look at her. "What other murders would I be discussing with Henry?"

A forceful nudge became his answer, along with an unhelpful clarification: "None of them."

⁂

Max mulled over his mother's list of admonitions, his shoulders drooping as he caught the streetcar. He understood the dark place from which that fear arose, as he had the same cache of dread locked away within himself. It came from the often-repeated experience of caring for a drunk and vicious Felix, unwilling to accept the care he obviously needed while making demands on his family they couldn't possibly honor, all while threatening the violence that made them tremble.

If this was how Max had behaved, even in small part, he could forgive his mother the irrationality of the morning. His memories of the night remained fuzzy, but he'd interviewed all the Hagenbeck employees in the saloon. Doing so had required drinking with most of them, and Max could not hold his liquor. He rarely drank, hated the idea of it. It was a policy he should have followed last night before he wound up stumbling home and forcing Mutti to relive the worst moments of her life nursing him back to health, rubbing his back over a bucket, wiping his fevered brow with a wet cloth, forcing water and food down his gullet with astounding patience. That she spoke to him at all this morning should nominate her for sainthood.

He vowed to do better—no more drinking, and above all, no more drunkenness. He owed her that much, for all the years she'd endured his father's abuse, when Max wasn't strong or brave enough to defend her. He would not saddle his mother with more pain.

For now, he would have to endure the consequences of the poor choices he'd made at the cowboy bar as his head throbbed with every step he took along the Pike. The concession's entrance stood open, no longer roped off, and Max didn't see any sign of the Jefferson guard officers. What he did see, a few feet beyond the entrance, was Lorenz, smiling and chatting cheerfully with Oscar, who flashed a knowing grin at Max's approach.

"Rough night, Max?" Oscar smirked and tipped his cap before heading off toward the back of the Animal Paradise to start his day.

Lorenz watched the other zookeeper fade from view and turned to Max, saying much too loudly, "I must have missed a good night. I've never known a strapping German lad like you who couldn't hold his liquor. Heard you got pretty chock-a-block."

"Did you catch Lizzie?" Max asked, hoping to redirect the conversation from his indiscretions. He slid into the shade cast by the arena stands to hide his pulsing eyes from the notice of the screaming sun.

"Yeah," Lorenz said jovially. "The old girl gave us a pretty good run. Made it all the way to the Olympic Village before Rube got her talked down."

"Maybe he shouldn't take her to the bar."

"Some elephants don't belong in bars, it's true," Lorenz said. "Much like some men, though I doubt that will stop them. Probably won't stop Reuben from taking Lizzie out on the town, either."

"You're probably right about that." Max wished he could join Lorenz in his joking banter, but the deep ache of melancholy displaced any frivolity he might otherwise have enjoyed.

The traces of amusement slid from Lorenz's expression in response to Max's silence. "It must have been a very rough night indeed. Cheer up, my young friend. The sun is shining, the crowds are expected to break records today, and we are open for business. It couldn't be a happier day."

It could be, Max thought, if perhaps there'd been no murder on the Pike that had put an innocent man and woman behind bars.

"Oh," Lorenz added, holding up a hand to delay Max from turning to his work. "You might want to know Inesh has been returned to us, which is good news for the shows."

Max's gaze met Lorenz's and Max's troubled heart might have floated from his chest. "Shenani?" he asked, the words barely audible.

Lorenz responded as if he hadn't heard. He pulled his hands together in a single clap. "The show is saved. The snake charming act is such a highlight, I didn't know how we'd go on without it. The big cats will be missing some exciting elements, though. It's always a crowd pleaser when Shehani enters the cage with the tigers, but Rube can work something out, I'm sure."

"You mean Inesh is free, but Shehani is still in jail?" Max spoke up this time, his question causing Lorenz's eyebrows to knit together.

"Yes, she is, which might be a problem. Inesh is upset, of course, but he's a professional. I think we can count on him. Evidently it came down to a question of motive."

"What is supposed to be her motive?" But Max didn't need an answer to that question. He'd heard it posited by beer-soaked Hagenbeck employees, one after another, the previous night. It was no secret that Pete had been relentless in his badgering of the poor woman, who'd so clearly wanted nothing to do with him.

"Oh," Lorenz said. "You know, Pete was never particularly kind to her."

"He wasn't kind to anyone. By that logic any one of us might have killed him."

"Yes, well." Lorenz fidgeted, transferring his weight from one foot to the other. "I'm sure the police will sort it out. In the meantime, I have work to do, as I'm sure you do. In our business we like to say that the show must go on!" With that, he turned toward the concession's business office, waving a dismissive hand as he went.

Thus dismissed, and without a well-formed retort, Max walked dejected toward the ostrich pen to feed the birds and ready them for their day of carting around the record-breaking crowd.

The pleasant May day did welcome the expected large crowd to the fairgrounds and many of them to the Pike and the Animal Paradise, its arena filled to capacity for each show. Between his pounding head, roiling stomach, and heavy spirit, Max could not manage to enjoy it, though he did appreciate the endless tasks that demanded his focus. He could almost forget the tragedies of the previous days.

Midday had long passed by the time Max worked his way back to the reptile swamp, the one part of the concession to bear any marks of the gory events, rumors of which had attracted rather than repelled visitors. Police-erected poles supported a large tarpaulin that blocked the boardwalk across the swamp and the wall of vivaria beyond. A large sign explained that the animals here were temporarily unavailable for viewing for the benefit of their own health and safety. Nothing indicated that it had been a crime scene.

Max read the sign several times and then, without consciously deciding to do it, pulled back the edge of the tarpaulin and eased past it to the boardwalk. He stepped carefully around a few spots stained red with dried blood and scanned the water for the gators. He spotted the first, the top of its scaly head barely above the water, lying in wait, he supposed, for its next victim. If Lorenz's pleas on their behalf were unsuccessful and fair officials forced the gators' removal, Max would never have to care for these scaly, ancient monsters, a truth that didn't disappoint him. He studied the curious creature as it lifted its snout, mussy and wet from the muck. It made no sudden moves, appearing entirely non-threatening but frightening nonetheless. Max shivered and scanned wildly for the second beast.

He had to walk forward several steps before he spotted the animal. Its snout lay on the bank across the water from the elevated boardwalk which stood at least two feet above the surface of the water. The second gator drew its tail back and forth in the water as he watched, slowly and steadily, not at all agitated by his presence. One foot reached out onto land beside the long snout, but the rest of its body remained submerged, with only the controlled and deliberate movement of the tail indicating it was there at all. The snout, he could have easily missed in the foliage of the enclosure.

So focused was he on the animals that he didn't see Oscar emerge from the shadows. "Don't touch anything."

"What?" Max nearly jumped at the sound, realizing for the first time how deadly silent the reptile swamp was, as if the goings-on in this spot had rendered the space impenetrable to the noises of the fair that existed beyond its fabric boundaries.

"I said not to touch anything. The police were very clear about that. It's one of the reasons we can't open the swamp to the public yet."

"I thought it was because they are afraid the alligators will eat the fairgoers."

"Well," the man wiped his brow with a dingy handkerchief. "That, too, I expect. But no, they aren't finished with their investigation, and they don't want anyone cleaning up any evidence."

"What are they expecting to find?" Max asked, and then another, happier thought occurred to him. "They don't think Shehani did it."

"I can't say what they are thinking, but I was here earlier when that detective came back to look around. I wouldn't say he doesn't think she did it, but I don't think he's definitively tied her to it yet."

"So, there's a chance." Max bounced subtly on the balls of his feet.

"I wouldn't be so happy about it if I were you. What they do think is that someone on staff did it, and if not those foreigners, then it'll be one of us immigrants they look to next."

"They had another suspect, I thought," Max ventured. "Some gangster."

Oscar folded his arms over his beer belly. "I don't know anything about that. What I do know is I'll be keeping my head down, and if you're smart, you will, too. For one thing, you ought to stay out of here if the reptiles aren't on your list. It looks suspicious, you sneaking around."

"I was just curious," said Max. "And you were sneaking, too. You said you already took care of the reptiles today. They don't need that much attention."

Oscar unfolded his arms and leaned against the boardwalk railing. "The tarpaulin was out of place. I wanted to check to see that no one had come back here that shouldn't have. There used to be a guardsman posted. Not sure where he went."

"You're back here a lot then?"

"I keep tabs on the goings-on," Oscar confirmed.

"Were you around that night? When Pete was murdered?"

"I don't know what you're suggesting."

"Do you know who killed Pete? Were you here?"

Oscar shuffled and coughed, his entire demeanor changing as if he were closing up like the lid of a chest. "I saw nothing."

"But were you here, when the concession closed."

"I went home that night same as you, Max. Same as you, I swear."

"Do you think Shehani did it?"

"That little thing? No." He shook his head. "I wouldn't think a little thing like her even could, but then I wouldn't think I'd ever see a man could hypnotize a snake the way her brother can, either. I wouldn't put nothin' past a one of them."

"The police released Inesh. He didn't do it."

"No." Oscar surveyed the swamp, the gators as still as statues, before turning his gaze on Max. "He didn't do it. Neither of them did."

Chapter 26

Max released the pulley to slide the door closed after three black bears ambled inside for an evening meal of fresh Mississippi River catfish. Two of the animals cut immediately into the scaly flesh like dogs after a bone. The third, a smaller female, picked up a fish in her sharp teeth, moved away from her companions, plopped onto her haunches, and grabbed the meal between her enormous front paws in order to take dainty bites.

Max's own stomach grumbled for the first time that day. He stared vacantly at the eating bears for another minute before he pulled a shovel and a coiled hose off the shelf behind him. He dropped them both into a wheelbarrow before pushing it through the wide door to the right of the indoor bear cage. Max scoured the enclosure. Solid animal waste and food scraps went into the wheelbarrow. Then he hooked up the hose to the hidden spigot to wash down the hard surfaces, spraying the water toward the trench that separated the animals from the fence where concession visitors watched him work until they grew convinced there were no animals to see and moved on.

"Good day today, Max?" Reuben asked over the fence on the other side of the trench.

Max twisted off the spigot valve and stood to recoil the hose. He shrugged. "No one died today, which is something."

A laugh burst out of Reuben. He attempted to hide it with a cough.

"Yes, I suppose that is something. It's a shame, of course, about Shehani."

Max dropped the hose and stepped to the edge of the trench so his words might reach Reuben alone and not carry into the evening air to be plucked out by passersby. "She didn't do it. They won't be able to hold her."

He hadn't meant for his words to come out as a threat, but once he'd said them, Max didn't regret his tone. As much as he didn't want to think that Reuben could kill a man, no one could deny the animosity between the trainer and Pete. There'd been that odd comment, too, when Reuben claimed a nefarious connection with the county sheriff and the reckless decision to endanger Lizzie and by bringing her into a bar full of people. An unstable man would do such a thing.

"No, I'm sure they can't," said Reuben. "Poor girl wouldn't hurt a fly. It would be hard to find a kinder soul."

This last statement landed with sincerity in Max's gut, followed by regret at entertaining suspicions about this man who'd been nothing but kind to Max from the moment he'd stepped foot into the concession.

"Anyway," Reuben slapped the top railing of the low fence. "Looks like you're about finished up in here. Why don't you head home? You looked a little green around the gills today. I imagine a good night's rest would do you good."

"Thank you." Max didn't bother denying the day had been a long and difficult one. His head no longer pounded, and he wanted to try to eat something though the simple act of moving through his normal tasks had left him exhausted. Several hours and several animal shows remained until the concession closed, but he longed to go home and fall into his narrow bed in the attic.

Reuben Castang examined Max with round eyes that expressed an intuitive understanding of the needs of the man in front of him. Much as the animal trainer possessed an uncanny ability to interpret the motivations and limitations of the beasts with which he worked, his gaze probed into the depths of men as well. A tingling sensation spread through Max as he vacillated between the relief of having his needs met and the vulnerability of being so well understood.

His uncle's house stood welcoming with its windows open to catch an evening breeze and the shrieking sounds of happy children rambled through its rooms. They spilled out into the front yard to catch hold of the blinking insects his cousins called lightning bugs. They were magical little creatures—both the bugs and the children in hot pursuit of them. Max paused on the front walk to soak in their innocence and enjoy the revelry.

Dark curls bouncing, Martha ran to him and wound her small, soft fingers around his large, rough ones. "Come on, Max," she said. He allowed her to lead him into open grass where she pointed to a blinking bug clever enough to fly beyond her reach. "You're tall enough to get it."

Max reached up to the sky and scooped beneath the insect which landed, dazed, in the center of his palm. His other hand formed a dome over top, enclosing the creature in a fleshy cage.

"You got it!" the little girl said in delight. "Let me see!"

He walked to the edge of the yard and sat on the grass at the edge of the glow of the nearest streetlamp. Martha settled beside him. Her twin brother Otto arrived, too, breathless from his own fruitless attempts to capture his own firefly.

The two children leaned in close and slowly Max lifted his domed hand to glimpse a flashing light crawling about on tiny legs that tickled his skin. The insect climbed from finger to finger, finally rounding a knuckle to discover the sky beyond. Otto gasped as the creature spread wispy wings and took flight.

"You let it get away!" the boy complained.

Max clicked his tongue and pointed to flashing light rising steadily into the night sky. In the careful English he spoke with the children, he explained, "It wasn't ours to keep hidden away from the world."

The twins might have protested, but before they could, Claude hurried to them, his hands cupped together. "I got one!" He beamed. The older boy held it close to his impressed little cousins who squealed for him to let them see, reaching for a look. Claude moved beyond their reach, grinned and clapped his hands together, before presenting them to his cousins for inspection.

Each palm contained a speck of smeared, glowing innards. Otto shrieked and jumped back. Martha yelled for her Oma. Max's pulse accelerated, and he struggled to take a deep breath.

He was a half a block away, covered in a sheen of cold sweat, and bent over dizzy before he realized that Claude had called after him. Guilt needled him at leaving the children so without explanation, but Matilda or their parents or Frieda would look after them. What Frieda must think of him, he wouldn't entertain as he slowly regained his wits, pushed his exhaustion aside, and continued down the street away from the house.

The restaurant's outdoor lamps blinked out one by one as Max approached the only place he could think to go. He pushed against the locked door, and his cousin Hugh opened it for him.

"Max," Hugh said, in a tone that cautiously welcomed. "We're closing up for the night. What brings you here?"

"Is my mother here?" Max asked. He pushed past his large, friendly cousin toward the counter at the back of the restaurant, and as he did so, Mutti walked out of the kitchen.

"What are you doing here?" She scowled at her son, momentarily shrinking his resolve.

Into the silent space, Hugh asked, "Should I turn on some of the lights again, Aunt Emmi?"

"No," she barked.

Hugh regarded the two of them and then said to Mutti, "I'll leave you to lock up then. Max will walk you home?"

"No." Max said this to his cousin and then, embarrassed, attempted to explain. "She should walk home with you if you're willing. I'm not staying, I only needed to ask her a question."

Hugh nodded. "Sure. Yes. I'll be right outside." The bell above the door tinkled as he pushed his way outside.

Mutti appraised Max, no longer scowling exactly but clearly not pleased to see him. "You look terrible. Have you been drinking again?"

"Not a drop," Max said and saw her muscles relax in relief. "I was hoping you could tell me where to find Henry."

"I'm not his keeper," she said briskly, as she tended to be when he'd provoked her anger.

"I know that, Mutti, but I really need to talk to him, and I thought you might have some idea."

"Well, he's not here." Her tone was not as snappy as her words, the chill thawing, much to Max's relief.

"I can see that." He added a light chuckle to the words in hopes of smoothing the sharpness in his observation. "Surely you must have some idea what he gets up to."

"I don't know for certain, but often the nights he comes in here are the nights he's not working, which I assume means the times I don't see him are probably the times he is working."

"Thank you, Mutti. Really. I don't suppose you could tell me where he works?"

"You shouldn't bother him. Leave the investigating to the police."

"Mutti, please." He'd have dropped to his knees and begged if he thought it would help, but he knew her well enough to know she'd scold his melodrama. "Please, I need to help if I can."

Her resolve finally softened with a sigh. "He's a detective, Max. He works on crime scenes all over the city. But if it's his office you're wanting, it's in the Second District Station on Wyoming Street—Eighth and Wyoming."

He thanked her with a kiss on her cheek and she waved him through the door where Hugh waited. "Got what you need, Max?"

"Yes, I think so," he told his cousin, buoyed now by the hope that with Mutti's blessing, Henry Duncan would help him. Shehani would fly free, her bright spirit uncrushed by a careless world.

Chapter 27

The fair had brought much to the city—trains full of visitors, world attention, and a significant increase in crime. Nothing made this more obvious than the activity swirling around the police station at nine o'clock on a Friday night. Max found it exactly where Mutti had described, highlighted by a cluster of streetlamps in front and lights blazing through the many windows. Few buildings beyond the fairgrounds made use of electric lights, but Max could understand why the police station would be an exception.

The lobby beyond the front doors buzzed with activity, involving a number of uniformed officers as well as many people in civilian clothes patiently, and not so patiently, waiting their turn to step up to the front desk and air their complaints. Unsure where to begin, Max stepped past a man with a thick mustache and a large bowler hat in his hands and stood in a long line winding up toward the desk. He settled behind a gentleman in a top hat and fine suit with a woman in a peach-colored evening gown on his arm.

Max shifted from foot to foot as he slowly shuffled forward. The concerns of the people in front of him ranged from petty theft and noise complaints to reports of vandalism and even one attempted violent mugging. That was the claim of the couple directly in front of him who said they'd had their evening at the theater ruined at the knifepoint of a criminal. Max doubted the story, as the two appeared to him entirely unscathed, but the long-suffering officer behind the desk directed them through a door to his right with directions to an office in which they could give their statements.

"And what can I do for you, sir?" the man asked Max as he stepped up to the counter. The officer rose up slightly from his seat behind the desk to take stock of the line behind Max—a line that rarely grew shorter.

"Busy night?" Max asked, adopting his best sympathetic tone.

The officer squinted at Max. "They're all busy since the fair came to town. It's brought every kind of criminal element with it, including all the crazies who think they might have been the victim of a crime and the amateur sleuths who think they may have solved a crime."

"Well, I'm not here about any of that." Max swallowed, almost willing to believe his own lie. "I was hoping to get in touch with Detective Henry Duncan if I might."

The officer's gaze slid up and down Max's face. "What is this regarding?"

"Oh." Max didn't know quite how to answer. He had assumed that because he knew the detective by name that he would be admitted to see him without further questions. "Um, I work at Hagenbeck's Animal Paradise on the Pike at the fairgrounds, and I think I might have useful information."

The officer flipped through a stack of papers on his desk, squinting to read something. He didn't look back up to Max before he spoke again. "Detective Duncan isn't on the animal concession case. It's Detective Cullen you'll need to see."

"No," Max said, panicking. "Please, no, I have spoken with Detective Cullen. I would prefer Detective Duncan."

"And why is that?"

Max didn't want to say the next words, but he wasn't sure how he could get out of it. "He is courting my mother. As a courtesy, I would like to speak with him."

"This is a personal visit?"

"Yes, sir."

"Not regarding the incident on the Pike?"

"Not really, sir."

"Detectives are not to have personal visitors while on duty."

"I understand, sir, but I really do have something urgent to discuss with him."

The officer yawned and glanced again at the long line behind Max. With a shake of his head, he motioned Max to go through the door. "Second door on the left. If he's in the building, that's where he'll be."

Max pushed through the door before the frustrated officer could change his mind and entered a space no less hectic than the lobby he'd left. Officers, most uniformed but some in regular suits buzzed about, leaping from door to door in a row of offices. Outside the offices was a more open area with a series of desks, most unmanned at the late hour but all piled high with paperwork and teetering file folders.

The second door on the left stood closed but it contained a window, and Max could see Henry inside poring over something on his desk. Max knocked and the man looked up, surprise registering as he caught sight of the person interrupting his work. He motioned for Max to come in.

"Max," he said, standing with his hand outstretched. Max accepted the handshake and an invitation to sit in one of two chairs on the opposite side of the desk from Henry. "What brings you in tonight? Got something you need to tell me? Does your mother know you're here?"

Max felt his jaw clench. "She does, in fact. Is that a problem?"

"Oh, no, not a problem exactly. She mentioned earlier that she was hoping you weren't getting overly involved in the mess at the animal concession. You're not, are you?"

"I don't think so. A grisly murder shut down my place of employment and now a woman I know to be innocent has been arrested for the crime. I don't think I'm getting any more involved than I have a right to be."

Henry ran a hand through his hair and sighed. "Look, Max, I know this has been difficult."

"No. I don't think you do know. I want to help, if I can. I know you have to seek justice for Mr. Williamson, but I also want to maintain the credibility of the Hagenbecks who have been good to both me and my mother, and I want to help free the innocent woman who is behind bars right now only because she is foreign."

"And because, as I understand it, there is evidence against her."

"What evidence is that?" Max squared his shoulders. "Is it her brown skin?" He sniffed. "Or maybe it's her accent?" he said, stretching his lips to exaggerate his own strange version of American English.

"Max," Henry's words carried the weight of a warning. "I've been looking into the case a bit because I know it's important to you and because you are important to me."

"I doubt that."

"No, you are. You're the cherished son of a woman I admire greatly, and you are certainly important to me."

"If that's true, then help me. What have you discovered while looking at the case?"

"It would be highly unprofessional for me to share that with you."

"Because there is nothing, but if the murder can be pinned on a foreign woman without powerful friends, then it goes away. For everyone except the innocent woman and the people that care about her."

"You're frustrated. And probably overtired after the night you had last night."

Max squeezed his hands into fists, his fingernails digging into the flesh of his palms. "What do you know about the night I had?"

"I know that you went out drinking. Your mother was worried."

"I was drinking with the Hagenbeck employees so that I could ask them all about the night of the murder."

Henry closed the folder on his otherwise neat desk and slid it aside. "And did you learn anything?"

Max could have said that to a man, everyone from the Animal Paradise agreed that Shehani had a motive for wanting Pete dead. Instead, he mentioned the other assessment they all shared. "They agreed she wouldn't have killed him. It's not in her character."

"They might be right about that, but it is also a detail that has not escaped the notice of Detective Cullen and the officers working with him."

"Also," Max interjected, recalling Oscar's words, "if the intention was to use the alligators to dispose of the body, then the killer was unfamiliar with how much they could eat at one time."

"That could have been most of the people at Hagenbeck's," Henry said. "Would anyone who didn't take part in their feeding know that?"

"Most of us are cross-trained to better ensure the concession continues to run smoothly when problems arise."

"'You're telling me *everyone* working at the concession has experienced feeding the alligators?"

"Well," said Max. He scratched his chin. In reality, the gators ate every few days, and the task of feeding them hadn't yet fallen to all of the keepers, himself included. Shehani, too, rarely took part in basic animal care, as busy as the shows and promotion kept her. It was a stretch to suggest she possessed any particular knowledge of the alligators' feeding habits, but it was one Max decided he could make. "Many of us."

"That's precisely why Cullen released the snake charmer," Henry said. "Because he worked with all of the reptiles enough that he had taken part in feeding them. He knew precisely how much each of the animals would consume in one feeding. His confession made no sense."

Max sat forward, one hand on Henry's desk. "Inesh confessed?"

"Yes. He confessed, probably to try to protect his sister, but in doing so, he offered up a motive for her to have committed the murder."

Max curled his fingers into a fist and slammed it down. "Who else would have helped her? It *couldn't* have been her. She wasn't the only one with a motive. No one liked the man. Not Lorenz. Not Reuben. Not anyone."

"Calm down, please, Max," Henry said. "Look, I can't tell you much, but the case is not closed. Cullen got some new information from the coroner, and he isn't convinced he's got the right person."

"Is it the gangster?" Max asked.

Henry held up a palm. "I really can't talk about this. It's not even my case."

"So it is the gangster. Tom Egan?"

The detective closed his eyes and pinched the top of his nose. "This is a police investigation."

"I saw him with Pete that night."

"You saw him with Pete when he was alive." Henry dropped his hand and blew out a breath as if coming to a reluctant decision. "Egan is not the murderer. He has an alibi. He was seen in another part of town shortly after that and before the time the coroner is convinced Williamson died. Egan is a well-known character in the city. I don't doubt he was involved in some shady dealings with Williamson, but I'm afraid he didn't kill him."

"Then what does Cullen have to go on?" Max's head throbbed again, this time as if someone had tied a tight string around his brain.

"You keep asking me questions I can't answer."

"Can't or won't?" Max looked the detective straight in the eye. "Henry, I'm asking for your help."

Several moments passed in silence. Max continued to hold Henry's gaze as the detective chewed the inside of his cheek.

"Okay," he said at last. "You're not giving up, I see, and I suppose it can't hurt to tell you. The coroner noted some strange marks on the body."

"Alligator teeth marks?" Max said, eager to hear more, excited that Henry had agreed to tell him something.

"Well, yes, but you should know that they can look at the patterns of how the blood spilled on the victim and know whether those cuts were made before or after death. In the case of Pete, they were made before. That tells them Hagenbeck was right. The gators aren't responsible for the death. Something that might have been is a different kind of cut discovered in the skin right above his heart."

"He was stabbed?"

"In a manner. Something was forced into his chest, but it wasn't a knife. Too jagged and imprecise for that."

"It could have been something broken?"

"Exactly what the coroner thought." Henry brought his tented fingers to his chin, shifting his weight and causing his chair to squeak. "So, here's the really interesting part. The coroner had the same thought you did and so he was curious about what kind of broken object it might have been. He went looking. For example, if it had been wood, there may have been some kind of splinters on the torn parts of flesh. But it wasn't wood."

"No?" Max said, urging Henry on with his fascinating tale.

"No. In fact, at first he couldn't find any material at all, but when he looked closer, he noticed something he hadn't before. The skin around the very edges of the gash was irritated."

"That can't be too surprising."

"Not just from the trauma, though. It was definitely battered and bruised, but it also contained blistering."

"What broken object would cause blistering?"

"It wouldn't. The suggestion of the coroner, and what makes sense to me, is that there was a substance involved that he reacted to."

"Snake venom," Max said.

Henry stared at Max for an uncomfortably long time. "That's what the coroner thinks, and so does Cullen. The team at the crime scene found some collection vials but couldn't determine how the venom would have been delivered. Until the coroner located small shards of glass in the wound."

"It was a broken vial of venom. Someone forced it into his chest."

Henry raised an eyebrow, crossed his arms, and leaned back in his chair once more, "That was the detective's conclusion, too. You're good at this."

The praise lightened the weight that had settled onto Max's spirit. He couldn't help enjoying it a little bit, especially when the next thought occurred to him. "Where, precisely, did you say Pete was stabbed?"

Henry furrowed his brow. "I don't know. Why?"

"Because Shehani is small," Max explained. "She can't stand much over five feet tall. Pete was more than six feet tall. If someone stabbed him high in the chest, it couldn't have been Shehani."

Henry chewed his lip and frowned. "You're absolutely right, Max. The murderer would have had to be stronger and taller and, presumably, a man."

"So why is Shehani still behind bars?" Max sounded even to his own ears like a petulant child.

Henry put up a hand, urging Max to quiet down. "Because," he said, his words steady and calm. "there is a political game to be played here, and the reputation of the fair to think about. If there's no arrested suspect, then there's a killer at large at the biggest event in the world and the public will panic. That would ruin the reputation of the fair and of the city."

"And of the police department," Max added.

Henry shrugged.

"But there *is* a killer at large," Max said.

"Yes, probably, but most likely one that had a motive to kill only this one man. What we need to know is who had access to the venom. Who even knew about it?"

Max shook his head. "There weren't many of us that knew about it. When I mentioned collecting the venom to Lorenz, he didn't know what I was talking about. But it wouldn't have been hard to grab. It sits in glass vials on a shelf inside a cabinet behind the wall of reptiles. It's usually kept locked, but when the concession is closing up and last-minute care is being given to the animals, people aren't as careful. Anyone could grab a vial and smash it into someone if they were angry enough. They might not have even known what the vials contained."

Henry stood behind his desk and reached across to place a hand on Max's shoulder. "I think we need to go tell this to Detective Cullen."

Chapter 28

The grinding rattle of Detective Jerome Cullen's snoring could have awakened the dead. It assaulted their ears through the office door even before Henry's light knock, delivered with a raised eyebrow as he pushed his way in, Max on his heels.

"Jerry!" Henry's voice bounced off the four walls, filling the remaining space in the small room.

The detective jerked, his head rising from the cushion made by his folded arms on the desk. The man blinked and drew the back of one hand over his chin to wipe a thin line of drool. "Henry, what are you doing here?"

"Night shift," Henry said. "You?"

Cullen yawned and pulled a watch from the pocket of the jacket draped over the back of his chair. "Working late. I guess I fell asleep."

"Working on the Williamson case?"

"You gonna get on me about that again?" Cullen rubbed the back of his neck, and his eyes settled on Max. "Or are you interviewing my witnesses now?"

"Max is the son of a friend. He came to me with a thought that might be worth passing on."

Cullen yawned again and looked at Max. "Didn't I leave you my card?"

"You did, sir, äh, detective. I thought—"

"Don't read anything into it, Jerry. The kid is a friend. He works at the concession."

"I know he works at the concession." Cullen pinched the bridge of his nose. "That's why I interviewed him and left him my card in case he had any more light to shed on my case."

"You've made your point."

"Great. So, tell me, Mr. Eyer, what light have you to shed?"

Max eyed the door and wished he could be on the other side of it. Henry nudged him and Max attempted to calm himself. There was no reason to fear the detective on the other side of the desk, but now that Max stood in the man's office, he couldn't make himself say the words that would defend Shenani. A sense of failure clawed its way up his throat, burning like bile. After a pause, Henry spoke for him.

"What occurred to Max here was just how short your suspect is and how impossible it would have been for her to thrust the murder weapon into your tall victim's chest with enough force to kill him."

"Wouldn't have taken much force, though, if the murder weapon were poisoned," Cullen pointed out.

"But," Max said, surprised by the sharp defensive edge to his voice, "the venom wouldn't have slowed him down that fast. If he wasn't injured badly because of a lack of force, he'd have fought back. Was Shehani injured?"

"How do you know so much about this case?" Detective Cullen squinted up at his colleague. "Look, Henry," he glanced side-eyed at Max and corrected himself. "Detective Duncan, I've seen the report from the coroner and I appreciate you bringing this to my attention, but this is my case and I have considered it from every angle."

Henry placed a hand on Max's sleeve to stop him from responding. "We're not questioning your skill as a detective, Jerry."

"Aren't you?"

Henry didn't reply, and Max's limbs grew heavy.

"Look," Cullen said. He stood and pulled the coat off the back of the chair. "I'm going to go home and get some rest. I'll be back at this first thing in the morning, and I'll think about what you've said, but in the meantime, please consider this, Mr. Eyer. Hagenbeck's Animal Paradise is open, which means that you remain employed. It can only be open because the press knows were making progress on the case, something they understand because an arrest has been made. If one Indian woman spends a night or two behind bars while we get this figured out, I think it's worth it."

"She's Sinhalese," Max corrected. The detective looked at him as though he'd babbled utter nonsense. "She's Sinhalese from Ceylon. Not Indian."

"Okay, the not-Indian woman, then," Cullen said, slipping his arms into the sleeves of the coat.

Max's mouth fell open, the truth dawning. "You know she didn't do it."

"I know nothing of the sort."

Max spoke louder this time, eliciting a caution from Henry. "You know and you are leaving her in jail anyway."

"Someone has to be in jail." Cullen stepped around his desk and place a hand on the doorknob, a sure sign the conversation would proceed no further. "This is the largest, most spectacular fair the word has ever seen, double the size of the one in Chicago back in '93. We're safeguarding a hell of a legacy. A foreign woman with motive, access to a deadly poison, the means to administer it, and proximity to the crime sits in a jail cell doing her part to protect it."

He pulled open the door and motioned for Max and Henry to exit in front of him. As they did, Cullen said, "I hope you gentlemen both can understand that for now, she needs to be guilty, even if she's innocent."

Chapter 29

Inspiration struck Max in the middle of the night, fighting its way through sweat-soaked sheets and the half-delirium of sleep. Injustice loomed as a great, shadowy figure over every attempt to calm his mind until finally he'd sat up in bed, newly energized by a plan beginning to take shape.

"You are bright-eyed this morning," Frieda said, smiling at him as she poured a cup of coffee for herself, squirming baby on her hip. She set the coffee pot on the stove and grabbed a piece of toast to hand to the baby who she settled into a high chair at the end of the table. Squeezed in the pudgy toddler fist, the toast crumbled on its way to the child's slobbery mouth.

"I have a plan," Max said, though he explained no further, unsure how much Frieda knew of the tense situation at the Animal Paradise. The prospect of answering a long list of questions overwhelmed him.

"Ooh, does this have anything to do with your mysterious lady?" Frieda settled into her seat and began buttering her own toast.

As awkward as this conversational direction promised to be, Max preferred it to the more complete and complicated truth. "She's not married," he blurted, then grimaced, wishing he could pull back the statement.

Luckily, Frieda giggled. "She sounds perfect for you, then."

"How did you know there was a woman involved?"

"You are more transparent than you imagine, my friend. A woman can see such things. Also, your mother mentioned she thought you have interest in a woman she wasn't too sure about. Always a good sign."

"Is it?"

Frieda put down her toast and reached to brush a wispy curl from her daughter's forehead. "I think it can be. Mothers tend to be a bit threatened initially when their sons find someone really special. I assume she is really special?"

"She is." That was at least the truth. Whether or not he might have a future with Shenani, Max didn't know. There seemed to be a lot of barriers there, but then Reuben had mentioned a Hagenbeack who had married a Sinhalese woman. They lived in Ceylon, of course, but Max held no particular attachment to St. Louis or, for that matter, to America. He could just about envision the day when the fair ended and Lorenz and Reuben packed up the show to travel as a circus with their animals and Sinhalese mahouts in tow. Max could go, too. He could marry Shehani, and no one would even be the wiser outside of the circus itself where such a thing would surely be accepted. He smiled to think of it.

"Ah, Maxie, you are in love."

He smiled. "Mutti is the only one who ever calls me Maxie."

"I'm sorry."

"No, no, it's okay. It feels like, I don't know, almost that you are a sister to me when you use that name."

She reached across the table and took his hand. A dimple formed in her smooth cheek. "I always wanted a brother."

A few months earlier, the interaction would have tangled Max's insides, but his relationship with Frieda had become one of ease rather than awkwardness, and the warmth of their interaction followed him all the way to the fairgrounds where he focused on the important task at hand.

Shehani's wrongful imprisonment might mean security for the concession and for the fair as a whole, but it was necessary only because the real culprit continued to roam free. Max would demonstrate the innocence of the woman he loved by proving the guilt of another, and he had an idea how to do it.

He entered the fairgrounds at the Lindell entrance as usual, but instead of turning right to wind his way to the Pike, he took some extra time to head through the Plaza of St. Louis and south to the Palace of Education. The wide doors at the front of the palace remained closed with the fair opening thirty minutes away, but as Max surveyed the building, several employees walked around the side that ran along the Grand Basin to enter through side doors. He fell in step behind one man wearing a long coat and top hat. The gentleman held the door open behind him, a gesture Max particularly appreciated given his own rough attire, more suitable to cleaning up after animals than as a presenter in one of the great palaces. Perhaps the man assumed Max was a maintenance worker who belonged in the building.

He thanked the man and hurried away, walking as confidently as he could manage, as though he really did belong there. On his previous visit to the Palace of Education, with Mutti and Henry Duncan, Max had entered through the main doors. It took him a minute to gain his bearings, but before long he saw what he'd been looking for—a small, high table sitting at an angle against a framed display labeled Fingerprint System of Identification.

The table sat bare and alone with no one near it to assist him. Max planted his feet in front of it and waited. He would be late to work at the Animal Paradise, but this was more important. Reuben would have to understand. Max would simply explain to him that the fate of an innocent woman, of the entire concession, and even of the fair itself rested on what Max might discover.

Lost as he was, playing through this imagined conversation, Max did not initially notice when a man wearing the full uniform of the London Metropolitan Police approached the display. The officer tapped a finger on the table, and said, "Excuse me, sir. Could I help you with something?"

The same officer who'd inked Henry's fingertips three days earlier gave no indication that he recognized Max.

"I wonder if you could explain to me your system of fingerprinting."

The officer's head tilted to the side and consulted with a watch that he took from his uniform pocket. "The fair isn't open yet, son. How did you get in here?"

"I work here," Max said, and then clarified, "on the Pike, actually. It's going to be another busy day and I wondered if you could answer my question now."

He slid the watch back into his pocket. "It's a big question. Could you be more specific?" The man spoke with an accent similar to Reuben's, but thicker and more difficult for Max's ear to capture. He leaned close and observed the officer's lips forming the words.

"How do you..." Max thought for a beat about how to ask the question he most needed to know without alerting the detective to his intentions. "That is, I know how to take the impression of a fingerprint from someone with ink, but how do you discover a fingerprint at a crime scene that a criminal may have left behind?"

"Ah." The man grinned and pointed a finger into the air, working his way around to the other side of the table. He reached into a drawer below the tabletop and pulled out a small oval tin and what looked to Max like a cosmetic brush that Mutti might use to apply a light coating of color on her cheeks. "That is a great question, young man. And an exciting one.

The science of fingerprinting is rapidly developing, and the answer to your question depends on what kind of surface you're dealing with."

"What do you mean?"

The detective pointed to a clear glass plate sitting in the middle of the table that Max hadn't previously noticed. "The smoother the material, the simpler it is to find something useful. It'll be easier for me to show you." The officer popped open the tin which contained a dark powder that the brush picked up when he ran it across its surface.

"Go ahead and touch the glass with a fingertip. Do it in a few places if you like."

Max complied as the officer looked on and gave an encouraging nod.

"Now then, we take a fine particulate matter like this and brush lightly over anyplace a fingerprint may have been inadvertently deposited." While he spoke, the detective brushed across the glass Max had just touched. "The particulates stick to oils left by the skin, and because fingerprints are made up of distinctive patterns of raised ridges, the oils are deposited in those same patterns."

He set the brush and tin aside and removed a small cylindrical object from his pocket that he manipulated so that it shined a narrow light out of the end. "It's called a flashlight," he said, correctly interpreting the motivation behind Max's dropped jaw. "Ingenious little invention. It uses electricity generated by a battery. They don't last long, but they're very useful."

Max bent over the table and squinted at the glass. In the narrow band of light, a powder-covered smudge emerged and, upon closer inspection, he could see swirling lines forming patterns of arches and circles.

"You can see it, yeah?"

Max stood straight. "I can. That's amazing."

The detective clicked off his flashlight. "Now I can look at this under magnification and compare it with our files of fingerprints, which will allow me to correctly identify a potential criminal connected with the scene. It's some of the most reliable technology we have in crime solving today, and it is infinitely superior to eyewitness accounts and the Bertillon method of suspect identification."

The detective turned to the next display over, which included several framed panels mounted on the wall displaying illustrations of various profiles, head shapes, and facial features. He pointed to them and explained, "The Bertillon System uses precise body measurements to aid in identification of criminals."

While the detective spoke of the other exhibit, his back turned to his own display, Max reached over the table and plucked out a second set of powder and brush and dropped them into his pocket.

"The trouble is," the detective was saying. He turned back to look at Max. "People can sometimes have very similar measurements. Fingerprints, on the other hand, are entirely unique to each individual."

"That's fascinating," Max said honestly.

The enthusiastic detective nodded. "It really is. It also helps us to identify victims sometimes, too. It's a good idea to get your fingerprints on record, if you have a little more time."

Max shrugged. He didn't want to raise the man's suspicion by running off too eagerly, especially when presented with a good opportunity for an interesting souvenir. Eight o'clock had arrived. Fair visitors wound their way through the palace displays, and a line would soon form. If he was late for work already, he couldn't see that a few more minutes would matter greatly. Max agreed and held out his hand.

The detective reached into the drawer again to pull out two cards and an ink pad. Max swiped at a bead of nervous sweat on his temple, but the man gave no indication that he'd noticed anything unusual.

"Great. It'll be quick. We'll take a set for you to keep and one for us to file away." He winked and cocked a half grin. "In case you turn out to be a criminal."

Chapter 30

Max ran his thumb over the stained pads of his fingers, scrutinizing the whorls and ridges, the artist in him wondering if their unique patterns might have a story to tell, if this composition that could reveal a criminal might also stipulate what sort of man he was. This question took up residence in his mind sometimes but never yielded an answer. He knew only that his life had taken a dramatic turn from the course set out for him at birth—that of a potato grower on a small farm in a small corner of the world.

Rustling in his pocket with each step across the fairgrounds was a card filled with the stamped images of his fingertips, its twin now buried in the files of the detectives of Scotland Yard, a knowledge that had no business making him nervous, and yet his pulse raced at the thought.

More likely his agitation came from his tardiness. Visiting the criminology exhibit had taken more time than Max thought it would, and by now his absence from the Animal Paradise would surely have been noticed. When Oscar caught him walking past the ticket windows and through the front gate, Max registered the man's annoyance.

"I had to chase the damned goats." Oscar threw up his hands as he spoke these words through clenched teeth, his brow beaded with sweat either from the exertion of the ordeal or from anger with Max.

"How'd they get out?"

Oscar waved a hand in the air. The other held a bucket of dead fish.

"Hell if I know. Beasts were running loose around the arena this morning. Maintenance is trying to figure it out."

Max pictured the two troublemakers Flick and Flock prancing free around the concession—their true animal paradise—maybe for the entire night and couldn't help but smile. "Reuben sent me home before closing time last night. If anything was left open, it wasn't my fault."

"Nothing left open, far as anyone could tell this morning. No other animals got out of that enclosure. Little varmints are escape artists." Oscar set the fish bucket on the ground. A little girl who reminded Max of Martha let go of her father's hand to come peer at its contents, then swiftly backed away, pinching her nose.

Oscar stepped toward Max and pointed a finger directly at him. "It's not my job to chase them down."

"I'm sorry I'm late." Max retreated from the quaking finger. "I had an errand I had to take care of. For the concession."

Oscar dropped his hand and stared Max down, as if he could suss out the truth of this claim by gaping at him. The statement was true enough, Max reasoned. He meant to determine Pete's true killer so that Shehani could return and Hegenbeck's Animal Paradise on the Pike could leave this whole disastrous situation in the past.

After several beats, Oscar still hadn't spoken, the only sounds belonging to those of the Pike—the competing calls of the barkers overselling the delights of their concessions, the excited chatter of passersby, the barking of an ostrich enduring the cinch of a saddle.

Max ventured a question. "How far did you have to chase them? All the way to Mysterious Asia? Did they line up with the dancing girls?"

That engendered a chuckle. Oscar backed up. "Nah. They turned right this time. Made it all the way to Cairo before I caught up with them. One of them tried to eat my shirt. Nearly took my finger off. I don't know how you can stand those things."

"Thank you, Oscar. Goats are assholes." Max smiled, recalling the words Reuben had said to him about Flick and Flock who, other than maybe Lizzie the elephant, were probably two of his favorite animals in the entire Hagenbeck collection.

"How can I make it up to you?" Max didn't want to be known as a man who collected favors he never returned.

Oscar scratched his head. "I wouldn't mind some help with the reptile swamp tomorrow."

"Sunday? What are you doing to the reptiles?"

"The police have given us the go-ahead to clean up the scene. We can open it once the gators are removed. Lorenz found some place that's going to take them, and with the fairgrounds closed for the day, looks like tomorrow's the time to make a transfer and scrub down the boardwalk."

Max's shoulders stiffened and then relaxed as the meaning of these words sunk in. He leaned his head toward Oscar's and said quietly, "Are you saying the police are finished with the boardwalk? And they haven't cleaned up anything yet?"

Oscar laughed. "Are you kidding? They're not going to clean up a thing. We've been told we can move in now and do whatever we need to do. The mess is all ours to deal with. Besides, Lorenz would rather it was us anyway. He doesn't want any detergent in the swamp to endanger his animals. He cares about that above anything else. He might have put it above profits if Williamson hadn't always put his foot down."

Max chewed his lip. "They really didn't get along very well, did they, Lorenz and Pete?"

"Oil and water."

"But I suppose Lorenz did regret his business partner's death."

"Regretted the change in diet for his alligators, I dare say, though the creatures didn't seem to mind too much."

Max swallowed a chuckle. "Makes our job tomorrow easier, I suppose. Shouldn't be any body parts left over."

"Let's hope not." Oscar bent to pick up his bucket of fish. "I gotta get back to work. Got some hungry sea lions to get to." He headed off down the path with a casual wave behind him. "Have a good day, Max."

Max returned Oscar's wave and walked in the opposite direction toward Reuben's office to check for his assigned morning responsibilities, which he had little interest in completing. He scanned the handwritten list to determine which of the tasks could be put off and which needed his immediate attention. No animals would go hungry, of course, and as long as he gave each of his designated areas a brief once-over, he could clean more thoroughly later.

He checked the time. Max had barely more than two hours before he needed to be available to assist in the arena with the first show at noon. If he hurried, he could just manage to get the bare minimum finished up and have time to swing by the closed off reptile swamp.

As if he were in a trance, the memories stored in his muscles led him through his chores until at last he discovered a few spare minutes. Max hurried past the elephant enclosure where he pretended not to notice Reuben motioning to him as he and two of the mahouts encouraged one of the elephants toward the wide gate that would lead them out of their enclosure. Soon the animal would be planted in front of the concession entrance to aid the barker in drawing a crowd for the first arena show.

He passed the big cats next. The male lion Trieste perched, alert on the highest point of the largest rock, his harem of two yellow-haired lionesses resting below. Along the edge of the trench a tiger paced, stalking a young woman walking past with an ice cream treat. He suspected the big cat had no interest in the ice cream.

PARADISE ON THE PIKE

A small crowd mingled outside the closed off swamp, and when Max stepped across the rope to pull open the slit in the tarpaulin, a woman called out to stop him. "Excuse me, sir, do you work here?"

"I do," Max grumbled, dismayed at both the interruption and at the implication that the woman might be considering crossing the rope as he did. She seemed the type, as young as him, slim and pretty, with blonde hair that frizzed in the humidity, escaping from the knot at the back of her head.

She blinked long lashes at him. "May I ask what's back there?"

"It's a reptile exhibit," Max said, and when the young lady quirked one perfectly shaped eyebrow, Max recognized he had to offer more. "The animals are unavailable for now. For their own safety."

"For their safety, or the public's?" A man stepped forward from the milling crowd and asked the question. He had the familiarity of a frequent visitor, but Max couldn't place him for certain. The Animal Paradise remained one of the most popular concessions on the Pike and the gangster Tom Eger was not its lone repeat visitor. This question, too, implied that the man knew something more than the average fairgoer. Max didn't know how best to answer it.

"I don't know what you mean, sir. The animals were agitated and their health is the most important thing here at the Animal Paradise on the Pike. They have been given some much needed quiet and privacy."

"I heard there was an attack." Another man from the crowd said this through a thick mustache. A bowler hat, too big for him, sat atop his head, and he wore a satisfied smirk as his comment, more statement than question, produced a flurry of anxious glances around him. More people had begun to gather, their forward progress through the concession halted by curiosity at seeing a Hagenbeck employee in front of the forbidden enclosure, engaging with the public.

"Where did you hear such a thing?" Max asked in an attempt to avoid commenting on the rumor.

"Isn't it true this entire concession was closed for a full day recently, because there had been an animal attack?"

"There was no attack," Max said, and it was true. According to the coroner's assessment, the alligators were simply hungry, pointy-teethed innocents in all of this. "The concession was closed because one of the workers had an accident and we were all shaken up about it. Including the animals. The enclosure will be open again on Monday. There's nothing secret going on here."

"That's what you would say if there were something secret going on." The young lady who'd first addressed him said this as she placed a hand on the forbidding rope. It wobbled under her grip.

Max's back stiffened. "Maybe," he said, "but I'm telling you the truth."

"Then what are you going to do behind that curtain?"

Max shot a pointed look at her trespassing hand. She sneered back at him and didn't move it. "The animals in this closed exhibit need care regardless. And if you have further questions about it, I think you'd better speak with Herr Hagenbeck himself, or perhaps Reuben Castang, our head trainer."

The man in the bowler hat added, "Or your business manager Pete Williamson?"

Max hesitated, unsure how to respond, but certain now that he recognized the man. He had to be a reporter, which might explain why Max had seen him at the police station the night he visited Henry. Probably the man had been causing trouble there, too, sniffing around for a story. "I'm afraid Mr. Williamson is unavailable."

"Because he's dead, isn't he?"

Max refused to let the shock of the statement play out on his face, his jaw muscles tightening with determination. "Where did you hear that?"

"Please answer the question. Was Mr. Williamson killed by an alligator?"

"That sounds like a question better addressed to the police."

"Or was he killed by one of those Indians you've got running around?"

Max's hands began to shake, the tarpaulin to quiver. "I really can't answer these questions. I don't have time for this. I have work to do. I am very busy."

When the curtain flap closed behind him, Max bent over, hands on his knees and drew several deep breaths, still trembling. The reporter's questions and the agitated murmurings of the crowd reached him through the thick cloth, but no one attempted to follow. It occurred to him that he might pull back the flap, confirm their suspicions, and invite them in to see for themselves if the beasts were hungry.

He'd enjoy seeing the reporter speechless, the blonde fainting dead away at the suggestion. Max's hands stopped shaking and his breathing came easier. The curtain could not block out all of the noise, but it was a relief to be tucked away from the anxious curiosity of the fairgoers.

Let Lorenz handle questions from the press. No one would choose Max as spokesman for the Animal Paradise anyway, and especially not, by extension, for the fair. Reporters, he was sure, would love to sink their teeth into a sensational story of gruesome death at the grandest World's Fair ever seen, pinned on ferocious beasts and foreign savages, between which the public saw little difference. Max could not forestall such an inevitability with his often unreliable words. He could help most by keeping silent, and by forcing the investigation into Pete's death away from Shehani, but had to be quick about it. The one truly honest thing he'd said to the gathered crowd was he'd not had time for their questions. Reuben would expect him at the arena in a handful of minutes. Max had to hurry.

Despite the ruckus on the other side of the curtain, an eerie stillness settled on the boardwalk and he proceeded carefully, scanning the water for signs of the gators. He located the animals, each on the opposite end of their murky pond and neither interested in him. The body of the smaller of the two stretched partially onto the dry ground, its snout aimed away from him. The larger of the two, approximately nine feet in length, basked in a sunny patch at the edge of the water and offered no indication that it registered Max's presence.

With cautious steps, he moved along the boardwalk, moving around a dark-stained patch. Little else remained to tell the tale of Pete's messy end, though the handrail bore a good smear of the man's dried blood. Max examined the smear carefully. Unbroken, it clung to the grooves of the wood like a film and contained no obvious trace that anyone had put a hand into it.

Max paused at the end of the boardwalk, searching his brain for any idea about where he might discover a fingerprint that could betray a killer and lead the police away from Shehani. The wood surface, even if it had been touched, would not reveal a fingerprint so easily, a fact he knew from his conversation with the officer at the Scotland Yard booth. He needed a smooth material, one from which the minuscule, oil-coated ridges would stand out. He needed glass, like the glass front of a vivarium or perhaps a vial that held a deadly venom.

The glass that delivered venom into Pete's heart would of course not be accessible, as the shards Max knew of had been broken off in the body. A quick scan didn't reveal any forgotten scraps. Max looked at the water's edge. Something could have fallen in during a struggle. He crouched for a closer look and as he did so, the larger of the two alligators turned its toothy snout toward him, shuffling one clawed front leg.

Max stood, deciding that even if some forgotten piece of the murder weapon had made it into the pond, the water would have washed away any fingerprints by now. He backed to the far edge of the boardwalk away from the water, never taking his eyes off the larger alligator, which made no sudden moves but kept watching Max as he walked to the end of the boardwalk and examined the vivaria.

Behind the glass fronts, the vivarium residents moved little more than the gators had. Snakes, both large and small, deadly and harmless, coiled in their restrictive homes. Cleaned daily under normal circumstances, the glass now featured noticeable smudging on its smooth glass front, not surprising given the number of fairgoers who regularly tapped with grubby hands against the displays. Max decided against looking for prints on these, as most would belong to the innocent public.

Instead, he turned his attention to the supply cabinet on the side of the display. Normally locked, the cabinet door hung unlatched. The shelves inside held cleaning supplies as well as several of the glass vials and dishes used to store and dry venom. None of these contained the substances themselves. Max suspected the police had removed any that did, but undeterred, he used the supplies he'd lifted from the criminology exhibit to carefully dust each glass surface. Without the aid of the detective's handy little light, Max struggled to see any individual ridges, but the sides of three of the glass vials featured obvious oily deposits. These prints should belong to no more than a select few members of the concession's staff and, along with any prints on the vials the police held, would establish a connection to the crime scene. Unexpected prints could point to a killer, and more importantly, the absence of anyone's prints could go a long way toward exonerating them.

Max tucked the marked vials into his coat and, with a whispered hope that the curious crowd outside the exhibit had dispersed, he hurried down the boardwalk, glass vials tinkling in his pocket, and determined not to speak a word.

Chapter 31

Max opened the front door to his uncle's house to discover Mutti sitting on the stairs leading to the second floor and wringing her hands. She'd been waiting for him. How long he could only guess, but it had been a late evening at the concession. Reuben had asked for Max's assistance through the last arena show of the day, and then he'd helped settle the bears and the big cats into the indoor portions of their enclosures for the night. The grandfather clock in the sitting room would have chimed eleven before he walked in.

"Maxie," Mutti said, her tone carrying a silent plea he had no time to puzzle out.

"It's been a long day." He walked past the stairs and pushed through the door to the kitchen where a plate of dinner, courtesy of his thoughtful aunt or cousin, awaited him. The covered plate on the counter held little interest for Max, his stomach knotted as it was with anticipation. Inside his pocket, his knuckles brushed against the glass vials he hoped would point the blame for Pete's murder in a new direction and make it impossible for Detective Cullen to continue to hold Shehani. He thought of the magnifying glass Claude used to examine and torture insects and decided to circle back through the sitting room. With luck, he could find the glass in the toy box that stored the children's playthings.

The kitchen door opened a crack and Mutti peeked at him. "We need to talk." She pushed the door open wide enough to let herself into the room and with her came a shift in the room's atmosphere, as if a storm brewed in her wake. "It's about Henry," she said, and her cheeks puffed out slightly with a held breath.

Icy dread cascaded down his back. The last conversation he wanted to have with his mother was about the new man in her life. He wished her happiness, he really did. After all the evil she had experienced at the hands of his father, Max did not begrudge her that, but he didn't want or need another father figure at this point in his life, even if Henry seemed to be a decent enough man.

"Can we talk about it in the morning?" He placed his palm flat across his forehead. "I have a terrible headache. I just want to go to bed."

Her papery cheeks deflated. "Of course. Can I get you anything?"

Max shook his head. "No. All I need is rest."

His mother dropped into one of the kitchen chairs and massaged her temples as if she had a true headache.

"Good night then." Max injected his voice with as much strain as he could muster, placed a comforting hand against her upper arm, and walked out of the room, attempting to hide his excitement. Before climbing the stairs, he turned right into the sitting room and gently flipped open the lid to the toy box. The magnifying glass sat right on top. Max clasped the toy and took the steps two at a time up to his third-floor attic bedroom.

Over the next several hours, Max pored over the loops and whorls and arch patterns of each fingerprint he could isolate. Just as the detective had suggested, differences began to jump out at him, some obvious, others more subtle. It was a slow process that required a great deal of concentration. By the light of a single oil lamp that sat beside his bed, Max worked late into the night until becoming confident he'd managed to identify a small handful of unique prints and sketch the rough differences in the patterns he'd discovered.

PARADISE ON THE PIKE

Dawn had barely begun to streak the sky with the oranges and pinks of sunrise when Max looked up from his work and yawned, satisfied that his idea, once demonstrated to Detective Cullen, might help catch a killer, or at the very least make it more difficult to blame an innocent woman. Shehani's fingerprints, he felt sure, would not be among his collection, and if she could not be connected to the scene of Pete's death, then she could not be found guilty of his murder.

Max yawned again and he stretched the sore muscles of his neck and shoulders that complained of a long night hunched over the vials with no sleep, but he didn't have time to rest. Sunday morning had arrived, the fairgrounds were closed to the public, and soon the boardwalk exhibit would be scrubbed clean of any other potential clues. If his findings were to have any bearing on the case's outcome, Max had to deliver them to the police as soon as possible.

The police station stood ablaze with light in the dark of the early morning. Since the start of the fair, St. Louis had become a city that did not sleep, though its criminals did at least seem to slow down toward dawn. Max walked into the lobby, expecting to be greeted once again with a large crowd, but aside from an officer sitting at the large front desk, the space contained one other person. A haggard man clad in a long coat and in need of a good shave sat slumped on a bench beside the door that led to the detective offices, his chin resting on his chest. He didn't look up when Max walked in. The officer at the desk did.

"What can I do for you?" Not the same man who greeted Max on his first visit to the station, this officer was younger and much too chipper for the hour with an exaggerated smile and a ruddy German complexion.

"I need to see Detective Henry Duncan," Max said, wondering if the fatigue that tainted his voice would help or hurt his cause.

The young officer glanced down at a piece of paper on the desk. "I'm afraid Detective Duncan isn't in right now. Most of our detectives aren't in yet this morning." He pointed to the bench with the large man who'd begun to snore softly. "You're welcome to wait."

Max was about to decline when the door opened behind him and Detective Cullen walked in.

"Mr. Eyer," he said loudly as if attempting to compensate for obvious weariness. "First thing in the morning. To what do I owe this visit?"

"He's waiting to see Detective Duncan," the helpful desk officer said.

Cullen scowled at the young man. "I wouldn't mind having a word with him myself." Then he looked at Max. "Is this about the Paradise on the Pike case? Are you meddling again and trying to play detective?"

"I—" Max didn't know quite what to say. He'd wanted to see Henry first, to solicit his help in getting through to Cullen, because Max *was* meddling. He *was* playing detective. But the police had arrested the wrong person. What else was he to do? He swallowed his anxiety. "I think I do have some more information. Can we talk in your office?"

The detective closed his eyes and sighed, then waved Max toward the door. "Fine."

Cullen keyed his way into his tiny office and flipped on the electric light. "Sit," he said without the warmth of welcome before lowering himself into his own chair on the other side of the desk. "What have you got for me?"

Max took the smudged vials, carefully wrapped in a soft rag, from his pocket and placed them, along with his sketches, on Cullen's desk.

The detective squinted at them. "What is this?"

"Fingerprints from the vials in the reptile swamp the ones used for collecting venom."

Cullen blinked at him. "What are you talking about?"

"Fingerprinting. When a person touches a smooth surface, they leave oil behind from the raised ridges of their fingers—"

Cullen stopped Max with a look and his eyebrows pulled together, transforming his face into a mask of anger. "You removed these from my crime scene?"

"I didn't touch anything until you were finished with the scene and had given permission for the staff to clean up the space." Max could hear the thud of his own heart in his ears. "The alligators are being moved today and the exhibit will be cleaned. I am an immigrant who cleans up animal droppings for a living and, with all due respect, you and your officers are not likely to listen to me. I had to do something."

"And so how did you think to do this?" Cullen's whispered voice somehow filled the room's every crevice.

"I saw it at the fair. No two people in the entire world have the same fingerprints. There's an exhibit at the Palace of Education, run by Scotland Yard."

"Ah." The detective shuffled a stack of papers on his desk. "Scotland Yard. Well, then, that's something."

Max suspected this would be the best opening he would get, and so he launched into an explanation of what he'd done to pare down and sort the prints, demonstrating for the detective using the card of his own fingerprints taken by the Scotland Yard detective.

Cullen listened attentively until Max finished, then the detective pursed his lips and looked hard at Max. "So, Mr. Eyer, what exactly am I supposed to do with these?"

Max had given a great deal of thought to this answer, and he said with confidence, "Take the fingerprints of the victim first. The coroner can help with this. That way you can eliminate them from the bunch. Then collect the fingerprints from all your suspects and see if any of them match and can place them at the scene of the murder. It won't pinpoint the guilty person with certainty, but it might help you narrow your search. You could ask the detective at the crime exhibit to help."

Cullen examined the top page of Max's sketches, filled with carefully enlarged approximations of the ridges and grooves that made up an identity. The detective flipped his left hand, palm up, and squinted at the tips of his own fingers while his other hand tapped a slow, steady rhythm on his desktop, like the ticking of a clock.

A minute passed, maybe two, before Cullen balled his fist and said, "Thank you for this, Mr. Eyer. Now get out of my office."

Chapter 32

Even under the best of circumstances, Sundays filled Max with dread. When he was a child, the day had brought increased tension and the ever-present danger of Felix's explosiveness. For many years, Mutti had attempted to drag her stubborn husband to church. By the time Max turned six, she'd given up trying, though she still subjected Max to stiff, itchy clothes and interminable sermons he could never understand.

When Max turned eight, Felix decided his son had attended all the church a man need attend and the regular weekly struggle began again. Max didn't mind not having to wear the itchy clothes or pretend to listen to the droning preacher, but his heart ached to see Mutti lose the fight over his soul. He'd not quite turned ten when she gave up going to church herself. At the time, Max assumed she'd attended all the church a woman need attend. She hadn't even welcomed the preacher when he endeavored to visit them following Felix's death.

Now that she'd been reunited with her brother in St. Louis, Mutti had returned to Sunday morning worship with his family in a Lutheran church that looked like a castle and held services in German. Despite her encouragement, Max had yet to join them and had been grateful for the excuse of his job at Hagenbeck's Animal Paradise on the Pike. The fair might have closed for the Sabbath, but the animals needed to eat.

If he were honest, Max might have rather been singing hymns and sitting on a hard pew than strolling down the empty pathways of the fair. Not entirely abandoned, the grounds boasted some activity. Maintenance men made repairs, Pike workers living onsite milled about, savage peoples with nowhere else to go populated their native exhibits, and a small contingent of Jefferson guardsmen kept the ground secure from the general public. Still, compared to the enormous crowds during the week, Sunday brought desolation and bleakness to the fairgrounds.

At the main gate, Max flashed his employee identification to the guard who waved him in without looking at it. Detective Cullen's rude dismissal weighed on Max's exhausted mind, and the oppressive atmosphere of abandoned spaces around him filled him with an unease that stiffened in his legs and tightened in his chest the closer he got to the animal concession.

Hagenbeck's Animal Paradise was one of the few concessions on the Pike that boasted close to a full crew on a Sunday morning, though the presence of busy men unrolling hoses, shoveling animal droppings, and hauling fresh hay and buckets of feed did little to lift Max's melancholy.

The animals, too, seemed pensive, the elephants barely lifting their heads when Max entered their yard. Leopard, lion, and tiger made no move to stalk him along the edge of their trench as he walked by. Sea lions allowed fish to fall at their flippers rather than catch them in their jaws. After six days of performances, the concession, both men and beasts, needed a rest.

One o'clock arrived before Max finished his own essential chores. He sat on a rock beside the pond in the herbivore exhibit and rested for no more than a few seconds before he received a gentle head butt from Flick. He scratched the goat behind the ear and stood, attempting to rub some sensation back into his fatigue-burdened limbs.

"Well," he told the goat, "I suppose I can't avoid it any longer." Flick bleated encouragement and Max let himself out through the back of the enclosure to head toward the reptile exhibit.

The space had already undergone a transformation, with the canvas curtains removed and piled in a heap on the pathway. Finn, crowbar in hand, worked to pull apart the frame that had held it. A keeper named Tom polished the glass fronts of the vivaria, the spray from his bottle causing a stir among some of the occupants. Another keeper worked on the bloodstains on the boardwalk with a rag and soapy water. Oscar wore a pair of large hip waders and stood in the pond, trowel in hand, replacing plants on the far bank. Flashes of orange zipped through the water around his legs. The man looked up at Max's approach and followed his gaze to the water.

"They're koi fish," Oscar said. "Japanese, apparently. The Hagenbecks hold a lot of sway in the animal market. Fellas brought these beauties to fill in the space when they came for the gators. You missed all the fun there."

"Sounds like it," Max said. "But someone has to do the work while you play around in the water."

Oscar chuckled. "If you think this isn't work, grab a scrub brush."

Max snatched another rag from the soapy bucket. He leaned over the railing to scrub at the bloodstain on the far side, anxious to finish this last part of his work. Without shows to conduct and animal rides to coordinate, the concession became much easier to run on a Sunday. His bed called to him, but he also knew that with whatever spare time he had, he would return to the police station to continue pressuring Detective Cullen into action on the fingerprints in hopes of seeing Shehani freed. Perhaps Henry would be there this time and could help.

What should have been an uplifting thought, however, faded into worry when Max pulled back his rag for a rinse and saw the blood tinge of the bubbles floating atop the bucket. His fingertips, too, had been stained pink by his efforts, a taint that would not fully wash off no matter how long he rubbed his fingers together in the water.

A hand on his back stopped him. Max pulled his hand and the rag from the bucket and saw that Reuben stood over him.

"Max," the trainer said with a sad frown that did not suit him. "If you have a minute, we need you in Lorenz's office." Reuben turned to walk away before Max could wrap his tongue around a follow-up question. A glance toward Oscar, who shrugged, shed no light on the summons.

"Almost finished here," Max said through a hitch in his throat, though the trainer was already too far away to hear it. A call to Lorenz's office couldn't mean anything good. Suddenly dizzy, Max sat back on his haunches on the boardwalk where he stayed for several minutes, wishing he could capture the vision of a future in which he traveled with the Hagenbeck Circus, Shehani by his side, an image that swirled from his grasp into an unattainable black mist.

"You go ahead. We're just about done here anyway." Oscar's voice snapped Max back to reality.

Max complied as if in a trance, stood, and walked out of the reptile swamp toward the concession entrance. Lorenz's office, which had been shared by Pete, was located along the edge of Paradise on the Pike in between the front gate with its ticket booths and the restaurant. Max had rarely been inside, but it was a spacious office with a window that looked over the front walkway and the entrance to the arena. The door was rarely closed, but today it stood fast.

Max knocked with a trembling hand and when the door opened, he was surprised to see a stone-faced Henry with his hand on the knob. Behind him stood Detective Cullen, one uniformed St. Louis police officer, and a member of the Jefferson Guard. Lorenz sat at his desk, his hand tented beneath his chin. Reuben stood beside him and did not look directly at Max when he entered.

"What is going on?" The edges of Max's vision began to blur and he wavered on his feet.

PARADISE ON THE PIKE

Henry reached out a hand, catching Max's elbow with a gentle squeeze. "Max, are you okay?"

"Why wouldn't I be okay?" His voice quavered.

Henry surveyed him up and down with an unusual expression that Max might have sworn was pity, or perhaps even fear.

"What's going on, Henry? Did they discover something in the fingerprints? Have they been able to clear Shehani?"

Henry shook his head and Max's shoulders sagged. All the effort he had gone to clear the name of the beautiful Sinhalese girl and none of it would pay off, none of it had done any good at all.

Then Henry said, "Yes."

"What?"

"Yes, Max. Detective Cullen has identified the murderer. The fingerprinting you provided pushed the investigation in a new direction."

"That's great," Max said.

"Max," said Henry sadly. He spared a glance toward the other men gathered in the office before looking back at Max. "I wonder if we could step outside and talk."

Max let Henry guide him through the door, which shut behind them with a soft click.

"What is it, Henry? Should we sit? You look ill."

Standing in the cool shade of the upper walkway, Henry appeared unusually pale, his skin covered in a light sheen of perspiration. The distant bleat of a goat broke the silence of the empty concession.

Henry licked his lips. "I need you to tell me about the night of the murder."

"I've told this story already," max said. "I was with you and my mother."

"I mean after that. You said you needed to come back here and take care of some loose ends. What did you do?"

"I checked on the animals that are normally on my list—the herbivores and the ostriches. I played some with the goats because the more familiar they are with me, the easier they are to handle. I sorted tack for Reuben and then walked around a little and talked with some of the other employees."

Henry held his stare firmly on Max, encouraging him to continue, but the words stuck in his mouth as memories from that night tumbled over him, catching not on the details he'd shared but on the spaces between them, some as murky as the alligators' swamp water before it had been cleaned for its new vibrant occupants. The night had been like any other, he supposed, except that there was always something a little bit extraordinary about the nighttime in the concession.

When no longer on display, the animals of Hagenbeck's Animal Paradise behaved differently, more wild, as if humans wandered through their territory instead of the other way around. He enjoyed that sensation, as if he were a little more wild, too, and perhaps a little braver. The nighttime offered up new possibilities, the chance for him to say the things he otherwise might not say and to do the things he otherwise would not do.

But then, he'd also come for another reason, because after the fairgoers were gone, when the pathways were empty, it wasn't only the animals that were off exhibit then. Shehani, too, was no longer the exotic Sinhalese dancer in a pretty foreign gown with strange foreign ways. She became simply a pretty young woman who he liked very much. He loved seeing her that way and speaking with her, perfecting his English that had been so strange in his mouth but had become for him the language of Shehani. He'd stumbled upon her again that night on the path near the swamp, her long black hair luminescent in the light from the streetlamps. He shook his head, unable to untangle the details. He'd seen her arguing with Pete and the two of them had walked away. He wanted to believe she'd not been in the proximity of the murder, but she'd returned to the back of the concession to retrieve her brother and instead had found Pete who leaned into her, pressing her against the boardwalk railing.

He shook his head. "I don't know. It was a normal night. I talked to people and then I went home. Nothing unusual." Except that there had been something unusual. He could see it now, Shehani standing there, leaning against the railing above the swamp, her eyes on the alligators. Standing beside her had been Pete.

Max's voice must have hitched, because Henry grabbed his shoulder and shook it. "Max, I need you to tell me the truth. Were you in the swamp exhibit that night?"

"Yes," said Max, wrenching himself free. "Yes, for a while, I was."

"Were you alone?"

"I saw Shehani," he admitted. "And Pete was with her."

"What were they doing?"

A fierce protectiveness roared in Max. "They weren't doing anything. That monster grabbed her and kissed her and—" Max couldn't finish, but he didn't have to because as he fought back a round of dry heaves, Henry finished for him.

"He attacked her."

Max managed to nod.

"And then you attacked him."

"She's innocent, Henry. I swear it. He wouldn't have stopped until he hurt her. She had no choice but to fight back."

Henry wrapped Max in a hug and allowed him to cry there for a moment. Then, softly, "I know, son. I know. But she isn't the one that fought. The glass in the body wasn't the only glass on the scene. A piece caught in the victim's clothing, a large enough piece to contain a complete fingerprint. Your suggestion led Detective Cullen to look for it. He consulted with Detective Ferrier at the criminology exhibit and uncovered a match among his records."

Max pulled out of Henry's arms and drew a deep, halting breath. He could see it, finally, as Henry spoke. He'd known, somewhere in the back of his mind that Shehani was innocent, that he wouldn't let that monster hurt her the way his mother had been hurt by his father again and again when he was too small to do anything to defend her.

Max wasn't small anymore. He'd become barrel-chested and broad as Felix had been and developed strong muscles from farming and from caring for the animals. A hard thump with a shovel on the head of a man who'd spent half his life blind drunk on the vodka of his own making was all it took to spare the one woman he'd ever loved from continuing in her oppressive life. In the end, he didn't even realize he'd done it. Not until now did he understand the full picture, how Mutti must have known, had protected him, had run with him, making herself look guilty in the process.

He recalled the scene, watched his father crumple like a sack of the potatoes he'd always grown, and heard the final resonance of a hard head thudding against the hard-packed ground. The memory played out in Max's head, and his father's contorted features melded and shifted into the features of Pete Williamson, whose lanky body slid silently into a watery grave.

Max had been the one to break the vial of venom, to shove the jagged edges of the glass like a knife into Pete's breast. And just as Mutti had done, the other woman in his life who he truly loved had borne suspicion for him. While he twisted the poison into his adversary, as he'd hefted the man's body over the railing and lowered it into snapping jaws, she had run, sought solace with her brother, and had not uttered a word about what Max had done.

That was the part he could not tolerate. He'd spent months believing, even if he did not form the thought fully, that his mother had killed his father. Max had wanted nothing more than to protect her from that, not quite knowing that he could if he'd accept the blame as rightfully his. Now he wanted nothing more than to protect Shehani by doing the same.

He confessed, not only to the murder of Pete Williamson, but to that of Felix Eyer as well, a case brought to the attention of the St. Louis police by detectives in Hamburg after the body, with obvious head trauma, was unearthed on the construction site of Tierpark Hagenbeck in Stellingen. At the request of the Hamburg police, Detective Henry Duncan had agreed to investigate their prime suspect, now relocated to the United States and living with her brother in St. Louis.

"I did it," Max said, the news causing Henry to clutch at his own chest and close his eyes.

"I chose to forget. But it was me. I know everything. I'll tell you everything."

Epilogue

Max dreams of goats.

At the end of a long day making shoes for a pittance in the Missouri State Penitentiary, his mind wanders back to the Pike. There a pink skirt swirls as a dainty foot is snatched from danger, a snake uncoils to the ethereal melody of a master's flute, and an elephant plunges to detonate an explosive rain shower soaking a delighted crowd. But rising above it all comes the bleating of two goats.

They run, these goats he used to know so well but that he's recently come to better understand, forever compelling him forward to plead, to cajole. He offers food in his dream—crunchy carrots, bright strawberries. The creatures remain obstinate, trotting down the Pike, surefooted on rough cobblestone, past Asia and Japan and the Indian Cliff Dwellers, past incubators filled with tiny infants on display, and half-naked Igarots parading for the entertainment of the masses.

On and on the goats run in search of a true paradise—one not manufactured with false rocks and imported bushes and surrounded by ditches. In his dream, Max runs after them, breathless and never catching, almost rooting for their escape.

Inevitably he awakes frustrated, sweat-covered, and no less exhausted than when he first closed his eyes on the cage he now inhabits.

He wakes to a day that is the same as yesterday, to navigate the personalities and the politics that rule his strange new home. There he's fed and housed in a narrow space that is not his own. He has thankless employment. Sometimes he is led outside to pretend to taste freedom. Occasionally he receives visitors—his cousins, his mother, his detective stepfather, and always at night in his dreams, the goats.

Acknowledgements

I am grateful to so many people for helping this story along its way, including the archivists at the Missouri Historical Society, the librarians of the St. Charles City-County Library System, and members of the 1904 World's Fair Society whose knowledge of and enthusiasm for the Louisiana Purchase Exposition is inspiring. I'm also grateful to a team of excellent early readers including Andrew Galloway, Jeannette Vargo, Diane How, Susanna Goheen, Ruth McClintock, Amy Houke, David Lutes, and Cheryl Rowland. Their insights were invaluable in shaping the story. Thanks goes as well to my wonderful group of Coffee & Critique partners who never fail to mop up my messy prose and skillfully nudge me along. Special thanks go to fellow authors on the journey, David Wilson, Karen Tinsley, Ann Marti Friedman, Kirsten Claiden-Yardly, and Kate Pettigrew for much encouragement and a regular reminder that the often frustrating business of writing need not be a lonely one. I owe much thanks to Steve Varble who once again has designed the cover of my dreams, to Jeanne Felfe who made the book beautiful on the inside, and to Megan Harris whose editorial expertise is indispensable and who always puts the commas in the right place. A very special thank you also goes to Jerry "Pete" Longley for graciously volunteering to be killed off in a book and who in no other way resembles his fictional namesake. As always I am extremely grateful to my husband Paul and my entire family of encouragers who walk alongside me through the ups and downs.

Author's Note

I approached this story first for the animals and then stuck around for the World's Fair. As an undergraduate, I studied zoology and earned my Bachelor of Science degree assuming that I would work my way into the world of educational outreach at a zoo. Life had other plans, however, and instead I found myself drawn to storytelling and earned my Master of Arts degree in Literature and Creative Writing.

I wasn't convinced the two would ever fit together, but then while researching for my previous novel *White Man's Graveyard*, I met a charming orangutan named Jenny, a faithful friend and travel companion of one of my historical protagonists. Attempting to trace her story pushed me briefly into reading about the history of zoos and that's where I stumbled across Carl Hagenbeck, who brought his animal show to the Louisiana Purchase Exposition in St. Louis in 1904.

In the late nineteenth and early twentieth centuries, Carl Hagenbeck was the biggest name in the animal trade. He worked with live animal trappers all over the world to supply zoological gardens, circuses, and personal menageries with every exotic creature imaginable. He and those he worked with closely, including renowned English animal trainer Reuben Castang, pioneered more humane animal handling and training techniques.

Hagenbeck designed the world's first open animal enclosures, trading bars for trenches and strategic landscaping that more closely resembled natural habitats and served to break down barriers between animals and human visitors. Because of this he is often referred to as the father of the modern zoo. His design approach, which he implemented successfully at the 1904 World's Fair and perfected in his own Tierpark Hagenbeck, has made a lasting mark on zoological gardens throughout the world, including the St. Louis Zoo in Forest Park.

I think it's appropriate to celebrate that part of Hagenbeck's legacy. Today's zoos are partners in the business of preserving and caring for species, some of which are desperately endangered and in need of our special protection and attention. It's also true that many species were initially pushed over the edge into precarious endangerment by the very practices of the animal catchers who supplied the world's earliest zoos, circuses, and personal menageries. It was a brutal and sometimes gruesome business. That is also a part of the legacy.

And so, Carl Hagenbeck represents a mixed bag. There's little doubt he loved the animals in his zoos, his circuses, and his traveling exhibits, and that he did much to improve the handling, treatment, and safety of captive animals, but he also had a penchant for experimentation and showmanship resulting in highly unnatural behavioral modification and many attempts at strange, and ultimately sterile, crossbreeds, including the *zebroid* that appears in this book and today would be more commonly known as a zorse.

Hagenbeck was also an early proponent of *ethnographic exhibits*. As early as 1874, in order to maintain the interest of audiences, he began recruiting groups of people from less familiar corners of the world to be put on display alongside the animals that populated their homelands. In his memoir *Beasts and Men,* he discusses his first venture into what our modern sensibility understands as an extreme example of exploitation. He imported a family of Sámi (referred to by him with the more common European and now derogatory term *Laplanders*) from the Northern part of Norway to live alongside a herd of reindeer outside on the grounds of his early Hamburg zoo.

His dehumanizing descriptions of these guests who'd volunteered to live their lives as though not surrounded by what must have been the terribly disorienting bustle of a culture entirely unfamiliar to them is certainly disturbing from a modern perspective.

Hagenbeck continued to display humans alongside animals, often as part of traveling tableaus viewed throughout Europe with great success. It is little surprise then that part of his plan for the World's Fair in St. Louis included the importation of both captured Asian elephants and hired Sinhalese mahouts from then British Ceylon, now Sri Lanka.

Fair organizers did not bat an eye at this suggestion because in a World Exposition carefully crafted to promote industrial progress and Western superiority, thousands of indigenous peoples from every corner of the world would be on display. The largest such people exhibit was the Philippine Reservation, which included representatives of the Igorot People, who despite traditionally consuming dog meat only rarely and for special ceremonial purposes, were forced by fair organizers to do so daily in St. Louis.

I apologize to any readers who found that difficult to read about, but I felt it important to include because a large portion of reminiscences of the fair by those who attended make mention of it. More than anything else at the fair, this contrived and extreme demonstration of supposed cultural inferiority made a loud and lasting impact and well illustrates the exploitative design of the Louisiana Purchase Exposition. It's part of the legacy.

But of course, like Carl Hagenbeck, the 1904 World's Fair is a mixed bag because it was also the largest, most spectacular exposition the world had ever seen, originally planned to commemorate the centennial of the 1803

Louisiana Purchase. The enormity of the undertaking ended up requiring the date push to 1904. It was a land of dreams and imagination filled with enormous palaces, new ideas, and displays like nothing anyone had ever seen before. It introduced or popularized hundreds of new inventions, discoveries, and processes, including the brand new science of fingerprinting, presented as described in the book, by Scotland Yard and quickly adopted by St. Louis Police detectives.

In 1904 St. Louis was a city of immigrants. First and second generation Americans, the majority of them of Irish or German descent, made up a large percentage of the population. Max Eyer, his mother, his deceased father, and his St. Louis family members are all fictional characters, as are the detectives Henry Duncan and Jerome Cullen.

Lorenz Hagenbeck and his father Carl are historical figures, the latter of whom really did piece together land acquired from potato farmers for his new tierpark in the village of Stellengen just prior to the Fair. The innovative zoo opened only a few years later and is in operation still today in what is now the Stellingen neighborhood of Hamburg. I mimicked the Hagenbecks' personalities and opinions as I could from the writings and stories they left behind and from the perceptions of them shared by their contemporaries, but to some extent of course, they too are at least partially fictional. The same can be said of Reuben Castang, though he did have a way with goats and his accidental slide down the elephant chute comes from his own account, as does the incident of Lizzie the elephant playing tabletop in the Cowboy Bar.

For the sake of simplicity in the book, I streamlined the team that put together Hagenbeck's Animal Paradise on the Pike for the 1904 World's Fair, choosing to exclude a second main animal trainer, Charly Judge, and to reduce the number of American business partners from three to one. Pete Williamson thankfully is fictional, but I did take the inspiration for him from the unfavorable opinion Lorenz Hagenbeck and Reuben Castang expressed about one of the partners, a Mr. Williams, who both described as a bothersome dandy who knew nothing of any use about animals.

Reuben Castang spoke of a gangster who frequently visited the elephants at the concession in St. Louis. Tom Egan was a known gangster in the city at the time, though whether it was him, or anyone who was there for nefarious reasons, I do not know. I have no particular reason to believe that the snakes present at the fair were milked for their venom, and likely they were not, but Carl Hagenbeck does write of the process, precisely as it is described in the novel, and mentions that collected and dried venom was in demand for medical research and the creation of antivenoms. The implication that Egan may have used it for more criminal purposes is my invention.

The Sinhalese mahouts were present at the concession and did participate in much of the animal care, parades, and shows. At least one of the group of Sinhalese gentlemen was a traditional snake charmer. I do not know if there was a woman among the group, but there is a wonderful account of a pretty woman working at the concession who amazed the audience by dancing with the lions. I have found no records of the names of the Sinhalese participants. That in itself tells a tale, as I easily discovered records of many of the animals' names including all of the elephants, Trieste the lion, Flossie the dog, and the goats Flick and Flock.

To the best of my knowledge there was never a murder at the Animal Paradise.

Thank you for reading. If you have enjoyed this book, please help others find it by leaving a review.

Visit Sarah-Angleton.com for extras, including discussion questions and a truly immersive, era-specific Spotify playlist.

Also by Sarah Angleton

∞

Fiction
Gentleman of Misfortune
Smoke Rose to Heaven
White Man's Graveyard

∞

Nonfiction
Launching Sheep & Other Stories from the Intersection of History and Nonsense

About the Author

SARAH ANGLETON is a storyteller, blogger, and history enthusiast who once worked as a zookeeper and spent much of her time chasing after a fugitive goat. She lives near St. Louis with her family and if she ever gets the chance to time travel, her first stop will be the 1904 World's Fair. For now you can find her at Sarah-Angleton.com